MW00737181

Published by

Etched in Stone Publications

756 South Orange Avenue

Newark NJ 07106

www.Ghettofab.biz

Copyrights reserved in 1998
ISBN-978-0-9767987-2-9
Printed in Canada

Fingered for Murder

Written by Rodney Wilson

IS IT MURDER

WHEN AN INNOCENT MAN'S LIFE IS DESTROYED OR ALTERED,

FORCING HIM TO DO OTHER THAN WHAT IS IN HIS HEART,

WHEN ALL THAT HE HAS TAKEN A LIFETIME TO BUILD

AND CONSIDERED TO BE CONCRETE

CRUMBLES BEFORE HIS EYES?

IS IT MURDER

WHEN A SOUL IS TORMENTED FOR THE CRIME OF ANOTHER

AND IS IN NEVER-ENDING PAIN INSTEAD OF PEACE?

WHEN AN INNOCENT HEART CRIES OUT

WHILE JUSTICE TURNS ITS BACK,

ALLOWING SATAN TO STALK HIS FLESH LIKE A VULTURE.

CAN IT BE CONSIDERED MURDER

TO TURN A WARM HEART COLD,

MAKE A STRONG SOUL WEAK AND WRACKED WITH PAIN

OR WHEN A PERSON IS ROBBED OF THEIR SPIRIT OR DIGNITY?

IS THIS MURDER TO YOU,

AS IT IS TO ME?

OR CAN YOU POINT YOUR FINGERS TO A LESSER CHARGE?

FINGERED FOR MURDER

INTRODUCTION

OVERVIEW

Since I can remember, the human race has always crowded around to watch fights, or just after someone's been shot or killed. The human mind, though the most complex, still exhibits its animalistic instincts and emotions. These baser elements are appeal to, for example, television shows, movies, etc. They have produced popular entertainment based on shock value.

I am far from perfect, because I am a product of this society; but I have chosen to compile my experience into a literary format.

I see this formula as a blend of reality, fiction and to the young minds, a possible source of enlightenment.

ABOUT THE AUTHOR

Rodney Wilson, a resident of Newark, New Jersey, has been writing nearly as long as he can remember. For many years he wrote poetry and dreamed of being published. Much like the old cliches, one must endure many trials and overcome unbearable pain before one can write and be effective.

His inspiration to write this story came from tales that he heard, incorporated with others that he encountered. The author's vivid imagination, plus detailed violent memories and the justice system that he identifies as big business, made this an easy task.

The author's love for reading, writing and analyzing others and their written works gave him a strong incentive to see if he could do any better.

Being thirty-seven now, and a Black male in the midst of crime and poverty, he considers himself lucky to be alive.

TABLE OF CONTENTS

FINGERED FOR MURDER

A Tale of Mystery and Murder

By Rodney Wilson

1THE FRAME-UP

About eight-thirty in the evening, John left his apartment and headed toward the playground. Passing through people singing, throwing dice and hanging out, he whistled while he bounced his basketball continuously. During his stroll he came upon several young ladies who admired him as he passed.

"Nice legs," one said, flirting.

Smiling now, he drifted back into his private world and dribbled on.

As this tall brown skinned guy approached the dimly-lit playground, he noticed three sweat-drenched guys playing basketball. Unaware of what he would encounter, he proceeded toward the entrance. Suddenly, gunshots could be heard. He froze in his tracks and then took off running as if his life depended on it. He ran through the streets, looking back every so often, as if the shooters had seen him. As he frantically ran, everyone he passed along the way wondered what had spooked him.

Approaching home now, he was out of breath, but still clutching his basketball. He stopped to look around as he leaned against a tree and lifted his partially soaked shirt to wipe the sweat from his face. Now peeping from around the tree, he coughed and spit as his body shuddered with fear.

Moments later, safely in his apartment, he made sure every lock on his door was secured, proceeded to the back room where he threw his trembling body across the bed. Wondering to himself if one of the killers had seen him, the vision of this playground execution stayed with him till he dozed off to sleep.

Morning came and he awoke from the dead, grabbing his alarm clock from his nightstand.

"Eight-thirty-two," he grumbled as he read it.

Sitting up now, he was still completely dressed and sweating from the heat of the sun. But as it glared through the window and he was completely awake, his eyes were still wide with fear. So as he climbed from the bed he wondered if he should mind his business and go to work or play the model citizen and report what he had seen to the police.

Now, in the shower, the vision became more vivid. The nightmare began to run through his mind like a never-ending movie. The shots, the blood, the anger in which he had seen released, reminded him of a gangster scene.

"Oh, my God!" he shouted as the water beaded from his partially soapy body. "Are we all mad?" he then asked himself.

In that instance he stepped from the shower, dried off and raced to the phone, wrapped in a towel.

"I got to call the police," he mumbled to himself, thinking of the three guys executed. Sure of what he should do, he picked up the phone and dialed 411 for information. As the operator answered, he greeted her "hello" and asked her for the number of the Fifth Ward police station. After listening to the computerized recital, he dialed the number which was given. The phone rang about five times before it was finally answered.

"Hello, Fifth Ward police station, Detective Brown speaking."

John responded, "Yes, is this the homicide squad?"

"Hold on," replied the detective.

The officer hung up after he transferred the call.

John heard, "Hello, homicide squad, Detective Jones speaking."

"Yes hello. I'd like to report a triple murder," John quickly blurted.

The detective said, "First things first. I need your name, address, plus the location and time of the murder or murders."

John complied. "My name is Johnathan Jackson. I live at 534 South Fifteenth Street, Newark, New Jersey, and the triple murders took place in a playground on Tenth Street. As the detective took all the information down, John could hear him telling another. He then asked John if he could come in for questioning. He agreed.

Approximately ten-twenty that same morning, John dragged his tall frame from the building in which he lived. But as he walked, a dark-colored luxury car pulled up on him, and as the tinted window dropped, someone called out to him. Just as they did, he was quickly abducted. He fought for dear life as one of the guys in the vehicle brandished a handgun, hitting him over the head, rendering him unconscious.

"It's a pity you just happened to be in the wrong place at the wrong time. We should just kill ya ass, too, but you're going to wear dis shit!" stated one of the guys sitting in the car as he started to laugh. Putting on his gloves, he pulled a brown suede pouch from under the seat. Opening it, he pulled a nine-millimeter handgun from within it. He placed John's now limp right hand firmly against the surface of it. Having accomplished exactly what they had set out to, the guy put the gun back in the pouch as they tossed John from the car, leaving him in an alleyway in which they sat and then drove off.

When John woke up, he found himself lying face down on the ground with a throbbing headache. Grabbing the back of his head, he felt a lump and some soreness as he slowly stumbled to his feet. Bracing himself against a nearby wall, he tried to shake the pain as he wondered. If they were killers, then why was he still alive? So now, more than ever, he felt it was his civic duty to report this crime. Continuing on his journey to the police station, he rubbed his head as he thought, what the hell was that all about? The obvious didn't occur to him.

Once at the police station, he was directed to the homicide squad by an officer at the front desk. Entering a room with desks facing the walls to the right and left of him, but with only a few officers present, he stood staring patiently. He was greeted by a short, black, neatly dressed detective in a brown blazer.

"Hello, I'm Detective Jones, may I help you?" he asked.

"Yes, I'm Johnathan Jackson, I'm supposed to meet with you."

"Okay, have a seat," added the detective as he cleared a few things from a desk.

After being seated, John told his story and gave a vague description of the murderers in the execution. Afterward he spoke of his abduction and how they knocked him out and left him in an alleyway. Now two of them, the detectives listened and took down his statement in its entirety. As soon as he finished, they stood up, shook his hand and told him they'd contact him if they needed him further. Walking from the room and down the corridor, John couldn't help but think that he had been brushed off.

Outside, he shook his head in disbelief and walked away from the station. But at that same exact moment, a call was made to Jewels, a big-time drug dealer in the Newark area, from within the precinct.

"Hello, Jewels, I thought you were going to take care of that."

"Don't worry, I got dis under control; trust me," states the voice of the dealer.

"There's been a slight change of plans. I'll talk to you bout it later," he added.

On that note the conversation ended.

Back on the streets, John headed to his girlfriend's house, which wasn't far from the station. When he finally arrived on her doorstep, he rang her bell and waited to be buzzed in. Upon entering this tidy apartment, he leaned over to kiss his girlfriend, Tammy, and she smiled. She was a true sweetheart, inside as well as out. She was not a great looker, but her shoulder length hair accentuated her small frame and light skin. Comfortable now, John told her of his crazy encounters. He graphically described the triple murder, as her eyes widened. She gasped, then asked, "Honey, are you all right?"

"Kinda," he answered, as he paused then finished, "but it's got me shook."

He spoke of his abduction, explaining that they had knocked him unconscious and when he woke up, he was in an alleyway; face down with a throbbing headache. As he went on, she maneuvered under him and began to massage his temples. He soon relaxed and fell asleep.

The next day, Tuesday, August 22, John awoke with his head resting in Tammy's lap. The pleasant sounds of chirping birds serenaded him, as he squinted from the sun's glare. It dawned on him that it was a work day. Jumping up, he kissed Tammy, who was still sleeping, then raced out the door. En route home, he stopped at a coffee shop that he occasionally ate at, to get a newspaper. After purchasing the paper, he flipped through it in search of something pertaining to the shooting. Suddenly he stumbled onto an article which read: "Three killed on a basketball court and the community yells foul."

After walking several blocks and reading the entire article, he closed the paper and picked his head up. Continuing home in a rush, he turned the corner on Fifteenth and Madison, where he lived. Noticing two police cars and a detective unit double-parked in front of the building he called home, it never occurred to him that he was the unsuspecting soul they were looking for. Never slowing his momentum, he tried to rush past the clutter of police. But as he attempted to climb the stairs to his apartment, one of the officers stopped him.

"Are you Johnathan Jackson?" the officer asked.

"Yes," he replied.

The officer walked up to him as he said, "You're under arrest for murders, the murders of Darryl Ward, Kevin Chamber and Michael Evans."

The officer then reached for his cuffs as John looked at him in disbelief.

"What the hell are you talking about? Is dis some kind a joke?" asked a confused Johnathan, as he pulled away. "I'm the one who reported the shit!" he added angrily.

"Correct," replied the detective who spoke from the background. "But the only person seen in or around the park was you. Plus, we found the murder weapon in a dumpster not far from here. Now would you like to guess whose fingerprints were found on it? Yours! Mr. Jackson. Now take him away!" shouted the detective.

John shouted repeatedly as the officer cuffed him, "That's impossible! You hear me? That's impossible!"

Tears ran down his confused face as he struggled, giving them a tough time. They fought to keep him still, but he broke away, only to get beaten with nightsticks. Windows opened as people looked on, as the officers grabbed him and threw him in the back of a parked patrol car, then as quickly as it pulled off, the detective unit followed closely.

It was about eight o'clock that same morning, when they arrived with Johnathan at the precinct. Dragging him from the vehicle in through the doors, the officers tussled with him angrily. Upon putting him in a cell in the holding area, he yelled, "I'm innocent! The only thing I'm guilty of; is trusting the system!"

Restlessly, he walked back and forth in the eight-by-eight cell in which he was thrown. Cursing and mumbling to himself, he looked out through the bars. Minutes later, an officer entered the holding area and unlocked the cell.

"Mr. Jackson!" he shouted as he looked around.

John, who was standing in his face, quickly made it known that he was Jackson.

"This way!" directed the officer as he put the handcuffs on him before escorting him down the corridor.

Entering through an open door, John was confronted by Detective Jones as Detective Michaels sat in the background.

"Here he is!" stated the officer, as he closed the door and could be heard walking away.

"Have a seat," offered Detective Jones.

"You remember my partner, Detective Michaels, head of homicide," he added.

Michaels stood tall and distinguished in his blue jeans and white shirt, the darker of the two. Jones was a slight bit shorter loved to wear blazer and vest. At this time he had on vest and jeans. He picked up some papers from the table and began to look them over as he paced the room.

"Now according to your criminal history, you've never committed a violent crime. You haven't even been in trouble in approximately nine to ten years, or is it that you just haven't been caught?"

"Well anyway, was this in any way personal? You know, over a girl or something?"

John, angered now, finally responded. "Hell no, I didn't even know 'em. I told ya what happened!"

"Refresh our memories; tell us exactly what did happen that night."

John, remembering how the police like to play the good cop, bad cop routine, decided to say no more. Instead he asked for a phone call as Michaels shouted, "Get him out of my face!"

On that note Jones opened, the door and called for an officer, who then escorted John back to the holding area. As the two of them strolled down the corridor, John asked again, "Can I make a phone call?"

The officer nodded his head yes, as he walked with him to a phone across from the holding area.

"What's the number?" asked the officer.

"6-2-4-7-7-4-3," John answered.

After dialing and hearing it ring, the officer handed the receiver to John, who stood waiting. As soon as someone on the other·end picked up, he quickly blurted, "Hello, Tammy. It's me, John. I'm locked up!"

"What for?" she asked.

"They're saying I murdered dem guys!" he replied.

"Murder . . . John what's going on?" she asked in a worrisome tone.

"I don't know! Just get in touch with my brother and my family and tell them I need a lawyer. Someone's trying to frame me!" he added.

She didn't say anything for the next few minutes, as she recalled him speaking of what happened in the playground, a few days before.

"That's crazy, baby; don't worry. I'll make the calls then I'll be right there. What's your bail?"

John turned and asked the officer, who in turn, yelled out to another, who replied, "Fifty thousand cash."

Hearing this in disbelief, John told Tammy, "Baby, call my family and tell them I need a lawyer."

Disgusted, he said good-bye as the officer told him to cut it short.

Later, about six o'clock, Tammy had done all that she said she would and had arrived at the police station. By this time, John had been identified from a photo line-up as the one running from the park. Two middle-aged women, who lived across from it, positively identified him.

One of the women stated that he nearly ran her over. The other said she was sure it was he she had seen that night and to solidify it, she said she also knew him from his community involvement. So now the police were sure they had the right person.

In another part of the precinct, Tammy sat on a wooden bench in the lobby area, crying in disbelief. Detective Michaels, seeing this, walked up and then sat beside her as he asked, "What's wrong, young lady?"

She replied, "My boyfriend is being charged with murders he hasn't committed."

Realizing who her boyfriend was, Detective Michaels added, "He seems like a good person, so if what he says is true, he'll be free before you know it."

Then as she sat sobbing with her head in her hands, the detective rose from the bench and proceeded down the corridor.

Hours passed and then about nine o'clock that same evening, a tall, dark, sharply dressed man in a forest-green designer suit walked in. As he strolled up to the front desk with his briefcase in his hand, he opened his mouth to greet the officer.

"Hello, I'm Anthony Sharpe, counsel for Johnathan Jackson. May I speak with my client?"

The officer checked, then had John brought from the holding area to one of the rooms along the corridor, as another escorted Mr. Sharpe to the same.

Shortly after, John's brother, Rick, and his father, Leo, walked in, accompanied by Richard Lewis, who was a well-known bondsman and a dear friend to the family.

As the trio walked up, Tammy jumped to her feet in relief. "Am I glad to see you guys!"

At the desk, Rick spoke. "We've come to post bail for Johnathan Jackson."

The officer behind the desk responded, "He's in the back with his lawyer at the present, but you can post his bail while you wait, to speed up the process."

The officer led them through a door, where a female officer sat behind a thick glass partition.

"Yes, may I help you?" she asked.

"Hi, I'm Richard Lewis, bondsman. I'm here to bond out Johnathan Jackson."

He passed her some documents through a slot. She picked them up and then looked them over. In front of the computer, she began to type in the information according to the paperwork. Then she returned to the window to tell Mr. Lewis, "He'll be released shortly."

"Thank you," responded Mr. Lewis.

For the next fifteen minutes everyone sat in silence. Then came a loud crash, as two officers stumbled in, dragging a hysterical man who seemed to be badly beaten. Not far behind followed Detective Jones, who shouted as he entered, "Put him in the interrogation room."

The officers dragged the man into the back, as everyone looked on in amazement. Rick looked at this as if it was nothing new.

"Somebody's gonna kill that cop one day!" he stated, referring to the detective.

Mr. Jackson, a hip brown-skinned guy, who wore all the latest style and also had a lot of facial hair (a full beard), was sitting beside him, patted him on the back, remembering Rick's run-in with Detective Jones.

Jones picked him up in a drug raid, where he planted seventy-two grams of cocaine and beat him up when he denied it was his. Rick took it to trial and lost, ending up doing a year and a half in prison. Now that he was out, he worked for his father, along with Johnathan.

Twenty minutes later, John and Anthony Sharpe (his lawyer) came walking down the corridor, accompanied by an officer. Disgusted now, but still able to smile, John stood still as Tammy jumped up to embrace him.

"Baby, oh baby," she rambled as Rick and his father stood behind her, smiling.

Their father said, "Hello, son. I knew something was wrong, when the store was closed at eleven o'clock!"

"Dad, I didn't do it. I didn't kill anyone!"

"Come on, boy, I know better," responded his father.

Anthony Sharpe then assured the family he'd do his best to get John acquitted. Everyone grabbed their belongings and they all exited the precinct. Anthony waved good-night as he rushed in the opposite direction to his car. The entire Jackson family, plus Tammy, climbed into Mr.

Jackson's car and then drove off. Mr. Lewis hopped in the one behind them and did the same.

Driving now, Rick spoke of Detective Jones. "John, do you know Detective Jones?"

"How do you mean?" asked John.

You know, from the 'hood or something!"

"No," he replied.

"Well anyway, he's the dirtiest crook of a cop you'll probably ever meet!"

Just then, Mr. Jackson interrupted.

"Where are you guys going? I have to get back home before your mother gets worried. She's probably hysterical by now!"

Tammy then added a few words. "John's coming home with me."

"And you, Rick?" Mr. Jackson asked directly.

"Home," stated Rick.

Mr. Jackson then started backtracking, so he could get to Tammy's place, which wasn't far from the precinct. After dropping them off, Mr. Jackson pulled away as Rick shouted, "See you tomorrow, we have to talk."

Wednesday dragged in. John headed out and off to work. As he unlocked the security gates to his father's business, he lifted them up and walked in. Rick pulled up and followed. Rick, who was much shorter than John, but of a muscular build, started the task of filling up the soda box.

Loading the shelves one at a time, he whistled while John prepped the store to be opened.

Flipping the sign on the door from CLOSED to OPEN, they were ready for the new day.

Hours later, as customers entered and exited, suddenly the phone rang. John, who stood the closest to it, grabbed it after the second ring.

"Hello, Sandwich Spot."

"Yo, what's up, John?" returned the voice.

John not recognizing it at first, asked, "Who is dis?"

"It's me, Keith. Oh, you don't recognize my voice now?"

"Sorry, Keith, I'm kind of out of it this morning. I was accused of three counts of murder."

"What? Three counts of murder! How did that happen?"

"I went out like I normally do to play a little basketball Sunday night. Just so happens, I saw three guys get shot. I ran, then the next thing I knew, I was being locked up."

"What?" Keith stated again.

Stunned by the news, Keith didn't say anything for the next few minutes. Then he told John not to worry, that things would work themselves out.

"Where is your father? He asked me to help him with his books," stated Keith as he quickly changed the subject.

"He should be here shortly. Call back in about an hour."

After a few more words, John smiled and hung up, rushing to help a patiently waiting customer.

By one o'clock their father had arrived and was rushing back out to take care of some business. But as he did so, it dawned on John that he had forgotten to tell him something.

"Hey pop, Keith called," he shouted as he leaned over a counter.

Mr. Jackson, remembering that he had promised to bring his books and records to him, responded, "Call and tell him that I'll be there at five."

The door slowly closed behind him and the store had emptied out.

Rick struck up a conversation about the incident.

"So John, you probably don't know any of these cats. Their faces have changed since your hustling days. The ones that were killed had muscled in and started making a little too much cash. So the way I figure it, Jewels had them smoked. But somehow they're trying to say you did it."

John finally spoke. "But what's supposed to be my motive?

The phone began to ring.

"Hello Sandwich Spot, John speaking."

"Hello, baby, it's me, Tammy. Are you all right?"

"Yes."

"I'm coming to see you later."

"Okay, later. Bye."

Tammy hung up. Rick started right back in, just as he finished a sale.

"Now John, think, did you see anything?"

The phone rang again.

"Hello Sandwich Spot, John speaking."

"Hey John, did you relay my message to your father?"

"Yes, I did. He said to tell you, he'd see you before five."

"Thanks, I'll talk to you later. Stay strong."

Rick picked the conversation up again, as John hung up the phone.

"Someone had to see something."

This conversation went on throughout the workday.

Later at home, John was on the phone with his lawyer. Before they hung up from each other, he told John he needed to see him at five o'clock sharp. John shook his head as if to agree and then stated, "I'll be there."

Up now, he headed to the back of his apartment, where he entered the bathroom and closed the door. The sound of the shower running soon became the only noise in the entire place, after which he headed into his bedroom. Flipping on the lights, he began to get dressed. Sitting on the edge of his bed, he reached out to turn on his television, which sat directly in front of him. The news was on, and the newscaster talked about a triple murder that took place on a basketball court. They suspected that it was rival drug dealers fighting for turf. The police were questioning a suspect. Disgusted, he shut the television off as he continued to get dressed. He heard a light knock at the door as it echoed throughout the apartment. As he rushed to it, he shouted, "Who is it?"

"It's Tammy, baby."

Partially dressed, he unlocked the door and let her in.

"Hello, baby, how was your day?" she asked as she entered, closing the door behind her.

"Fine," he replied and added, "Let me finish getting dressed. I have to go see my lawyer. Would you give me a ride?"

She told him yes as she sat on the bed beside him. "You know I love you, right? You also know, I don't want anything bad to happen to you."

"I know, honey," he answered.

Forty minutes later, they had arrived at his lawyer's office and stood at the reception desk.

"Hello, I'm Johnathan Jackson; I'm here to see Mr. Sharpe. He's expecting me."

"Have a seat, Mr. Jackson, I'll tell him you're here," stated the receptionist.

She hit a button on the phone, as she proceeded to relay the message. "Mr. Sharpe, you have a Mr. Jackson out here."

"Send him in, I'm expecting him."

As John entered the well-decorated and ritzy-looking office, Mr. Sharpe cheerfully greeted him and offered him a seat.

"I'm glad you could make it; let's get right down to business. First, I have to ask you exactly what did you see? Start from the beginning."

John took a breath and began.

"Leaving my apartment with my basketball in my hands, I headed toward the playground. But as I approached the entrance, I heard shots and I froze where I stood. Then I saw the three guys with guns shoot the other three, and I ran."

"Did you get a good look at any of them?"

"No."

"Did you see anything else?"

"No."

This looks like some type of hit, but the problem is proving it. Being that they have your fingerprints on the murder weapon, we have to find a witness or a loophole. Do you have any idea who might have done this?"

"No."

"Well, I'll send my investigator to the scene tomorrow, and I want you to accompany him. I'll give him your phone number and address. Thanks for stopping by and try not to worry. I'll do all that I can to get you out of this mess!"

"Thank you, Mr. Sharpe," John responded appreciatively.

John left the office and went back out into the lobby, where Tammy was reading a magazine. At the sight of John, she dropped it to the table and rose to her feet. The two them walked hand in hand out the door, but not before saying good-bye to the receptionist.

As they walked down the hall, the elevator could be seen ahead, its doors open. It quickly became packed as they raced to crowd on it, along with everyone else. Descending to the lobby area, it emptied out just as fast.

Walking to the car Tammy uttered, "You know, there had to be somebody that saw something. I know it; I feel it!"

"That's what everyone else is saying, too. But it happened so quickly and I was so scared, I can't remember anything. Nothing."

The two of them climbed into her car and sped off. The conversation started again.

"Honey, you have to find out who framed you. If the guys were drug dealers that were killed, then most likely so were the killers. It was probably over money or turf."

"I agree, but the only way I can honestly find out, is to hang in the streets and find out who Darryl might have offended. That life I swore I would never return to, no matter how bad things got!"

"I know, baby, but this looks pretty bad. If you don't find the killers, everything points to you and you know there's no justice for us!"

A tear began to run down his right cheek. His face hardened as he said, "Baby why me? I've lived my life right for ten years and look, I'm about to go to jail for somethin' I had nothing to do with."

In that same instant she pulled up to where she lived, looked him in the eyes and told him, "I'm here for you, no matter what, all the way!"

Later on in her apartment, they made love and drifted off to sleep. Then suddenly, John jumped up in a cold sweat, eyes bulging and wide. He was having a nightmare and the realism scared him half to death. Tammy woke up, equally frightened from his sudden movements and noises. She comforted him as she asked, "What happened?"

"I had a dream about the shooting!" he answered.

"It's going to be all right," she added to comfort him.

The next day, August 24, at four-thirty in the afternoon, John stepped from the local number twelve bus, dropping him directly in front of the community center. He noticed a few of the regular kids throwing dice against the center wall. John, annoyed, marched directly at them.

"You guys know better. Clean it up and come inside," he said. "Let's go do something constructive."

In unison they replied, "Okay, Mr. Jackson, in a minute."

"Now fellows!" John shouted as he held the door for them.

Sensing that he meant it, the boys put away the dice and headed through the door. Entering the gym behind John, they stood looking for a second and then blended in with all the others running and playing. At the same time, John squeezed through kids playing basketball, screaming, racing and just hanging around, to get to the front stage.

"Listen up, everybody, listen up," John shouted as he climbed on the stage.

The gym slowly quieted down, as the other volunteers signaled to those who didn't hear. As all the kids focused on the stage area where John stood, he began to speak.

"Hello, everybody," John yelled at the top of his lungs.

The kids all responded. "Hello, Mr. Jackson."

"What's our motto?" asked John.

"Respect where we come from and those around us," they all shouted in unison.

"Okay, you can go back to what ever it was you were doing," John added in closing.

"Mr. Jackson, Mr. Jackson," shouted a light-skinned skinny kid as he raced across the floor toward John.

John stopped in his tracks as the kid paused to get his breath, saying, "I know you didn't shoot those dealers." Afterward he smiled and walked away.

John was now in shock, mainly about how fast and wide the news had spread.

"Hey! What's your name?" John yelled.

"Mark," the kid answered.

"What do you mean by that, Mark?"

The kid, who had walked back toward John, explained.

"My mom thinks you did it. But I know better. You're a good man, not like those guys on the corners and stuff."

John smirked, then told him he was a good kid and for him to keep up the good work.

After Mark's departure, John walked through the gym, picking up a basketball in the process. With the ball in hand he began a game with the kids. As he did so, some of the kids jumped on his back, as laughter broke out. Later, John talked with a few of the volunteers and then decided to head home. Finally there, he climbed the steps then entered the hallway area. Upon checking his mailbox, he found a letter from the Superior Court of New Jersey and tore it open. As he stood still, he began to read it. "Essex County vs. Johnathan Jackson, docket number 9003764. Please be advised that you must appear before Judge Long, room 402, County Courts Building, 190 High Street, Newark, New Jersey. Thursday, November 23, 1989. You will be arraigned on three counts of murder."

He closed the letter, regrouped by taking a deep breath, then continued up the steps that led to his apartment. Pulling his keys from his pocket, he quickly unlocked his door. Reaching around in the darkness, John searched for the light switch. After turning it on, he found that someone had ransacked his place.

Annoyed now, he stated, "Now my apartment's being violated, what's next? What the hell's next?" he shouted as he glanced around.

Grabbing a bat, he went from room to room. When he entered the kitchen area, he couldn't help but notice that the back door had been forced open.

"Damn!" he shouted as he continued and finished his search. He let out a slow sigh of relief when he didn't find anyone. Relaxed and leaning against a wall in the bedroom, he put the bat down.

Suddenly an arm eased out from a nearby closet, bluntly striking him across the head with a crowbar, knocking him unconscious almost immediately.

Waking up an hour later, John shook his head as his vision slowly came back into focus. Grabbing his face and head, he could feel the swelling as it pulsated painfully. Stumbling from room to room, he checked closets and all hiding places. Hoping to find nothing in his condition, he continued. Throughout his search he saw nothing missing, so he called the police. Sitting down with the bat in his hand, he tried to gather himself.

Twenty minutes later, a loud knock could be heard throughout the place.

"Hello, who is it?" asked John nervously, as he gripped the bat tightly.

"Police!" the voice responded.

John staggered to his feet, leaving the bat alongside the couch. Still dizzy from the blow to the head, he stumbled to the door. After opening it, he noticed that one of the officers was a woman. While inviting them in, he continued to pat his face and head with a cold, wet face cloth.

"Are you okay?" asked the female officer as she noticed the bruised area about the side of his face.

"I'll be all right," John answered as he grimaced in pain.

Roaming through the house, the other officer began to note things on his clipboard.

"Your name is?" The officer asked.

"Johnathan Jackson."

"Now where did they come in at?"

"They forced open the back door," John said, pointing to it.

"Could we see it?" The officer asked.

"No problem, follow me," added John as he led them through his apartment.

In the kitchen area, the officers looked over the doorway and, once again took notes. The molding hung and the door sat slightly off. John just looked on in disbelief.

"Is anything missing?" The female asked.

"Not that I can see." John stated.

"Okay, Mr. Jackson, you take it easy. If you need a copy of this report, you can stop by the precinct tomorrow or any day after. Ask one of the clerks" stated the male officer as they made their way back through his place.

John slowly closed the door as the two of them walked out, then dragged himself over to the couch to relax.

Two hours later, he woke up, still fully dressed and slobbering from the mouth.

"Damn, let me get up," he mumbled as he rose.

Remembering the damage that was done to the back door, he searched for some tools to repair it. Finding a hammer and some nails beneath the kitchen sink, he started to tack the molding back in place. After tightening the screws in the lock and making sure everything was secure, he headed through the apartment and out the front door.

Back at the family's business, he arrived as his father and his staff were swamped with customers. After the chaos was over, his father noticed him leaning on one of the counters.

"Hey John, what's up?" asked his father with a grin.

John turned to face him and his father's happy expression became one of concern.

"What happened to you?" he asked as he came from behind the counter and walked up to John.

"More of the same," replied John, sounding somewhat depressed.

His father started to examine the swelling as John went on to say, "I went home and got knocked in the head, in my own place!"

"For what? Are you all right?" asked his concerned father. "You need to move, at least until you find out what's going on!"

After speaking, his father hugged him and tried to cheer him up, but he drifted into space. He decided to head to Tammy's place before it got too late.

It was dark outside when he arrived. She pulled up seconds behind him. Seeing this, he sat on the stairs and waited for her to park and lock her blue hatchback. Smiling at him, she quickly noticed his face and raced to the porch, where he sat.

"Baby, what happened to you?"

"It's been a long day, can we go up stairs first?" asked a battered Johnathan.

She agreed, so she started up the stairs with him following her. After she unlocked the door, he followed her inside.

Sitting in the living room and relaxed, he was ready to discuss the incident with her.

"So what happened?" Tammy asked as she sat down beside him, sipping a cup of tea.

"I got mugged inside my own apartment," replied John as he turned to look her in the eyes, fuming from all that had happened.

"You need to put something on that swelling," she said after getting a good look at his face, then rose and headed into the kitchen to get some ice. Upon returning, she put the ice, which was wrapped in a cloth, against the side of his face.

John continued. "I need to move, I need to rest, I just need some peace!" Looking into Tammy's eyes, he then said with a puzzled expression on his face, "I can't figure out what they wanted or what they were looking for."

Meanwhile, inside a vacant apartment in a run-down building from which Jewels and his boys hustled, he and Jimmy talked and laughed loudly.

"Yo, I broke in right, but check dis, I had to hide 'cause that joker came home. He was boiling when he noticed dat his place was tore up, so he searched the place with a bat, right! I was sure he was going to find me, but I was ready for him. But he didn't and then he finally relaxed. That's when I knocked him in the head, kid! I got what you wanted and some keys from a hook, dat looked like spare house keys, den I bounced," stated Jimmy, excited.

"He'll probably change the locks anyway," added Jewels.

"Yo, who the hell cares, kid, if I got to get back up in there, I'll break shit again."

They both burst into laughter again. Jimmy was an ugly cross-eyed kid, who was genetically gift with a natural physique. He stood about five foot eight.

Friday morning at work, John leaned over a glass counter with his head resting on his two folded arms. Hearing footsteps, he rose up. Noticing a slim, studious person who dressed like he jumped fresh from a catalog, John fought back a smile. It was Keith.

"What's up, my brother?" asked Keith with a look of concern on his face. John stood straight up and responded, "Not much."

"What do you mean not much? Look at your face. You look hurt! What's going on?" Keith remarked.

John came from around the counter and invited Keith to come outside so they could talk. Just as they did so, two customers entered. Rick served them, then sat down and watched them talk through a window.

"Look, John, I know this is rough and if there's anyway I can help, you just name it," stated Keith.

"Right now, I don't even know where to start," replied John.

As the two of them stood outside the store talking, kids began to crowd in and Rick yelled to John for help.

"I have to go help Rick," stated John as he rushed inside.

"I have to go to work anyway, talk to you later," added Keith. He then got, into his car and drove off.

After punching in at work, Keith was greeted by his boss, Mr. Krasdale.

"Hello, Mr. Payton, how are you today?" he asked.

"Fine and you?" returned Keith.

Mr. Krasdale continued towards his office, which was located in the back. Keith, not far behind, stopped at his desk. He sat directly behind a beautiful young lady named Karen Wells. Sitting, he started the task of filing client information.

An hour later, a car pulled up, gleaming in the sunlight. A large figure rose from the driver's side and walked in the front door. Karen rose from her seat and met this person almost at the entrance. Keith, buried in his work, never even noticed. He came and went before Keith ever looked up.

Back at the store, John headed out and off to the community center. Shortly after he arrived and was greeted by the kids, he went through his normal routine. He was playing basketball with a few of them, when he noticed a small kid with braids who seemed lost and out of place. He told the others to keep playing as he headed toward the seemingly lost soul. Not wanting to scare him off, he approached him calmly.

"Hey, why aren't you playing basketball or something?" John asked with a smiling face full of sweat.

He answered, "I don't like basketball."

"Okay, what's your name?" John asked, changing the subject.

"Alvin."

"Alvin, what do you like to do?"

"Nothin'," he said angrily. "Can a young brother get some space?"

Alvin walked away. As he did, John watched. A kid named Mark walked over to John.

"He's got problems. Ever since his brother died, he does nothin' but mope. His mother and father are separated. His mother drinks and stuff. So he hates to go home and when he does, she beats on him and takes his money."

"How does he get money?" John asked.

"He hustled for the guys that were killed!"

"What happened to his brother?" asked John as Mark sparked his interest.

"He got killed in a shootout with the police, so they say."

John looked across the gym, focused on little Alvin as he headed for the exit. Running behind now, John began to shout, "Alvin."

He turned around, looked at John, turned back and continued walking. John chased him down outside the center, put his arm around him and smiled. "Are you hungry?" he asked as he walked with him.

"I got money, I can get my own food!" stated Alvin.

Sensing Alvin had a lot of pain and anger in his heart, John said, "Okay, let's just go get something to eat."

They walked into a local sandwich shop named Slices of Heaven.

After ordering and sitting down, they waited for their food to be brought to them. Shortly after, a young lady carried it over to them. As they ate, John looked over at Alvin, who had been forced to mature and survive at any cost.

"How old are you?" John asked with his mouth half full.

"If you're going to question me, I'm out!" stated Alvin. "What are you, some kinda cop?" he added.

"No, I'm what you see, a working stiff and a volunteer. All I want to do is help," stated John.

"I can help myself!" replied Alvin as he continued to eat his sandwich.

After they finished eating, John handed Alvin his number and told him to call if he needed anything. John watched Alvin as he bounced down the block and smiled at him as he looked back. Continuing on, Alvin disappeared. John shook his head and hurried on his way.

Arriving home, John slowly and cautiously opened the door to his apartment. Flipping on the lights as he entered each room, he checked out the apartment thoroughly before relaxing. Hitting the button on the phone answering service, he lay back in his recliner and listened.

"Hello, Boo, it's Tammy, call me when you get in." (BEEP)

"Hello, Jay, it's Rick. Yo, call me back. . . peace." (BEEP)

"Yes, this is Mr. Woodson, Mr. Sharpe's investigator and assistant; I'm going to the scene today and Mr. Sharpe asked me to take you along, but I realize you're not in. Call the office and we'll go another day. Good day. (BEEP)

"Hello, this is Anthony Sharpe, I need to talk to you at your earliest convenience. (BEEP)

"Hello, baby, it's mom, just checking on you." (BEEP)

John roamed from the bedroom to the bathroom doing odd chores, continuing to listen as the messages finished up.

Suddenly, "This is Terrance Smith, meet me at nine o'clock, at 167 Rosehill Terrace. Just you! I have information that can get you off."

Quickly looking at the clock, which read seven-thirty P.M., he showered and headed out the door, only to run back in to call Rick, just in case something went wrong.

"Hello, hello, Marie, is Rick there?" he asked half out of breath.

"Hold on," she told him.

"Yo, what's up?" grumbled Rick softly.

"Wake up, I need you to take me somewhere."

"Where?" asked Rick.

"Rosehill Terrace, I got to check something out."

"Okay, I'll be dere." (CLICK)

John went downstairs to await Rick's arrival. As he waited, he watched a few kids as they passed drugs and the police as they raced behind a stolen car. In the midst of all this his brother pulled up.

"Yo, let's go."

John jumped up and headed to the car. After getting in, he directed Rick as he pulled off. He told him about the message that was left on his answering machine. Hearing this, Rick decided to detour and stop by his place to get some protection, before continuing on.

But while they journeyed to Rosehill Terrace, Jewels had walked in on the end of Terrance's conversation. Quickly sending Jimmy to John's apartment to erase the call from his machine, Jewels shot Terrance, then left. The police soon arrived at Rosehill Terrace and cautiously entered the house.

At that precise moment, Jewels had one of his boys put a new message on John's machine from a nearby phone booth.

Back at Rosehill Terrace, John and Rick finally arrived. Seeing all the flashing lights, they slowly turned around as they wondered what was going on. Noticing that they were at the address where they were to meet with Terrance, John told Rick, "Let's go home."

"Yo, Rick, I think someone's seriously trying to set me up!" John shouted.

"Why?" asked Rick.

"I don't know, but I'm going to find out!" answered John.

"So bro, whatever goes down, you know I'm rolling with you!"

After their brief conversation, Rick pulled up in front of John's place.

"Come up for a minute, I want you to hear something," directed John.

Rick shut his car off, climbed out, locked it up, set the alarm, then headed up the stairs behind John. Once inside, John rushed over to the answering machine, hit the play button and prepared to listen.

"Listen," he said as he played the messages.

(BEEP) "Yo, John, this is Terrance, about that money for dat, you can come get yours whenever."

John, now in shock, rewound the machine and played it back once more. The same message repeated itself.

"That's not the original message or the voice," he shouted.

Hitting fast forward, John listened, but there was nothing. Reading the number of messages, which was one, he became puzzled. "Someone's definitely trying to set me up!" he shouted.

Rick stood in the middle of the room, more baffled than John as he stared at him. John snatched the tape from the machine, threw it on the floor and crushed it with his boot.

"Damn, why me?" shouted John, looking for an answer.

Rick put his arm around John, walked him over to the couch and sat him down. There was a long silence before John spoke again.

"I'm going to stay with Tammy for a while, but I'm keeping this place. I'm just changing my locks.

"Damn. Just think, if we hadn't doubled back to your place, we would have arrived at Rosehill a few minutes earlier, in the middle of that mess. How the hell are they doing this?"

John, beginning to unravel from all of this, punched a wall, flipped furniture and cried out hysterically.

Rick grabbed him and said, "Look, man, you have to maintain, at least till we can find out somethin'.

John took a deep breath then said, "Okay, I'm all right, you go ahead home before Maria gets worried. Go ahead, get out of here!" he insisted, practically pushing Rick out the door.

"Okay, but I know you, you're up to somethin', ain't you?" added Rick.

"Yeah, some sleep," jokingly stated John.

Rick smiled suspiciously as he walked out the door.

John locked it behind him and then headed to the window to make sure he left. Rushing to his bedroom closet, he grabbed his black boots, sweatshirt, jeans and a black cap. Quickly putting them on, he headed out the door and down the stairs.

Approaching the bottom, he noticed a shadow of a person sitting on the porch. Slowly and cautiously opening the door, John exited the building as the figure turned around.

"Damn you, what are you doing here?" shouted John.

"The same thing you're doing here, so let's do it together," answered Rick.

"Where did you that change of clothes?" asked John, noticing that he had on a sweatsuit, opposed to the jeans and plaid shirt he had on earlier.

"I keep a few pieces in the trunk of my car," Rick stated then continued, "Come on, let's go."

Rick went on to add as they approached the car, "You need me!"

They drove off and to the "strip," the place where all the hustlers hung out. They parked three blocks away, and then walked down to a building on it. In this particular building, Rick's ex-girlfriend had resided for some time.

Upon entering, John asked, "Where are we going?"

"Angie's apartment," stated Rick.

"Isn't she a fiend?" asked John.

"Last I knew, yeah. But this ain't for pleasure. We need her window to see the whole strip," Rick pointed out.

The two stomped up the flight of steps, then up to her door.

After knocking, they listened, but heard nothing. Rick knocked again and this time a light squeaky voice answered, "Who is it?"

"It's me, Rick."

The door opened slightly, a chain lock prohibited it from moving any farther. A small face appeared in the opening.

"Hello, Mr. Longtime-no-see, what brings you here, stranger?" asked the person behind the door.

"Can I come in?" Rick asked.

"For what?" she questioned.

"I need your help with something," he added.

"What makes you think I'd want to help you?" she asked, attempting to slam the door in his face.

Pushing the door, Rick continued on; "Because you're good-hearted. Please, I need your help."

She noticed John standing beside the wall, out of view.

"Who is he?"

"That's my brother, John, you don't remember him?" Rick answered.

She looked him over, then again at Rick. She closed the door to remove the lock and let them in.

Entering her apartment, Rick made a few comments.

"I see you've got things back together and you look great, too!" She was a fair-skinned petite woman with long braids in her reddish hair.

"Save the bullshit," she angrily returned, then continued, "If you took the time to call, you would a known that I've been though rehab and I've been clean for about a year now. Plus, I have a part-time job at the supermarket. But ya so into Miss Thing, you can't see straight."

"Her name is Maria!," Rick bluntly stated.

"Whatever," responded Angie as she went on to ask, "What's up?"

"Look, Angie, can I trust you to keep this between us?? And in return, I promise we'll take care of you."

The room got quiet.

"I'm listening," stated Angie patiently.

"We need to use your place, because we can see the whole strip from your window. We want to get to know all the faces, who's who, and how we can get in the mix," stated Rick.

"What you're asking is a lot. You're asking me to participate in something that brought me down and that I'm solely against. Not only that, Jewels, Silk and their runners aren't the type of guys you'll want to mess with," cautioned Angie.

"Angie, if you help us, I'll personally give you two hundred a week to start," Rick pleaded.

"Look, Angie, I know I've hurt you in the past, but I promise, baby, they'll never know you had nothing to do with anything," added Rick.

"I have to think about it," she spoke softly.

John passed Angie a card with his number on it.

"That's my pager number and this is my home number," he pointed out and then added, "I get off at three and I'm usually home by four."

After reading the card, she said, "I'll call tomorrow, either way"

Rick walked to the window once again.

"Yo, Jay, come here!"

Looking out, John could see the whole strip.

"That's Jewels."

John noticed a big, dark-skinned guy in a black leather jacket, with a bald head. Watching Jewels walk up in the building with four others, trailing him, John became angry. Backing away from the window, he gathered himself as Rick checked his watch.

"It's eleven o'clock, let's go."

Leaving, John told Angie not to forget as she closed the door. She told him she wouldn't, then told him good-night.

Exiting the building, they noticed a green Benz, then Silk as he climbed from within it. It was like a movie star had arrived, as he walked from the car to the building across from Angie's. He strutted in a thin silk French, with his bald head gleaming as his specs glared.

Stunned for a moment, Rick mentally drifted away in envy of him, until John tapped him on the shoulder and said, "Can we get out of here?"

Rick, still amazed, began to walk away with John at his side. Heading up toward their car, suddenly three police cars flew by with their sirens and lights flashing. Turning around, both of them stared down the street to see what was going on. As they watched, the police stopped right where Jewels' squad had stood.

"Everybody up against the wall!" shouted one of the officers as two of the dealers ran. Just as they did, a patrol car gave chase, as one of the detectives did so on foot. Disappearing through an alleyway, twenty minutes passed before the detective emerged. Breathing heavy and coughing, the detective stood bent over, trying to gather his breath and then threw his nightstick out of frustration. The patrol car circled the area to no avail. John and Rick turned and continued walking toward their car. John stopped at a phone booth and called Tammy.

"Hello, baby, I'm coming over, wait up for me."

In the car, not much was said. Rick dropped John off at Tammy's and he continued home.

The next afternoon, shortly after work, John arrived home. Before he could do anything, he received a phone call.

"Hello, is this Johnathan Jackson?"

"Yes."

"This is your lawyer, Anthony Sharpe, just calling to remind you we have to get together so we can prep for your trial. Oh yeah, you still haven't met with my investigator. Please take this seriously, because the State sure will!"

"I know, and I'm sorry, but I've been stressing," replied John.

"Fine, but if you think murder isn't reason enough to find time, you'll really be stressing, if the outcome isn't in your favor! It's up to you. I'm here, and if I were you, I'd be here Monday about four-thirty!" rambled Mr. Sharpe, pushing his points home.

"Okay," John answered understandingly.

"Don't disappoint me. Talk to you Monday" added Mr. Sharpe.

(CLICK)

Wondering how one man could juggle so much, John sat in thought. He decided to call his mother. After two rings, she picked up and he said, "Hello, Ma, how are things going?"

"Well, I've been worried about you. You're hardly ever home," stated his mother.

"I have to give you Tammy's phone number. Do you have a pen handy?" John asked.

"Yes." She could be heard searching, then she said, , "Go ahead."

He recited the phone number. "Six-two-four, seventy-seven, forty-three. You can catch me there anytime I'm not home."

"Okay, you take care of yourself."

"Love you, Ma."

"Love you, too, bye." (CLICK)

As the clock read five forty-five, John headed out to a nearby hardware store. Once there, he purchased some new locks and security devices for his apartment. His pager started to beep, but as he read the number, it wasn't one he was familiar with, so he walked on. Then it dawned on him, when he thought of who it might be.

"Angie was suppose to page me today," he mumbled to himself. Quickly stopping at a phone booth, he dialed the number on the screen.

"Hello, did someone page me?" he asked as someone picked up the phone on the other end.

The voice spoke. "Hello, John, this is Angie, how are you today? I told you I'd call and yes I'll work with you guys."

"Okay, give me at least a week to put something together," John told her, stressed.

She agreed and then hung up.

Later on at home, after putting all the new devices and locks in place, John sat down to relax. He seemed to feel better, a bit safer. He loved Tammy, but he enjoyed his own space. Drifting off to sleep, something suddenly came to him. Someone was searching his place for something. Anything, that would make his case open and shut. Now wide eyed and awake, he began to look around, wondering what they could possibly use. He walked through each room wondering what? What could they use? Continuing on till the phone rang, he gave up upon answering it.

It was Tammy, and he relaxed as she spoke.

"Honey, I'll be working late tonight, till about eleven, so call first if you decide to come by."

"Okay, baby, I love you."

Then, just as he put the receiver down, it occurred to him. Maybe they had tapped the phones. So he tore the phone apart, but found nothing. He searched the house up and down and still found nothing. Disgusted, he fell back across his bed, shouting, "What? What?"

Realizing that it was getting late, he decided to let it go for the moment.

Twenty minutes later, the phone rang again. "Yo, big brother, let's go out for a few drinks. Hit a few spots; it's Saturday night."

"Nah, that's okay," responded John.

"Come on, man, you got to mingle to get to know dese cats. You have to get familiar with the whole environment," stated Rick.

John, not really wanting to go, agreed anyway. He looked at his clock to check the time, It was nine-fifteen.

"Come pick me up at ten o'clock," stated John as he struggled with his thoughts.

An hour and a half later, John and Rick were entering a bar on Frelinghysen Avenue named the "Tootsie Roll." Upon entering, they were confronted by a half-nude woman, who danced provocatively in front of them. As the two of them maneuvered around her and roamed, they saw quite a few more doing the same thing. Some were sitting in guys' laps, others wriggling wildly while guys fondled them. After seeing this, John told Rick he had to go.

"Rick, I can't do dis; if Tammy found out she'd have a fit!"

"Come on, stop being a wimp, enjoy yourself!" shouted Rick, who then yelled to the bartender, "can we get two beers?"

After the bartender brought them their beers, Rick paid him and passed one to John. Rick sat at the bar lusting, but John rose from his seat and marched out. Rick followed, shouting, "If you don't get with the program, you'll never fit in."

John, realizing that he was right, followed him back inside. Rick then bumped into one of Silk's boys, whose name was Dre. Now Dre was short for Andre. He was a stubby short kid with a lot of heart.

"Yo, man, what's up with you Rick?" he asked as he smiled and embraced him.

"I'm all right, you know how us cats is," answered Rick, grinning as he took a few sips from his beer.

"Good, glad to hear it. You take it easy," added Dre as he eased away and through the crowd.

"Yo, Jay, that was one of Silk's people, his right-hand man. Over there, that's Biz, he's big across town where you used to hustle," Rick told John as he pointed to another and said, "That's Jewels, the cat you saw from the window the other night."

John took a long, hard look, long enough to notice every bump, blemish and hair on his face. He continued to look as women took dollar after dollar from Jewels as he held them out.

Now arriving at a club in Orange called the "Soundroom," they paid the cover charge and made their way in. This was a hangout for all the hustlers and the women who played them. They sat around there for a while, long enough for Rick to get drunk.

Knowing this, John took away his keys, then helped him out to his car, and drove him home. John rang the bell several times. He knew he had to wake Maria out of her sleep. So he stood on the stairs, holding Rick up and waiting patiently.

A light came on, as a petite shadow of a figure appeared at the door. The door opened, and Maria stood, blocking the entrance, then moved to allow John to drag Rick in.

Dropping him on the couch, John began to walk out, when Maria, who could pass for Spanish or Black because of her wavy hair and dark complexion, spoke out.

"He knows he can't drink, but he always wants to. I hope he has the worst hangover of his life."

John laughed, then told Maria to remind Rick that he had his car and for him to call him in the morning.

"Night, night," John added as he headed out.

"Good-night," she returned softly.

Once in the car, John drove off looking at his watch.

"Damn, it's one-thirty. I better go home. Tammy's probably sleep." So he headed home.

The next morning, with the sun shining brightly, John woke up to a loud, repetitive knock. Jumping up, he shouted, "One minute, wait one minute!" Gathering himself together, he rushed to the door. "Who is it?"

"Me, damn it!" replied the angry but familiar female's voice.

"Oh, man," John mumbled as he rubbed his eyes.

"Open this door, John," she added impatiently.

"Okay, okay," he replied as he fumbled to do so. "What's wrong with you?" asked John as he opened it and she barged in.

"What's wrong with me? I was worried all night. I called you, paged you; I had no idea where you were! You had me worried to death. You could have at least called."

"Okay, I'm sorry!" John rushed to say.

"Where were you?" she asked, still angry.

"I hung out with Rick. He got drunk, so I took him home and that's that! Calm down, baby."

"You don't understand, you're having all these problems, so I worry because you . . . you fool!"

Walking out now, still boiling in anger, she slammed the door behind her. She could be heard crying as she did so.

John raced down the stairs behind her to console her.

"Look, baby, I understand. It won't happen again, I promise." He hugged her and escorted her back up the stairs and into his apartment. Still comforting her, he walked her over to the couch, where they sat until she stopped crying.

Seeing this, he told her, "As long as I've got you; my world will always have sunshine! For you're all I need."

She smiled and then punched him. "I hate you!" She told him with a slight smile.

"No, you don't," John laughingly pointed out.

Getting up, he headed toward the back to shower. When he emerged from the bathroom, the place was filled with the aroma of eggs and bacon. Smiling, he walked into the kitchen area and hugged her from behind.

"I'm going to marry you, right after I get out of this trouble."

He smiled again as she pushed him away.

"Move you fool, let me set the table so we can eat."

Then, just as they sat down to eat, the phone rang.

"Let it ring," stated Tammy, holding him in his seat.

"Honey, I have to answer the phone, it might be Rick. I have his car."

She let him go and he got up to answer it.

"Hello . . . hello . . . hello. Whoever it was, hung up."

But as soon as he sat back down, it started to ring again. He grabbcd it quickly.

"Hello."

"Hey, John, I have the worst headache of my life," his brother began.

John smiled to himself as he thought of what Maria had said.

"I just called to tell you there's no rush with the car. I'm staying in. You know why, otherwise I'll have to hear her mouth. Talk to you later, bye."(CLICK)

John headed back to the table and sat down and finished his still warm breakfast.

The day slipped by quickly. John and Tammy watched television, talked and then made love as they fell asleep in each other's arms.

2 THE HUSTLE

It was about seven o'clock one cold evening, when John could be seen walking up the avenue. He ran into a few friends he used to hustle with back some years ago. After shaking their hands and giving them the peace, he couldn't help but notice how bad they looked. Trying to slip away before they could beg, he started to step, then it came.

"Yo, John, can you spare a few dollars, brother?" one of them asked.

Shaking his head in disgust, he replied, "Honestly, I don't have it."

As he turned and started walking away, he could hear them calling him all types of names. He shook his head and continued on. That's when he heard one of them say, "That's why you're going to jail, fag!"

Pausing for a slight moment, he once again continued on. Suddenly, two guys he had never seen before hurried across the street in his direction. John, shook up, considered running, but froze. Then he noticed a small-framed woman pointing him out from across the street.

She yelled, "There he is! That's him right there!"

The two figures came directly at him. One began to speak.

"John, we need to talk," he demanded as if there was no other option. They told him they were armed and would kill him if he tried to run. Asking him to step into an alley, they stared at him expressionlessly.

John hesitated, and the smaller of the two tall men told him, "Either ya step into the alley or you die here; it's your choice."

Not feeling as if he had one, John did exactly what was asked.

"Now, before we kill you, who ordered the hits?" asked the two of them in unison.

"What hits?" asked John, scared to death, knowing that he was talking about the playground murders.

"Oh . . . I see you're on some dumb shit! Well, I've got some bullets with your name on them. They're called dum, dum!" The thug who made the statement pulled a gun from his waistline and waved it in John's face.

John wised up and tried to talk reason with them.

"Look, do I look like a hitman?"

His teeth started to chanter from the cold and the fear that consumed his body. As he looked at the two of them eye to eye, they stared him down, thinking.

They looked at each other. The two of them put their guns to his temples, then dropped them back to their sides. The thinner of the two spoke. "I'll tell you what, you help us find their killer or killers and we'll let you live."

A nervous, shook-up John replied, "You have my help, completely."

As sweat dripped from his face, his heart raced with fear. He swore on everything living that he'd help, seeing that these two angry soldiers meant business and was out for blood.

"Why should we believe you?" asked one of them angrily.

John, barely able to speak for stumbling and stuttering, mumbled, "I couldn't hurt a fly, I swear to you!"

Not sure, but somewhat believing him, they put away their guns and begin to relax their tense arms.

"Tell you what, since you seem sincere and your ass is on the line, I want you to work for me. My name is Tony," stated the smaller of the two, who stood six foot, 235 pounds, with a small Afro and fair skin.

John heard this and wanted to say no, but said yes for fear of his life.

Smiling now, Tony looked around, then asked John to give him a way to get in touch with him. John gave him his pager number, then Tony told him it wouldn't be healthy to play games. The duo headed back across the street to a parked black van.

John, still shook up, just watched as they pulled off and blew the horn. He looked around and then started to walk once again. Scared to death, he marched home as he thought of the mess his life had become.

Tears streamed down his face as he mumbled to himself. "I've tried to put my past behind me; I've lived life righteously, I've done nothing but pour my heart into everything I've been involved in. So explain to me why this is happening, Lord, explain this to me! Is it a trial for all of my past wrongs, some sort of lesson that you wish me to learn?" At that moment, he dried his eyes with the back of his hands, straightened up and continued on his way.

He then received a message on his pager. It was Angie. Being that he was close to home, he figured that he'd wait till then to call her back.

Once home, he pulled off his coat and sat down as it dawned on him that he had to see his lawyer at four. Noticing that it was four, he decided to call and tell him he'd be a little late.

Later, upon arriving, John was expected, so he was directed into Mr. Sharpe's office.

"Now, Mr. Jackson, like I told you back in August, we have to work on a defense. We have to find someone who saw something! Did you see anyone else?" asked Mr. Sharpe.

"No," John quickly replied. "I just ran, strictly out of fear that one of them saw me. Okay?" he added.

Okay," agreed Mr. Sharpe. "I have your criminal history in front of me; from what I can see, you haven't been in trouble in seven or more years. You've held down a steady job and you're a community volunteer. Now, what I need from you is a list of people who will speak on your behalf. But at the present, I need to view the scene and see if anyone saw anything."

After leaving to visit the scene of the crime, the two arrived and viewed it. Mr. Sharpe went over things as John stood where the bodies had fallen. Mr. Sharpe also asked people passing by about the incident. He continued asking others as he walked through the area, but no one knew anything. Giving his business card to a few of them, he told them to call if something came to mind.

After getting back in the car and driving off, he dropped John off at home and went about his way.

At about eight-thirty, John's pager and phone rung, as he laid resting in the living room. Damn, can I get a moment to myself; he thought as he glanced at his pager then picked up the phone.

"Hello."

"Yes, is this John?" asked the voice on the other end.

"Yes, it is."

"This is Tony. So when do you want to start? It's your call."

"Meet me at the grocery store on the corner of Fourteenth and Avon, in about thirty minutes," John instructed.

After hanging up, John paged Rick, who called right back.

Shortly afterward, Rick arrived and sat blowing his horn. John hurried to the awaiting car. Upon reaching their destination, Rick parked, then they jumped out and headed toward the corner. Rounding it, they bumped into Tony.

"Yo, what's up, my brother; follow me," stated Tony as he headed out toward the curb.

With John and Rick following, Tony walked up to a black Mazda van. The back door opened; Tony climbed in as John and Rick hesitated.

"Get in!" stated Tony sternly. He added, "We can't afford to sit here, with our van load like dis!"

John thought to himself, he's right. Fourteenth and Avon's one of the hottest corners. So he jumped in with Rick, following as the van hurriedly pulled away from the curb.

"So, who's your friend?" Tony asked.

"He's my brother Rick. He's going to help me take care of business, if that's all right with you," replied John.

"Fine. Handle your business as you see fit, but I'm still putting one of my boys down for insurance reasons. Meet my left and right hands, Eric and Kelly. Oh yeah, my brother, Seventeen Shots."

Eric, who stood about five-foot seven with a small gut and a full beard, usually wore jeans and plaid shirts. Kelly, on the other hand, was short, about five-foot three and loved to dress in khaki's and polo shirts. Seventeen Shots stood six foot two, 278 pounds of pure power. He was as strong as a bull.

"Now that everybody's been introduced, let's get down to business. Where are you parked?" asked Tony as he told the husky six-footer he called Seventeen Shots to pull off.

"Fourteenth Street, down from the store," stated Rick.

As they drove up to the car, Tony passed John a package and told him of its contents. Also, that its net value was two thousand dollars. Coming to a stop, alongside Rick's bright red Mustang, John fastened the package in place about his waist, then he, Rick and Kelly exited the van.

Tony cruised away as Rick started the car and pulled off as well.

"Hold up, fellows, I have to call Angie to see if she's still down. We've been putting it off so long, she might not be wit it." stated John as he searched his pager for her number, which he had locked in. After finding it, he motioned for Rick to pull over as they approached a phone booth sitting directly on the corner.

John jumped out and raced to make the call. As the car idled, he could be seen explaining. A patrol car passed slowly, so he figured he'd better cut it short.

Back in the car, he told them she was almost ready to say forget about it.

Arriving on the strip, they saw it was alive as usual. Not pausing for a second, they hurried straight up into the building. John knocked on the door to Angie's apartment. After hearing the pitter patter of feet, the rattling of opening locks, then finally the opening of the door, they all walked in. Upon entering John clarified the situation.

"Angie, sorry 'bout things. Okay? And, oh yeah, this is Kelly. He'll be working with us, too, that's it!" Kelly nodded and smiled.

"I hope so," she stipulated.

Rick and Kelly walked over to the window and began looking down toward the clutter of people, forming their course of action accordingly.

"Now first, we have to gather some fiends (junkies) and the best, way to do that is to let them sample the goods," Kelly stated and raced out the door.

When he returned he said, "I have two of them outside waiting. What's up?"

John removed the packages that were neatly taped around his waist and put them on the table.

Kelly spoke once more. "Take them a bag each. Make sure they let you know how good the product is before they leave your site."

Rick hurriedly took a few bags of heroin and disappeared out the door and down the stairs.

John, somewhat disguised, walked over to the window and watched his brother's every movement. Rick passed each one of the junkies a bag, then stood patiently awaiting their response. As one of them sat in plain view, the other disappeared into the hallway. Sniffing the contents hit after hit, the one in view threw up, as the other came from within the building smiling as he shook Rick's hand. John knew right away it was on, even before Rick came back in through the door out of breath.

"Yo, they're saying it's the best thing out dere," Rick stated as he gasped.

Kelly spoke again. "Take them a little at a time, spoon feed 'em."

Everything went smoothly and at the end of the night, they had accumulated seventeen hundred and ninety-three dollars.

"We're gonna get paid!" shouted Rick as Kelly smiled and laughed.

John just stared out the window, shook up from having to go back to a lifestyle he swore he would never do. No matter how many times he tried to tell himself he was doing it to save his own ass, he truly couldn't see it. Looking up at the clock, he noticed it was twelve-fifteen A.M., as Angie eased over.

"Why are you doing this? I can see it ain't in you."

John responded, "I just have a lot on my mind, thanks for your concern."

"Hey fellows, let's go! I have to go to work tomorrow!" he went on to say, as she walked away.

"Don't you want your cut?" asked Rick, still smiling.

"No, you guys keep it," John told him.

Kelly and Rick split the money and then put the rest away to give to Tony. As they all gathered together and prepped to leave, Rick walked over to Angie and gave her a hundred dollars, then kissed her on the cheek and told her thanks.

After leaving the apartment, John was dropped off, as Rick and Kelly continued on.

Later that same morning, half asleep, John dragged through his daily routine. He headed out the door and off to work, with everything on his mind. The work day flew past, ending as quickly as it started. Afterwards, he went straight home, shut the ringer off on the phone, and went to sleep.

When he woke up, he felt refreshed. He turned on the television and sat back. Tammy came to mind and he thought, let me call my baby. Looking at the time, which was five-fifteen P.M., he figured she should be home. He dialed her number and a sad voice answered.

"What's wrong?" John asked.

"You're what's wrong! You don't come home, you don't come by, you don't even call now! I could have died and you wouldn't have known! I had an accident last night and couldn't get in touch with you. I paged you and everything," she carried on.

"Are you all right?" he asked.

"Yes, but the car's totaled," she explained.

"Baby, I apologize. I just had some things to do last night. Are you all right! John repeated, as he felt bad.

"I'm okay, honey, could you at least stop by? I miss you."

"Anything for you! Bye."

An hour later, as John sat at Tammy's place eating and talking, his pager went crazy. He rose from the table to use the phone, which hung from the wall. As he did, she told him that they needed to talk. He dialed the number, and it was Tony.

"Hey, John, ya meet me at the pool room on Springfield and Twentieth Street in about an hour." (CLICK)

Afterwards, John called Rick and Angie, as Tammy stared in his face. Just as he hung up the phone, she spoke, "I know you're trying to figure out who's framing you, but don't get caught up."

"I'll try my best," he assured her.

Later at the pool room, John and Rick were shooting a game, when Tony, Kelly and Eric walked in.

"What's up? They shouted, as they gave each other the peace.

"You guys did good for a trial run. Now we're going to get down to business," stated Tony with a slight smile. "Listen, there's a Honda around the corner and here's the keys to it. He handed the keys to John. There's also four thousand dollars in merchandise, a Tech nine and a Glock under the rear seat. Now listen to me carefully. I want you two," pointing to John and Kelly, "to take that car to the building you guys are working from. Don't park in the front any more; we have to be more discreet. Rick, Eric and I will go talk to Jewels, face to face, you know, make him an offer he can't refuse." Tony laughed as he finished the last part of his instructions with that statement.

Shortly after, John and Kelly looked from Angie's window and saw Rick's car pull up, as Jewels' boys reached for their guns. Getting out of the car, Tony said, "Hey Ice, where is Jewels?"

Realizing who he was, Ice extended his hand to meet Tony's. The rest of the fellows relaxed.

Ice told Tony, "Hold up, I'll go get him for you."

Disappearing into a darkened hallway, he left them standing there waiting. When he returned, he announced that Jewels would be right down. Minutes later, he came from around the corner to Tony's left, catching him off guard.

"What's up?" Jewels asked, as he approached with his two henchmen, Smoke and Slim.

Tony, who turned to greet him, said, "Jewels, let's me and you talk, one on one, man to man."

They separated themselves from the crowd and headed across the street. Tony spoke first.

"Yo, somebody killed my man Darryl and I have every intention of finding out who. I just hope it wasn't you!"

"Is that the reason you wanted to talk to me?" asked Jewels, kind of disturbed.

"Partially; I'm going to find his killer eventually, but right now, I'm putting a new team out here. If you don't like it, tell me now!"

"Tony, look, we both have come a long way; there's enough dough out here for the both of us. So, if that's how you want it, I'm no obstacle."

They shook hands and then walked back across the street and back into the crowd.

"Fellows, let's get out of here," commanded Tony.

Jewels, Slim and their squad walked up into the building. John and Kelly both backed away from the window, wondering what had been said.

Meanwhile, up in an empty apartment that Jewels often worked from, he told his team what the deal was. He directed them to give Tony a little room to make a little money. He then dismissed everyone except Smoke and Slim. As everyone exited, the trio headed to an apartment up another flight of stairs. This one was well furnished and livable. They entered, lounged and laid back.

"Tony's fishing for information on Darryl's murder, so let's give him something to fry," Jewels stated as he broke his silence.

"You mean lead him in another direction?" asked Slim, somewhat unsure.

"That's exactly what I mean!" answered Jewels.

He picked up the phone and called his man, telling him of his conversation with Tony. In closing, Jewels told him to make it rough on them and that he'd know who he had working by morning. He also told him, he had to find a crash dummy, to leak out false information.

As they conversed, John was on the phone also, returning a page from Tony.

"Everything's cool, just watch your back. I don't trust that character," Tony stated.

Rick barged in eager to get to work. John, near to the stash, got enough to get things started. He gave it to Rick, who raced out the door, to give it to his workers.

John walked over to the window and looked out once again. This time he saw a little kid, the one from the community center. He watched him for a few minutes as Ice, Jewel's boy, pushed him away. Shortly after, he stared as Alvin walked up the street. John rushed out the door, as Angie and Kelly raced to the window to see what was going on. They looked left and saw Rick standing two buildings down, watching his workers. Looking right, they noticed that John had stopped a kid. Angie thought perhaps it was a nephew or somebody. Down on the street, John asked Alvin what was going on. Alvin, in a saddened tone replied, "Nothing. You won't understand."

"Try me," said John.

Alvin spoke as they drifted farther away from everything on the strip.

"Yo, man, my mom gets high and I try to help her, but she be beating on me and taking my cash. It would be cool, if she brought food and stuff. But all she does is buy that shit! My little sister be hungry all the time, that's why I hustle, man. Darryl used to give me money for doing little stuff, like going to the store. He used to take me places. He was like a big brother. Now he's dead!" he exclaimed on a depressed note.

"How old are you, if you don't mind me asking?" John inquired.

"I'm thirteen."

"I tell you what, why don't you hang out with me," suggested John.

"Nah, no thanks, I gotta get cash!"

"Don't worry about dat, I'll take care of dat," John answered.

Taking Alvin back to the apartment with him, John led the way as Alvin looked across the street at Ice and his boys. Entering the building, they had to step aside as Rick rushed down the stairs.

"Hey!" He smiled as he ran past them and out the door.

"Who was that?" Alvin asked.

"My brother," stated John, as they walked up the stairs and into the apartment.

"Hey everybody, this is Alvin. Alvin, this is Angie and Kelly."

"What's up?" Alvin mumbled.

"Have a seat," Angie offered as she flipped through the channels on the television, hoping to find something more suitable for a kid. Alvin frowned in disgust as she smiled and walked away.

Kelly pulled John into the kitchen.

"Hey, we don't need no kids in our business! Get rid of him!" Kelly stated angrily.

"No! He knows about the game already and he might know who murdered Darryl!" replied John, who then continued. "All he needs and wants is a big brother. I'll take full responsibility for his actions."

"You think little man knows somethin' about the murders?" asked Kelly, who had calmed down.

"I think so, he ran with him. I'm not sure, though. I don't want to pressure him, because if he does, he can help clear me and at the same time find Darryl's killers."

Rick burst in.

"They're raiding, the cops are raiding!" He quickly shut the door behind him, then raced to the window. Looking down at the police, Rick watched as they rounded up five others, including one of the guys that worked with him.

Shortly after, they let everyone go.

"Good, he didn't have anything on him," stated a relieved Rick.

Little Alvin hearing this, asked, "You guys hustle?"

At that moment, John looked over at him, noticing the confusion on his face.

"Hey, Alvin, how's about you and I taking a walk?" asked John, as he grabbed his coat.

Four blocks and about ten minutes later, John and Alvin began to talk.

"Look, I can't begin to explain to you the whole situation," started John.

"I don't understand. All the kids I know think the world of you. I'd never figure you to be a hustler or a hood," stated Alvin.

"I'm not."

"So what's going down? You work for the police or somethin'?"

"No, that's not it, either," answered John. "Come on, let's go shoot a game of basketball. The lights are on and my house ain't far from here," John added smiling.

"No! I don't go in there no more, not since Darryl was killed."

Coming upon a Chinese restaurant, the two of them stopped in and ordered. Remembering to get enough for everyone, John paid for it, then they headed back. When they finally arrived back at the apartment, all the product was gone and Rick and Kelly were counting the money over a table in the living room.

Alvin stared at them, then he and John went into the kitchen and placed the food on the counter.

"You'll musta read our minds, 'cause we were just talking 'bout going to get somethin' to eat," Kelly stated with a smirk.

"Here's your cut," Rick announced, as he passed John a knot of money.

Angie pulled some plates from the cabinet, placing them in front of each of them, as they sat at the table. She divided the food among them. As they all ate and laughed about this and that John couldn't help but notice that Alvin had a smile on his face. He thought to himself, all this kid needs is a family and some guidance. A little love and he'll be all right. Then he shouted, "Save some food and put it aside, so Alvin can take it home to his sister!"

About one o'clock, a half-hour after everyone had eaten, John announced that he was tired and had to go to work the next morning.

"Let's go!" he said as he turned to see Alvin asleep on the couch.

Angie, noticing also, asked John if he wanted her to wake him.

He paused and then said, "Yes, his mother might miss him, but I doubt it."

She shook him a few times, till he finally woke up.

"Come on, Alvin!" shouted John, hoping his voice would startle him.

"Don't forget the food!" John added, as Alvin dragged into the kitchen to grab it from the table.

After they exited the apartment, John and Alvin went out the back way, as Kelly and Rick made their way to the front.

As Rick and Kelly came out the entrance, Jewels watched from a window across the street.

"So that's his team?" he stated under his breath. The shade closed, as he let it go and walked away from the window.

Out back, John and Alvin pulled off and headed down Bergen Street.

"Now where do you live?"

"Off of Madison, on Seventeenth Street," Alvin answered.

John reached Madison and then drove up till he hit Seventeenth Street.

"Make a left. It's the brick building right there." Alvin pointed it out as John made the turn.

Driving up in front of the building, John brought the car to a halt. He reached into his pocket and pulled out forty dollars and gave it to Alvin.

"Make sure you give your sister some of that food," he added.

Alvin thanked him and then headed into the building. John sat watching and waiting, till he knew Alvin was in safely.

Moments later, Alvin waved from a window and John pulled off.

The next morning, November eighteenth, John had his work cut out for him. He worked non-stop as he watched the clock. Tammy came to mind, so he decided to give her a call.

"Hey baby, I miss you. Why don't you leave early and I'll come get you."

"Okay, but how are you going to do that? You don't have a car!"

"Don't start asking questions. I'll be there around three forty-five."

They both hung up.

At three-forty, he pulled up in front of the tall building downtown where she worked. She was a claims adjuster at one of Newark's largest insurance providers. As she walked from within the narrow hallway that separated the two sets of doors, she smiled as she headed to the car.

Climbing in, she expressed how nice the car was and also that he'd better be careful. She kissed him and he asked her, "How was your day?"

"You know how that game can be," she stated.

"I know, trust me, I know," he answered, as he pulled from the curb.

"Where are you going?" she went on to ask.

"It's a surprise!"

Later on at the hotel, sitting in a Jacuzzi, Tammy spoke: "Now this is the John that I remember! You took me out to dinner, a movie and now I have you all to myself. No phones ringing, nothin!"

His pager started beeping, but he smiled and ignored it. The two of them climbed from the Jacuzzi, dried off, then laid down on the bed. He applied lotion and massaged her body. Then she did the same. As she massaged his back, she could feel the tension in his muscles. As he moaned from the pleasure he felt, she went on. Afterwards, he grabbed her and together they let their passions run wild.

At two o'clock, when John finally woke up, he found Tammy with her head resting on his chest. He kissed her on the forehead, then laid back, thinking, I wish we could just run off together. He drifted back to sleep. The next time he opened his eyes, it was four A.M. He woke Tammy up, telling her it was time to go. She sat up in the bed and held her arms out for an embrace. John walked over and held her tightly.

She whispered in his ear, "Thank you."

John smiled as he stated, "Let's get out of here, before we end up back in the bed."

"At least take a shower with me!" she added. So he did, then they got dressed and left.

Later that Sunday, John called everyone to let them know he was all right, after which, he went to the nearest florist to get some flowers for Tammy, leaving them by her door, with a note.

When meeting with Rick and Kelly at the poolroom, that evening, he noticed that they had Alvin with them.

"Hey, what's up? What happened to you yesterday?" Kelly asked with a grin.

"I had to satisfy the wife. She felt that I was neglecting her," stated John.

"Who you? Not you!" added Rick as he continued. "Man, you're the most caring guy I know."

"We had a great day yesterday. We made seven grand," intervened Kelly. Waving some keys in the air, Kelly went on to say that Angie gave them to him, for the apartment.

"So imagine what we can do today! Little Alvin cleaned house. He really knows the streets."

Kelly patted Alvin on the back, but John interrupted.

"Hold up, you guys had Alvin hustling?"

"It's not like he's new to it!" responded Rick.

"That's not the point; he's just a kid!" added John, as they all headed out the door and to their cars.

Alvin said, "I'm not a kid, I know more about the strip than all of you!"

John looked at Alvin, then at Kelly and Rick, as he shook his head and said, "He should be in school or something!"

"What's with you and this goody-two-shoes attitude? Either you give it your all . . . or nothin!" demanded Kelly.

"I'm in this for one reason and one reason only! That's to find Darryl's killer! That way, I can find out who's framing me!" shouted John.

Everyone got quiet on that note, then climbed into their cars. Alvin jumped in with John and they drove off. En route to the strip, Alvin spoke out.

"You're the one they're blaming for Darryl's murder? That's deep!"

"Why is that?" asked John.

"Jewels talked about Darryl all the time. How he was starting to get in the way. He even talked about running him off the block, but Dee was nobody's punk! Nice; sorta like you. He had all the ladies and dat bothered Jewel."

John said, "You've pretty much worked with both sides, huh!"

At Angie's, they set up shop, but she was nowhere to be found. Everything was running smoothly, when all of a sudden there was a lot of yelling and sirens. John and Kelly both rushed to the window to check things out. They noticed that the officers had Rick and three others face down on the ground, cuffed, while they searched the area. Two narcotics detectives came from within one of the buildings. At the same precise moment, Alvin burst through the door breathing heavily.

"Lock it!," shouted Kelly.

"What happened?" asked John.

"Police came from everywhere! Rick gave me the money and the drugs that he had just took downstairs. I ran through 207 (the building next to the one Angie lived in) and out the back, then into this one! Dat's why Peters and Brown came from dis one!"

Kelly yelled, "Come here! Detective Peters just hit Rick!"

They all rushed to look, but were too late, as the unmarked car and the patrol cars pulled off. Rick stood against a wall outside for a few minutes, before walking through 207. Shortly after, he could be heard knocking at the door.

"That's probably Rick, but check the peephole first!" cautioned Alvin, still somewhat shaken.

Kelly looked through the peephole and saw two people, Rick and Angie. He quickly snatched the door open and let them in.

"Yo, Rick, what happened out there?" asked John.

"Man, Five-O came from everywhere! Lucky for me, Alvin saw them first. He yelled to me, I gave him the shit and he jetted! That's the reason they slammed me on the ground! The short cop, Peters, told me he didn't want to see me out there again and then attempted to beat my ass, but his partner stopped him. I also noticed they didn't mess with nobody but us and our customers.

Angie cut in. "I see you guys are having fun today."

"Where are you coming from?" asked Kelly, after her statement.

"Excuse me; I don't believe I owe you an explanation! You're not my man! But if you must know, I was at my girlfriend's place, downstairs."

During the course of this conversation, John stood at the window.

After about an hour, Kelly went out to finish what Rick had started. John, who turned from the window, looked for Rick, but only found Alvin and Angie watching television. He asked Alvin to take a ride with him, then told him, "I want to meet your little sister, if that's all right with you."

Arriving at Alvin's home about ten-thirty P.M., they entered through an unlocked door on the first floor. Proceeding on, they smelled a foul odor in the air. Walking through to the back of this spacious dump, Alvin called out to his mother and sister.

"Ma. Theresa!" he shouted.

A pretty little girl came running out of one of the rooms around a pile of clothes and an old torn-apart television to hug Alvin.

"Ma, its Alvin! It's Alvin and a friend," she shouted, filled with excitement.

His mother shouted back from within the room.

"Boy, what did I tell you? Don't be bringing none'a ya sorry behind friends to my house!"

John turned to head back in the direction from which he came, but Alvin grabbed his arm.

"Don't worry about her, she won't get up. All she does is lay in dat bed and yell, unless she needs something or feels like beating on one of us."

As Alvin spoke, his sister's smile lit up the room. Her soiled dress and sneakers screamed to be washed. John's stomach started to turn as he looked around, calling their mother a slob to himself. Marching back through the filth, they stepped over clothes, mattresses, along with a lot of other things. Once they reached the front door, a sign of relief appeared on John's face. Waving good-bye to Alvin's sister, John placed his arm around Alvin, as the two of them headed back to the car.

That night, after they arrived back at Angie's, they saw Jewels outside arguing with Silk. Silk came around periodically for certain reasons: to check on his boys and to make sure nothing went wrong. As they argued, Dre and two others pulled out their guns.

"Dre said, "Look man, y'all don't want it, so stop threatening our customers. 'Cause the next time we come, we're airing y'all out (shooting them up)!""

Jewels, Ice and a few others stood in fear, caught totally off guard and unarmed. However, as this was happening, Smoke and Slim crept up through a darkened hallway, with their sub machine guns in hand. But just as they stepped out into the light, Silk and his boys were pulling off. Ready to spray the vehicle up, Jewels signaled for them not to. So they just watched them drive off in a green Chevy truck.

While all of this was taking place, Rick and Kelly had finished up and were heading upstairs together. They quickly split up the money and everyone went their separate way.

A few days later, November twentieth, John did a day's work and was ready to leave as his father came in. He headed out, as Rick stayed around to help out for a few more hours.

Shortly after, John reached home and started checking his answering service. He noticed he had ten messages, so he hit the play button to listen.

(BEEP) "John, it's Tammy. Bye."

(BEEP) "John, Anthony Sharpe again, get in touch."

(BEEP) "Tony! Just checking with you."

As the messages continued, he went into the kitchen to fix himself something to eat. Suddenly, he heard an unfamiliar voice clearly state, "Watch yourself! Don't slip!" A burst of laughter followed.

John replayed it, but still couldn't identify the voice, so he decided to turn it off and flip on the television. Then he picked up the phone to call Tammy, his mother and his lawyer. Keeping his calls short, he eventually got around to his lawyer, who reminded him of his court date. He also told him that he needed five thousand by the time of the arraignment and his balance would be fifteen thousand. He explained to John that his father supplied the retainer, which was five, and said he would cover the entire bill.

John, hearing this, quickly objected. "No! I'll take care of it!"

"Are you sure?" asked Mr. Sharpe.

"Yes!" John replied, as they traded good-byes and hung up.

John dozed off as the television played program after program.

On November twenty-third, Thanksgiving, everyone was invited out by Tony. Most were late, due to other family get-togethers. But when they finally arrived and were seated in an elegant restaurant, Tony ordered champagne and poured everyone a glass personally. He held his glass high, proposing a toast to big money and good living, and most of all, he hoped that they'd all make it to the same table the next year. Tony, Rochelle, Raymond and his family, John, Tammy, Rick, Kelly, Alvin, Angie and Wallace, all ate and laughed, enjoying themselves on this day of thanks.

Friday, the very next day, John had to appear in court for his arraignment. As he sat outside the courtroom waiting for the proceeding to start, his lawyer walked up, sharply dressed as usual.

"Hello, Johnathan, I was expecting to see you sooner!"

"I have your money," John quickly stated, assuming that's what he was referring to. "I'll give it to you later," John went on to add.

As the two of them walked into the courtroom, they sat down as others filed in behind them. The court clerk read off a list of names to be arraigned, before the judge came out. There had to be about thirty others scheduled.

At about nine-thirty A.M., the judge entered the courtroom. The bailiff instructed everyone to rise, then to be seated. After everyone sat, the clerk called the first name.

"State vs. Tyrone Allen." A tall slender man approached the front.

By ten-thirty, they had finally called John's case.

"State vs. Johnathan Jackson."

His lawyer tapped him, and together they rose and approached the bench.

At a table directly in front of the judge, they stood patiently. There was a microphone at both ends, one for them and the other for the prosecutor. As the prosecutor spoke, John looked him up and down. This cheap suit, slinky, bald, glasses-wearing snake is going to try put me away, he thought.

The prosecutor spoke. "Hello, Your Honor, I'm Mr. Galileio, chief prosecutor for the State."

Mr. Sharpe, jumping right up as Mr. Galileio finished, said, "I'm Mr. Sharpe, from the law firm of Sharpe, Simpson and Smith. I'm representing Johnathan Jackson."

The judge asked, "How does your client plead?"

"Not guilty, Your Honor." stated Mr. Sharpe.

The judge gave John a trial date for July 30, 1990.

"Thank you for your time and patience," Mr. Sharpe added as he smiled and walked from the table.

John drifted into thought as he walked. I've got my hands full and we have nothing. Nothing that can clear me.

Mr. Sharpe brought him back to earth as he expressed to him that they desperately needed to find something that would stand up in court.

"You've given me character witnesses and my investigator is gathering all the reports I need. I even have the statements of all the State's witnesses. But still, we don't have anywhere near what we need to clear you!"

"I'll have something by the time of the trial, I promise you. I'm not going to jail for a crime I didn't commit!" replied John. Their discussion ended as they stepped onto the elevator.

Descending to the lobby area, they exited the elevator and headed their separate ways.

By twelve-fifteen in the afternoon, John had arrived home, early for him. He headed back out after changing into something more comfortable and throwing on a heavier coat. The weather had suddenly become extremely cold. Fighting the winds, he jumped in his car, and within minutes, he had arrived at his father's business.

Upon entering, Rick asked, "What happened?"

"Nothing; my trial date was set for July 30," John stated as he walked behind the counter.

"Dad didn't come in yet?" he added.

"No, but he called," answered Rick.

Grabbing a cake and something to drink, John sat down and waited for their father to arrive. Customers walked in and out. Rick worked and attended them by himself, till two o'clock, when an employee named Ray-Ray finally showed up to give him a hand. He punched in and went right to work. At three P.M., their father came through the door, dragging and carrying supplies. Rushing over to assist him, John and Ray-Ray took the packages, as Mr. Jackson stopped to take a breather.

"Woo, these old legs aren't what they use ta be!" he stated, as he scratched his balding head and was out of breath.

Ray started putting the goods on the shelves, while John and his father sat behind the counter talking.

"So son, how's things going?"

"Fine Pop.

"Do you need any extra money? I know you decided to pay your lawyer yourself. He called and told me. Now, how can you afford to do that? I hope your not thinking of doing nothing stupid."

"Don't worry, I can handle it."

"Don't go do nothing stupid. I'm here if you need me," finished Mr. Jackson. He stood up and headed to the back to his office. John rose seconds after him and headed out the door, but not before saying good-bye to Rick and Ray-Ray.

Driving aimlessly, John smiled because he hadn't done this in years. He passed through the Avenue, through downtown, did a little shopping, etc. After which, he went to surprise Tammy at work. By the time he had arrived, she had left, so he drove out to Market Street to catch her at the bus stop. Noticing her right away, he stopped and yelled out, "Hey, sexy, you look cold, need a ride?" Smiling now, he laughed, then called her name and she turned around.

Seeing who it was, she raced over to the car. Quickly jumping in, she gave him a big wet kiss.

"Damn, I should pick you up everyday!" he stated as she rested her head on his shoulder, smiling.

"Why are you so happy today?" He asked, smiling to himself now.

"Because I miss you! I was thinking about you just as you pulled up."

John continued to smile as he came to a red light, then added, "You always remind me of what's important, every time I see you or hold you."

Driving, he quickly pulled over by a small hidden store, jumped out of the car and ran in. Tammy looked up at the sign, then read it out loud.

"J&J Electronics, specializing in pagers, cellular phones, jewelry, etc. . . ."

Coming out of the store, John had a cellular phone in his hand.

As soon as he climbed in the car she asked, "Aren't we starting to live a little large?"

"No, I'm just tired of jumping in and out of the car every time I need to use a phone. There's time, like when I'm on the highway, that there's no phone in sight and I need to return a page."

"But, what about those cellular bills? I heard they can be expensive."

"This one has no bill! It's on illegally. I just return it when it's turned off, and for seventy dollars they'll reconnect me."

"You're getting in deeper and deeper. I sure hope you can get out when the time comes, because I'm not going to let you ruin your life and especially not mine. Now take me home, so I can show you what I have planned for tonight."

"Tonight! Not tonight! I have a lot to do; I have to take care of a few things. But if I can, I'll drop by for a minute, okay?

"Don't worry about it, I'll save it for another time," She stated, pouting.

After John pulled up in front of her apartment, she exited slamming the door and without saying good-bye. Then she stopped at the stairs as he sat in the car watching. Turning to look back at him, she said, "Be careful, I love you."

He pulled off, feeling somewhat bad, but knew he had business to take care of.

After he had taken his lawyer a portion of his fee, he stopped by the community center to say hello to the kids and the counselors. But as he did, Brian, the head of the volunteer program asked if he could speak with him for a moment. Now Brian was a light-skinned, skinny, baldheaded guy who always wore specs.

The two men walked into a little room off from the gym area.

"Close the door behind you," stated Brian.

After doing so, John asked, "What's up?"

"Well, John, as much as I hate to do this, I have to let you go as a community volunteer."

"Why?" John asked with a confused look on his face, but knew the reason.

"Well, besides the trouble you're already in, there's rumors to the effect that you're selling drugs in the community also. So, we all think it's best that you leave the program. I'm sorry, John." Brian dragged on in a sad tone, then said, "I personally believe that you're innocent, but this isn't solely my decision. I have no control over this," he added, seeing the hurt in John's face.

The room got quiet as John held his head up and his face seemed to harden and become expressionless. He exited the room as the door shut behind him, leaving Brian standing behind his desk, saddened by the fact that he had to be the bearer of bad news.

Brian exhaled and then marched out also. Crossing back through the gym, John ran into Mark and a few other kids who were regulars there.

"Mr. Jackson, Mr. Jackson. Come play a game of basketball with us!" they yelled.

Not really in the mood, but not wanting to disappoint the kids, he told them okay. He played game after game, and the laughter of the kids reminded him why he enjoyed the center so much. It was his outlet, a place where he could be around kids and touch their lives. To him, it made him feel as if he was making a difference. After their last game, when everyone seemed exhausted, John asked them to sit in a circle. In the midst of doing so, one of the kids asked a question.

"Mr. Jackson, my mom says you're a bad person, a loser. Are you?"

Mark told him to shut up.

John paused, looked around briefly, noticed Brian at one end of the gym, then turned his attention back to the kids. "No I'm not a bad person, or a loser, but listen carefully. Sometimes life throws us a curve ball and you put into your swing your all. But it rips past you." He acts it out, swinging his hands as if he was holding a bat. "Before you know it, the next thing you're doing is heading back to the dugout, sad, with your head in your hands. Then the same guys that commended you for yesterday's win, now look at you as if you're a disgrace. No one wants to pat you on the back anymore, maybe a few, but not many, especially when you're losing. Everyone wants to be supportive of the winners, the heroes, the quote, unquote, shining examples, which is easy. But what we must learn, is anyone can be a good winner. Anyone can sit in the crowd hissing and booing others, saying they're no good. But the true winners are the ones that can lose and take the ridicule and smile, absorb the pain and still be able to go on and believe in themselves. When everyone else has doubts, they never let it stop them, because part of being a winner, is knowing at some point or another, losing is part of the game and part of life."

Mark spoke out.

"That's deep, but what does that have to do with you?"

"You see, in the community and more so in their eyes, I was good, a winner, someone to admire. I changed my life for the better. I became a volunteer working with you guys. Cut and dry, to them I was a success, a shining example, someone who made a change from bad to good, so they loved me. But now due to rumors, lies and other circumstances, I'm a loser in their eyes. So instead of being supportive or at least understanding, they step away. They no longer stand in my corner or cheer me on. But what counts is that I know, in my heart, I'm still a winner. Still the same person they all once loved, but you see as a loser, I can no longer fill the seats. All the fans understand is the score and what's printed. Not remembering the qualities that made the winners, but clinging to all that convicts them as losers. Understand?"

The kids all smiled as they rose from the floor, then one by one, hugged John. They made his day.

As they walked away a few of them turned to say, "You're still a winner in our eyes!"

John smiled, as he began to walk toward the exit and some of their parents rushed in out of the cold. The kids started straightening up the place as Brian yelled out.

John smiled to himself as he mumbled, "Kids."

Then Mark shouted, "Tie the score, so we can beat them in extra innings!"

Hearing this John waved and then looked at his watch, which read eight-thirty.

Stepping outside, he noted it was snowing. So he buttoned up his coat and headed to his car. He smiled again, thinking of the kids. There's some hope for the future after all.

As he got closer to his car, his expression quickly changed, noticing that the side window was broken and all the glass was on the seat. He shouted as the snow drifted downward. "Damn!" But as his eyes roamed, he noticed that the only thing missing was his radio. "Damn, I forgot to take the damn radio out!"

Mad at himself now, because normally he took it and placed it in the trunk of the car, he slammed his fist into the side of it. Totally disgusted, he called Tony on his cellular phone and began to tell him what happened. Deciding to put the car up until morning, when he could fix it, he drove off to Tony's house.

Only having seen his house once or twice, he imagined it like a scene from the movie "Scarface." Upon driving up, Tony was standing on the porch sipping from a cocktail glass. John walked up the walkway toward him as he began to burst with laughter.

Tickled he stated, "You live in the stolen car capital of the world. I can't believe you left the radio in the car." Still giggling between sips, Tony put his arm around John as he reached the top step.

"Yo, let's go inside, out of this weather," stated Tony.

Entering through the door, Johns eyes widened.

"Take off your shoes and coat and get comfortable," demanded Tony.

Noticing that the carpet was off-white, John lightly uttered, "Damn!"

Wandering into the living room in amazement, John seemed overwhelmed.

"Have a seat," Tony offered.

John sat on an off-white leather chaise lounge, which was placed in front of smoked-glass table on an off-white marble stand. Sitting, he stared in awe at the matching marble fireplace and the eye-catching decor that surrounded him.

Tony handed him a drink that he had brought from the bar that sat in the background.

"Here try this."

Tony grabbed the remote and turned on the huge sixty-inch screen, then dropped down on a nearby couch.

"Now John, I've been wanting to talk to you anyway. This little mishap gives me the chance to do so one-on-one. Now I know how business is, but you always seem to be distant, gone, somewhere else."

Looking at the huge television, John took a small sip from his glass, then spoke.

"I'm basically doing this to clear myself. I have no desire for this lifestyle or the fast money. I've tried it this way and made good money, not as good as you though," John stated, glancing around.

"I was getting' it, till I caught my first drug charge and sat in the holding pen. Thirteen days was enough to make me realize what was most important to me. My freedom! Besides, it hurt me to see so many of my, I mean, our people fucked up, on drugs, crime and it's political wave," John preached.

Tony patiently awaited his last words, then clapped loudly. "Bravo, I like you. You're a smart brother, but wise the hell up. The man doesn't care who he steps on to get his, so why should you?" Tony remarked.

Noticing that Tony was a little tipsy, John smiled.

Suddenly a door could be heard opening, then closing. The sound of shoes patting against the floor began to grow near. A woman emerged from the kitchen area, a vision of beauty. As she held her bags in her hands, she leaned over the couch to kiss Tony.

"Hello, honey," she said as Tony introduced her to John.

"John, this is my wife, Rochelle. Rochelle, baby, this is my man John."

They traded hellos and then as she walked away and up the stairs so did John's eyes and imagination. Her bowed legs, her hazel eyes, her everything had him lusting.

Tony cleared his throat to get John's attention back and then spoke.

"She's beautiful, isn't she?"

Damn near spilling his drink, John stutteringly responded.

"Very . . . much . . . so."

Now feeling somewhat uncomfortable, John looked at his watch.

"Damn, it's eleven-thirty. I've got to check on the boys, They paged me a number of times."

"A number of times," repeated Tony, tickled with laughter.

John began to look as if what Tony was doing and saying was getting the best of him. Tony was so drunk, he really didn't care, he just laughed harder.

Tony stopped laughing long enough to say, "I like you; don't be so touchy, though." He then burst into another loud cry of laughter.

John, annoyed now, asked him if he could use his phone. Tony answered yes as he tried to stop laughing as tears poured from his eyes. John called a cab and within twenty minutes he had left Tony's house.

Arriving at his place a little after twelve, John prepped for bed. But before he did, he called Angie to see how things were going.

Kelly picked up, and told John how Jewels had flipped out about two hours ago, due to the fact that one of his boys had been picked up in an earlier raid. He went on to say that the guy they caught had two thousand dollars of drugs on him and that Jewels stated that no one could make a dime, except his boys, or else!

"So where is Rick?" asked John, concerned.

"Outside gettin' money! Where else? Oh, don't worry, he's strapped!" replied Kelly, sensing John's concern.

"Plus, me and Alvin are going downstairs to help him finish up," he added.

"No! Tell Alvin I said for him to stay put. Okay?"

"Okay, it's all right. Get some rest," Kelly told John, reassuring him.

"All right, I'll see you guys tomorrow," stated John as he calmed down.

After hanging up with Kelly, something just didn't set right with John. Rushing, he put his clothes back on, then raced out the door. After running down the stairs, he realized he didn't have a car. So he ran back into his apartment, grabbed the phone and started calling for a cab. The number was busy, each time he dialed. Busy.

He called back to Angie's with the gut feeling that something was wrong. He impatiently paced back and forth.

Angie answered and she yelled hysterically, "Rick, Kelly and one of Jewels' boys got shot! The ambulance and the police are outside."

Slowly moving the phone from his ear, John screamed, "Not my brother!"

Just as he cried out, Angie called to him through the receiver. "John."

He calmed down just a little as he put the phone back to his ear, hoping for the best. She continued by relaying what she could see from her window. "From what I can see from here, Rick's alive."

But after a long pause, she stated that they covered Kelly with a sheet after several attempts to revive him. Now in a saddened voice she went on to add, "Jewels' boy is laying against a wall; he's alive, too."

John took a deep breath and then mumbled, "Thank God Rick's alive." He also prayed for Kelly, but knew by her description that he was dead. Not wanting to believe it, John stated, "I just spoke to him, not twenty minutes ago."

Before Angie could respond, he dropped the phone and ran out of his apartment. Racing down the stairs, he looked for a young car thief named "Wheels", hoping if he found him, that he was driving or had a car nearby. Not seeing him anywhere, John rushed back up the stairs and into his apartment, where he continuously called different cab services, until he got through.

"Hello, can I get a cab to 534 South Fifteenth Street? Please hurry!"

Ten minutes later a green cab came down the street.

When it stopped, John jumped in.

Two-ten Clinton Ave. There's ten dollars extra in it, if you hurry!"

The cab driver put the pedal to the floor as he hurried on. Growing closer to John's destination, flashing lights and sirens could be seen everywhere. Seeing that they could not get any closer, he paid the driver as he expressed his thanks. Jumping out a few blocks from the scene, John rushed down the remainder of the way. As he did, he noticed that the police had everything sealed off with the yellow tape. So as he came to a halt and squeezed through the onlookers,

He noticed a white sheet, spotted with blood, and a body beneath it. Blood covered the sidewalk, and the police told everyone to back up. Tears raced down John's face as he looked around for his brother.

Someone tapped him. It was Alvin, who then told him, "They took Rick to the hospital. He's hurt bad. He got shot in the shoulder and twice in the stomach. But he seemed all right, he'll live."

They both focused on the body beneath the sheet, Kelly's body. He just lay there, still, never to move again.

As the crime lab and the coroner finished up, John put his arm around Alvin. They walked away with their heads toward the ground, glassy-eyed and furious.

Upstairs in Angie's apartment, John, Alvin and Angie sat in silence. Angie's eyes were bloodshot from crying.

John sat, realizing this was exactly what he thought it would amount to. Hesitantly, he called a half-asleep and drunk Tony. As John explained to him what had happened, a loud crash could be heard as the phone struck the floor. Screams of anger followed as the line went dead. Before they knew it, Tony was impatiently knocking at Angie's door. She rose from where she was sitting. As she looked through the peephole, seeing who it was, she let him in.

He entered with tears in his eyes and then stated, "Whoever did dis, gotta pay! Kelly was like a brother to me."

As this was being said, John closed his eyes as he reminded himself why he doing this, so he wouldn't get it confused. He thought to himself, I've got to find Darryl's killer and save my behind before it gets worst. The sooner I do that, the sooner I get out.

Little Alvin looked on as he fought back the tears.

John leaned over to comfort Angie, followed by Alvin as he pulled him from the couch. John put his arm around him, calling to Tony as he said, "Let's go to the emergency room to check on my brother."

Tony, totally devastated, rose to his feet with a look in his eyes that could kill an army. John seeing this said nothing, because he knew there was nothing that could comfort him through this time.

As they headed out the door, Angie yelled, "I'm coming too!" Rushing out behind them, she locked the door and caught up with them on the staircase. As the four of them exited the building, they noticed that there was a patrol car directly in front of the doorway. Walking past, they all climbed into Tony's van and drove away.

In the waiting area of the emergency room, they all awaited news about the outcome of Rick's surgery. Not knowing for sure whether or not he was going to make it, they all sat in silence, while their surroundings grew louder.

Hours passed as everyone fell asleep except John. He sat up thinking about all that Tammy had said to him, about getting in too deep. As time passed, he sat lost with his head in his hands, twittering his fingers, as he recounted his life.

A doctor entered the area where they all sat and asked for the Jackson family. They all rose to their feet with the exception of Alvin, who was fast asleep. The doctor said, "I'm happy to inform you that Ricky

Jackson is going to be fine, He's resting as we speak. We retrieved all the bullets and closed all the wounds. The best thing for him now is to rest." The doctors asked John for a little more information, besides what was furnished through his wallet and identification.

John home now, showered, sat down and before he knew it, it was time to go to work. So before he got too comfortable and sleepy, he stood back up and marched out the door. Dragging himself down the stairs, he tried to figure out a way to break the bad news to his parents.

At work, John began to pull the gates up and head into the store. His father pulled up right behind him and followed. He started hysterically asking questions, with a confused look on his face.

"What happened last night?"

John, exhausted and looking for a way to put it, just blurted it out.

"Rick was shot last night."

"Where?" His father asked, concerned.

Not wanting to tell him, John told him anyway.

"He got shot on the strip."

"The strip? his father angrily shouted. "What the hell was he doing on the strip? That shit again! You boys just don't learn, do you? Maybe the both of you will learn when you've got bullets in your skulls! Then it'll be too late."

He threw up his hands in disgust as he walked out the door. Just as he did, he turned around and asked, "What hospital is he in?"

John told him as he continued out the door to his car.

John figured he'd better call Maria and tell her, too, if she hadn't already heard.

On the phone, he told her and she acted as if she was expecting his call. She sat silently on the phone, then asked which hospital he was in and ended the conversation right afterwards.

After work, John talked with his father, who did everything but ignore him. So, on that note he left and headed to the hospital to see how his brother was doing.

When he finally arrived home, he sat staring at the walls thinking of his brother, Kelly, and all that his father had said to him.

"Kelly, damn, why?" he mumbled as he thought. He sat in silence for a while and didn't break it until he decided to call Tammy. Just as he started to tell her what had happened, she responded exactly as he thought she would. John, not being in the greatest of moods, decided to tell her he'd talk to her later.

After he hung up, he heard a loud knock at the door. When he opened it, he saw Tony, Eric and a new guy, whom they introduced as Wallace. John opened the door wide to allow them to come in. As the trio got comfortable, Tony began to speak.

"Yo, your car is outside. I had the window fixed. Now about what happened, I'm sending Eric, who you know and my boy Wallace, from across town, to work with you." (Now Wallace, who stood six-foot two, with curls and a fade, a neatly shaped beard was a thuggish pretty boy.) "I also brought some headsets, one for each of you. I want Alvin on the rooftop, strictly as a lookout."

"No, Tony, keep him out of this!" stated John.

"Look, yo, he knows these streets, plus being a lookout puts him in no real danger. He's small and he'll be on the rooftop, in a vacant apartment or in the window with a scanner. He'll be all right," Tony added as he drove his point home, then went on again.

"I want you (meaning John) and Eric to work the streets. You can control the money; let Eric hold the burners (guns). Wallace will bring you whatever's needed, by communication through the headsets. All communications will be handled through these headsets, understood? We can't afford to lose anyone else!" Tony finished, as he held one of the headsets in the air as an example.

Everyone agreed completely, then vacated John's apartment and headed out to their cars.

Tony shouted out to them, as they piled into the Honda, while he opened the door to the van.

"Yo, everything's in the car, drive carefully."

After they all were in, they pulled off right behind Tony.

On the strip, they set up for anything and everything. Jewels and his boys carried out their business as usual. That's when something occurred to John. What was Jugs (Jimmy) doing on this side of the street?

He never comes over here. He normally sticks right up under Jewels and never converses with anyone outside of their clan. Puzzled now, he grabbed the drugs, as he and Eric both walked out the door, John, with his baseball cap pulled tightly over his face, for fear that someone might notice him.

Downstairs, they distributed the drugs among their workers, after which John put the remainder in Angie's mailbox in 210. He then hurried back to 207, where everyone sat in the hallway. Slipping on their headsets, Eric hid his gun behind the stairs. The night drifted away, as they all watched things to make sure they ran smoothly.

Suddenly, a voice came through the headsets. It was Alvin.

"Back up, the police are coming down the avenue. I think they're closing off shit!"

Hearing this, John and Eric stepped into 207, then into a vacant apartment. Just as they did and peeked from a window, they noticed that the police came into the same building. Thanks to Alvin, they found no one. The two of them looked at each other, as they spoke almost simultaneously.

"Someone's telling on us or setting us up!"

They continued to watch, as detective Brown and Peters walked from the building. As they left, they glanced across the street, but everyone had disappeared. The two jumped in their unmarked car and drove off slowly. Communications started immediately.

"Is everyone all right?" asked Wallace.

"Everyone's cool," answered Eric.

Alvin spoke. "I'll walk through the building and out through the back, then around to the front, to make sure the coast is clear."

Everyone waited till Alvin came around the front. When he finally did, he nodded his head to signify yes, then went into 207.

John sensed something wasn't right, then suddenly Alvin's voice came over the headsets.

"They're in the back of 207, running the plates on the Honda. There's also an officer standing in the entrance. I'm going inside now; stay put."

A good distance away, in Jewels' car, Jewels and Jugs talked.

"What man, dem jokers could have murdered me!" stated Jugs angrily.

"True, but I trust 'em! He had to do it like dat, to make it look good. If he had shot them and you were left there standing, how would that have looked?" Jewels carried on.

"You used me as a stunt dummy, that's why you gave me dat vest! What if he had missed? You told me they'd pull up, jump out and rob us, not shoot us!" shouted Jugs.

"You're my man, I wouldn't let that happen! I need you!" continued Jewels, as he smiled.

Jugs pushed open the door and climbed out of the shiny car, slamming the door behind him. Jewels smiled, as Jugs walked away, angry.

Slim, who was sitting quietly in the back spoke up.

"What if they woulda smoked Jugs?"

"You're saying dat like he's not expendable," stated Jewels, as he turned to look in Slim's face.

"Cool out, Jewels, we came up together," added Slim, not at all agreeing with him.

"It worked, didn't it?"

"Yes!" answered Slim.

"He's alive, isn't he?"

"Yes."

"So what's the problem?"

"You're becoming the problem!" ended Slim, as Jewels pulled off and he sat in the back rolling a cigar.

The sight of snow, in addition to the cold, had everyone bundled up and running for shelter. John and the boys had finished with close to ten thousand cash and had divided it into shares, placing the remainder of it away in a travel bag beneath some clothes.

Wallace walked out to the car first and announced through the headset that things were safe and clear. The sky seemed bright as it was cluttered with white flakes.

Everyone came down the stairs and piled into the car, as Wallace sat in it with the engine idling. Heading from the parking area, Wallace noticed another set of lights as they lit up. Wallace sped off, and as he kept glancing in the rear view mirror, he caught a glimpse of two white guys in an old, four-door, gray, Grand Fury. "It's Five-O, fellows, hold on," announced Wallace, as he put the gas pedal to the floor.

As the unmarked car followed, Wallace ripped around and headed in the opposite direction, leaving the officers totally stumped.

Laughter broke out as they continued speeding, running right through a red light and nearly crashing into another car. Still racing with energy, they pulled in front of the building in which Alvin lived. Alvin climbed from the car, after hugging John tightly, then bounced across the street, through the scarred, barely-held-in-place doors.

Once inside, he signaled to let them know he had gotten in safely and they pulled off. Minutes later, Wallace pulled up in front of the building where he and Eric resided, which was on Twelfth Street, off Sixteenth Avenue. The two hopped from the car with the travel bag, as John moved over into the driver's seat.

John pulled out, as he looked at his watch, which read two A.M.

"Damn! I've got to get home earlier," John said to himself aloud.

The next day, which was Sunday, John had a day off. Knowing this, he relaxed in thought. Within minutes, he rose and walked over to the window. He put his head out to embrace the cold breeze, which freed him from the heat he was in. He felt hopeless at the start of this new day, as he sat on the window ledge thinking. Why is my life so complicated? Dropping his head in disgust, he stayed that way for about an hour, before jumping up to call Tammy at work. She picked up the phone.

"Hello, Quaker Insurance, Tammy Williams speaking."

"Hello, honey," John softly uttered.

Realizing it was John, she asked, "How's your brother doing?"

"He's getting better, but that was yesterday. I'm going to see him in a little while. I hope he's out of I.C.U. by then," answered John. He went on to add, "The reason I really called was to apologize for hanging up on you, and to also tell you I want see you tonight."

Not wanting to give in too easily, she told him she'd think about it and had to get back to work.

After hanging up, John started towards the back of his apartment to get dressed.

Suddenly his pager started going off, but he couldn't figure out where he had left it. Searching under clothes, through the sheets, he found it attached to his belt, which was on the pants he had on the day before and left at the foot of his bed. Grabbing it, he pulled it from the pants and viewed the number on the screen, then called it back instantly.

Quickly picking up, Tony told John that Kelly's wake would be the following day at seven P.M., at Terry's Funeral Home. Then told him to bring him the car the first chance he got. John sat wondering what it was that he had planned, but refrained from asking.

"Okay, after I come from seeing my brother," John answered. Concluding their conversation, John continued to get dressed and by ten o'clock, he was on his way to the hospital.

When he finally arrived and entered the room, Rick was awake. Noticing John as he walked in, Rick smiled.

John, seeing that all the tubes had been removed, let out a sigh of relief.

"Hey, big brother, I made it!" stated Rick with a grin. I couldn't let you down, you need me!" he added.

Grabbing his brother's hand, John expressed to him how much he loved him by kissing him on the cheek and embracing him. Shortly after he took a seat, his mother and sister Myra walked in. One after the other, they hugged John, as they noticed that Rick was in much better shape.

Myra, younger and outspoken, stated, "Daddy and Sharon came up and stayed for awhile yesterday," She looked at John's face.

"Who's running the store?" asked John.

"Ronald! He took a few days' leave from his job to help out and to visit with his brother," Mrs. Jackson replied, then continued on to say, "John, you're a smart young man. Why can't you understand that this life is that of the devil? You can't keep living like this! Why wait till you get shot, go to jail, or worse, get killed?"

"Mom, you don't understand, you see, everything I have is on the line. I have to somehow clear myself," John stated, justifying his reason for his lifestyle.

"You'll be found innocent son. Trust in the Lord. He works in mysterious ways!"

"I'll be found innocent if I can find those guys' killers! That's my only hope; cause all the evidence points to me!"

His mother hugged him.

"Son, I wish you wouldn't do this."

John, realizing the pain he was causing his mother, hugged her tightly. After he let go, she sat down next to the bed, in which Rick lay.

Within minutes, John had kissed his sister on the forehead, told Rick good-bye, and was out of the room and on his way. Now more confused then ever, he just wanted to give it up, but knew he couldn't. He had to find out exactly who the killers were.

Leaving the hospital just about lunchtime, he called Tammy and invited her out, as he was already in the area. They met at the pizzeria on Market Street. After being seated and finishing up their lunch, John told her that his brother was doing a lot better and that he could be out of the Intensive Care Unit as soon as they could get around to him.

John reached out, taking her hand, as he told her, "I'm going to find the information I need in the next few months, no more playing around. I know who's behind all of this, but without proof, it won't stand up in court." Kissing her hand, he smiled, as the two rose and left the pizzeria.

After driving her back to work, she opened the door to exit the car but not before asking, "Will I see you later?"

He replied, "I'11 stop by."

About two P.M., John could be seen driving the car to Tony's house.

Upon pulling up, he saw Tony has some guys washing his van and his wife's black Mercedes. John pulled in the driveway behind them. Getting out, he approached the front door. But as he got closer, the door opened and Tony came walking out.

"Yo, what's up, John?" Tony shouted, as if he were surprised. "My main man!" he added, as he turned John around and the two of them walked back down the walkway, then away from the house.

John popped the question that he had been itching to ask. "How do you hide all your income?"

"Well, you grease a palm here, open a business there, invest a little, spend a lot."

As the conversation carried on, one of Tony's partners from another part of town pulled up in a green BMW. He blew his horn to get Tony's attention.

"What's up?" the driver shouted, as he rolled down his front passenger window.

After shutting the car down, he climbed out, carrying a duffel bag. Approaching Tony and John, they turned around and the trio headed back up and into the house.

Once inside, John was introduced to Raymond, who was the driver of the BMW. He stood five foot seven, bald and looked more like a businessman than a hustler.

The trio headed up the stairs to a side room, which had a money counter sitting on a desk.

Tony announced, "Okay, let's see what the gross is this week!"

On that note, Raymond dumped the bag of money, which was in neat bundles, onto the desk. Taking one rubber band off at a time, Tony ran them through the money counter, after which, he marked them accordingly.

When it all had been counted, Tony pulled out a calculator and added it all up.

"Seventy-five thousand fellows, not bad!" Tony stated with a slight smile.

John looked on in amazement, as Tony and Raymond quickly packed it all back up. Everyone exited the room, with Tony trailing and closing the door. Raymond dragged the bag, as Tony instructed him.

"Take that batch of money and find some new investment property. You know what to do with the rest!"

Raymond shook Tony's hand, followed by John's, and he told him it was a pleasure to meet him. Afterwards, he turned toward the door and left.

"Now John, about that car; we have to sell it. So I'm going to give you eight thousand dollars, in the form of a cashier's check, so you can get another one." Pulling the check from his shirt pocket, he continued, "Go down to McCarter Highway, to Luxury Wheels and ask for Michael. Tell him Tony sent you; he'll take care of you."

John headed out the door after sliding into his boots.

By eight o'clock, he had pulled back up in a blue Acura Integra, with Wallace, Eric and Alvin following close behind in the Honda.

Jumping out, they all headed up the walkway. Wallace led the way, Alvin trailed, smiling.

"I finally get to meet Ton Capone!" Alvin shouted.

At the door, Wallace rang the bell a few times.

Someone peeked through the peephole and then pulled the door open. It was Tony, but as he did so, he told them to meet him around back as he was having his carpet cleaned.

They all sat in a sheltered area, with a few tables and chairs. As the dogs barked, Tony yelled to them to quiet them down. They spoke of the shooting and they all came to the same conclusion; the robbery was a set up, but by whom? They all had their suspicions.

Later that evening, as John and Alvin drove to the strip to meet with everyone, they rode past Jugs.

"Hey, I thought he was in the hospital!" stated Alvin.

"I thought so too!" added John.

They slowly rode by. Jugs, who noticed them right away, ducked down a side street. John spoke out after a long pause. "Something's just not right. I can feel it!"

Shortly after, they pulled alongside Rick's car, which sat in the parking area in the back of 207. Looking around, John also noticed the Honda, which meant that Wallace and the gang had beat them there. He and Alvin ran up the stairs to share the news. After telling Eric and Wallace what they had seen, John went back out to check things out.

Standing in the entrance to 207, John stared across the street at Jewels and his boy. He thought of ways to infiltrate his operation. Then it occurred to him: you get to people easiest through their weaknesses. Turning away, walking back through 207 into 210, he began to think harder. He thought to himself, enough is enough, as he thought of his obsession to bring Jewels to justice. Fight fire with fire, is what ran through his head.

As he entered Angie's, everyone had on their headsets and were situated and ready to go.

In that instant, John spoke. "Slow your roll, wait! Slow your roll! Listen, I want to catch one of his boys going home. So after everything's done, let's follow Ice and torture him.

Wallace responded, "That's not a good idea, because if we torture him and don't kill him, we've got beef!"

Eric smiles and added, "Let's just murder them all! Why the hell are we playing with dem?"

John spoke. "I'm sure we all feel about the same, but we've got to do this right, so we don't get caught up. So get Ice and shake him up, okay? Then let the cards fall where they may."

Wallace turned away mumbling. Alvin sat in the background smiling, as if he was in on it also. John saw his interest and told him, "You stay right here! Understand?"

Alvin didn't respond, he just looked and pouted.

After the strip was empty and there were no people on the streets but the bums and scavengers, John, Eric and Wallace sat and watched Jewels and his boys leave.

Jewels did so first, in his champagne BMW 535i, while Ice, Slim and Smoke stood guard. Slim drove off as Smoke followed. Finally, Ice pulled off in his black 300 ZX. John pulled off slowly behind him, unnoticed.

"Don't let him notice you," Wallace stated as John drove. "Because there's no way we can keep up with that thing!" he added.

Hearing this, John kept his distance, as he followed him into a parking lot across from an apartment complex.

John, Wallace and Eric all jumped out, after putting on ski masks and gloves.

Maneuvering among the cars in the lot, they finally came across the 300 ZX as Ice was pulling a bag from his trunk.

Wallace yoked him up, putting his gun to his head, covering his mouth with the same hand he initially grabbed him with. "If you so much as flinch, I'll murder you!" stated Wallace.

Dragging him to the passenger side of his own car, Wallace pushed him into the backseat. He climbed in behind him, never lowering the gun for a second. Wallace told Eric to get the keys out of the trunk lock, so they could get going, while John hurried back to the Integra.

Both cars sped off, as Ice broke his silence.

"You guys are crazy! When Jewels finds out about this, he'll have you murdered!"

"Like he had Darryl and Kelly murdered?" asked Eric as he drove.

"What make you think he'll find out or even find you?" Wallace then asked.

A long silence filled the air, as they pulled up and parked on a dark street. After everyone was out of the cars, they walked through an opening in a fence. Ice was held tightly at gunpoint by Wallace. After traveling through one yard after another, Ice broke free and tried to run.

Wallace unloaded as John stood in shock and Ice's body tumbled over into the dirt.

"Let's get the hell out of here!" yelled Eric as he looked around.

As they all ran and jumped in the Integra, they left the 300 ZX behind and sped off. Windows in nearby buildings lit up, as dogs begin to bark, and yet another person had been murdered.

The next morning, as John woke up, he was still tired because he hadn't slept much. For in this murder, he was an accomplice. He was thinking to himself, now I'm part of the problem, no longer part of the small percentage called the solution. Now if I'm trying to save my own ass, why am I digging a deeper grave? If I provide the shovel, but do not dig the actual dirt, aren't my hands just as dirty in a court of law?

After dwelling on the thought for a moment, he got up and went into the bathroom. Looking in the mirror, he turned on the water and let it run into the sink. Staring at his own image, he began to splash the water against his face.

Later on at work, John was still having flashbacks about the murders and the cold look on Wallace's face. Snapping out of it, he started to attend to waiting customers as they came in. Within minutes his pager went off.

It read: "911, 911."

Figuring it to be Tony, he picked up the phone and called his house.

"Hello, Tony? John asked as soon as someone picked up.

"Yes," he responded and continued, "Yes, John, what happened last night? I called Wallace and Eric, but they were nowhere to be found! I paged them and you and only you called me back! Angie said she didn't know what went down, but she was sure something did. So what happened?"

"We tried." John, not wanting to talk over the phone, told him he'd get in touch with him after work. As the two hung up, Tony's pager beeped, and John started to think of his brother. He decided to tell his father he needed to take the rest of the day off. He wanted to see his brother.

After his departure, he arrived at the hospital around twelve-thirty. Upon arriving at the front desk, he found that they had moved Rick to a different floor, due to the fact that he was doing much better.

Entering the room where Rick lay, resting, John noticed Maria and his mother, laughing about something Rick had probably said. When Rick spotted John he shouted, "Come give me a hug, big brother!"

John leaned over the bed and did just that.

"I love you," Rick whispered in his ear.

"I love you, too," John returned as he raised back up, then hugged Maria and his mother.

A few minutes later Maria spoke. "Well, me have to go back to work, so me see you later, honey." She kissed Rick and then made her exit. As she did, so did their mother, but not before embracing them both.

"So what's up?" Rick asked John with a smile.

John hesitated for a moment, for he was unsure about what he was about to speak about. He just let it roll slowly from his tongue.

"Well, you do know Kelly died, don't you?"

"No, I didn't. No one told me. I assumed he was in another room somewhere. But I should have known. Every time I did ask all I got was, 'he's all right, you just rest.'"

"Well, anyway, Kelly died and Jugs is out on the streets as if nothing happened," John stated.

"Why was he over there anyway?" asked John.

"He came to ask us to serve one of their regulars. They were out of product. He told us that he needed a fix bad," Rick explained.

"It was a set-up!" John stated loudly and angrily.

"But why would they shoot him, too?" asked Rick.

"So it would look like they had nothing to do with it," answered John.

"Come on, John, who's willing to get shot, just so something doesn't look like a set-up?" asked Rick, trying to make his point.

"Come on, think like Jewels thinks. He always covers his ass! In order to do that, he needed someone over there, so it wouldn't look like he was rolling on us. Jugs probably wore a vest, plus who is Jugs?" John rambled on.

"A nobody!" answered Rick, who was sitting up.

"Exactly, so if he slipped up and killed him, it would be no loss to their organization," John stated as he drove his point home.

"Now you see how he thinks?" added John.

"You're starting to sound scary. I think it was just a question of being in the wrong place at the wrong time," Rick went on.

"You don't get it! They never came to us before, why now?" John stated, smoking mad, because his brother couldn't see the forest for the trees.

Rick rejected the assumptions and allegations, because he refused to believe someone would get shot just to make something look a certain way. John marched out the room and exited the hospital, still angered by his brother.

Later the same day, as the temperature dropped and John sat in Tony's house, he explained the same theory to Tony, Wallace and Eric. He pointed out that he and Alvin had seen Jugs the day before. Wallace and Eric, who had heard about this already, sat in silence, and Tony had a puzzled look on his face. Everyone saw, in a weird, twisted, Jewels' type of way, that it all somehow made sense.

"So what do you suggest we do?" Tony asked, trying to keep his cool.

"We know, being that Ice is dead, Jewels will be looking to point a finger, so let it be at Silk. It clears us of blame, plus they did have an argument about a week ago, stated John.

"How do you plan to do that?" asked Wallace.

"We put the word on the street that Silk hit Ice," John answered.

About eight-thirty P.M., after viewing Kelly's body, the gang now more than ever wanted revenge, so they put their plan into effect.

Back on the strip, they watched as Jewels flipped out on the other side of the street. John watched as he hurried to finish selling the drugs he had left. A voice came over the headsets.

"Yo, John, I'm going to creep into the building while they're all unorganized and try to listen to their conversation," Alvin's muffled voice was heard and then faded out.

"Be careful, little bro!" stated John with concern.

Alvin crept into the building, passed a door where he heard loud yelling, and stopped to check the door of the apartment next to it. It was open, Alvin, surprised, went inside, closing the door behind him. Inside, he sat by the wall that stood between the two apartments and listened.

"It's not going down like dat! So Silk thinks he can get away with dis? That's it, he's finished, call Hits!"

The sound of footsteps walking across the floor was all Alvin heard, for a moment. The footsteps stopped, then there was a long silence, then voices were heard again.

"Hello, Danny?" Another long silence, then someone spoke again. "This is Slim. It's Silk's birthday."

Alvin pressed his ear to the wall to make sure he heard everything. He tried to listen a while longer, but there was nothing else said that seemed relevant. So he exited the apartment and headed back across to Angie's.

After entering, he told Wallace that somebody said something about it being Silk's birthday.

Wallace, putting two and two together, announced through the headsets that Jewels was going to have Silk killed.

"Who did they call and talk to? Did you hear the name?" quickly asked Wallace.

"Some guy named Danny," answered Alvin.

John and Eric listened over their headsets, but the name Danny set off no bells in their heads. So they continued and took care of business as usual. As they shut down, they waited and watched once again.

This time, they just trailed Slim, to see where he rested his head. After about a twenty-minute drive, he pulled into a restaurant parking lot, then went inside and sat down. Seeing this, they drove past and headed home.

On December second, five days later, John lay resting in his apartment reading Wednesday's paper. As he did so, he came across an article:

Drug Dealer Murdered

Twenty-five-year-oldKenneth Tombs, better known as Silk, was murdered as he drove his Mercedes into a telephone pole. The actual cause of death was two bullets to the chest and head area. He was pronounced dead at the scene. No suspects have been apprehended.

John cut the article from the paper and posted it on the wall next to the one about the execution. Looking at the clippings he thought, both of them in some way offended Jewels and now they're both dead! In both cases, he made it look like someone else did it.

John paused for a moment as he pondered the situation. Who is Danny? He must be a hired hitman or something.

As he ate his breakfast, he finished reading the paper, then the phone rang and it was Rick. "Did you read the paper this morning?" he asked.

"Yes," replied John.

"I know who you think did it, Jewels right?" Rick stated.

"If you know, why ask?" John answered.

"I'm coming home Sunday!" Rick added.

"That's real good," replied John.

"Well, I see you're kind of distant today, so I'll talk to you later. Okay, big brother."

"All right, bye," responded John.

John thought to himself, are woman always right? She told me I was getting in too deep. Now it's no longer a question of saving my ass, it's a question of will there be enough of it to save? Will the person I've become be forever, leaving who I truly am murdered like those that I read about or have witnessed being killed?

By twelve o'clock, he had drifted into a deep depression. He drifted so far he failed to hear the phone ring.

There came a knock at the door, a familiar one. It was Tammy. He let her in and she didn't have to ask if anything was wrong, she could see it in his face. She decided to ask anyway.

"Baby, what's wrong?" she asked as she touched him gently about the chest.

"Stop babying me, I'm not a child!" John shouted as he grabbed her hands and removed them.

Tammy, shocked by his reaction, stepped back and away from him.

"Okay, grumpy, I'll leave you alone!" she stated as she headed to the couch and sat down.

"Well, at least let me tell you my good news!" Tammy stated as she patted the couch beside her, as if to tell him to come sit next to her. "Now I know you're not ready for this, but let's get married anyway," she blurted out with a smile as she looked him in the eyes and held his hand tightly.

John responded with a puzzled look on his face. "That's the good news?" he asked.

"Yes! Let's get married and work toward a better life together," she added.

"I'm going through hell right now! Feeding me slices of heaven will only make things wore, when the pie is gone and I hunger for that which is no longer there!" stated John angrily.

"What do you mean?" she asked.

"I mean, if and when I do go to jail, I don't want to leave a wife and a child out here in this cold, cold world! I want to be there," he stressed. "I'm scared!" he explained.

"I understand. I understand!" she told him.

He laid still with his head in her lap as she embraced him as if to ease his pains, for his pains were hers.

Meanwhile, in another part of town, more specifically at Jewels' home, he sat in his spacious living room with Slim and Smoke. As they sat, they discussed Silk's workers.

"Either they work for us or they have to leave the block. Simple as that!" stated Jewels.

"But if—-"

Jewels cut Slim short as he tried to speak.

"There is no buts, either they flow, or they go!" added Jewels.

The phone rang, and Jewels told Slim to answer it.

"Hello, is Mr. Simon Parks there?" asked the voice on the other end.

Slim handed the phone to Jewels.

"Hello, this is Simon."

"Hi, Mr. Parks, my name is Milton Allen; I work with the Children's Athletes League of New Jersey. What we'd like to know is, would you like to sponsor one of our football teams this year?"

"No, I haven't the time or the patience," stated Jewels, as he cut the conversation short by adding, "I'm very busy now, bye!"

He started talking to the guys once again.

"Now, where were we? Oh yeah, Slim, take five grand from last week's gross and make arrangement to have it deposited in Danny's account. Then take the receipts and all the statements to the accountant, after collecting everything from the steakhouse, jewelry store and the liquor store."

Slim grabbed everything and left. Jewels, who was intelligent, but even more heartless, had the makings of a hard-nosed businessman. He often walked in on investments, such as a failing business and revived them. Others he just chanced, if he believed in them, incorporating them under "White Picket Fence, Inc." He laundered most of his dirty money through this corporation, often paying good money to those who helped him keep his name lily white, from his lawyers to his accountant, Karen Wells.

About three o'clock, Tony had called a meeting of his own. As everyone sat down, he stated, "We pretty much know Jewels is behind dis, so what we need to do is catch him in the act. That way we'll have the evidence to clear you (referring to John). After that, he's finished" Tony pounded his fist in his hand, as he looked about the room and at everyone.

Leaving afterward, they all headed to Kelly's funeral at Terry's Funeral Home. When they arrived the ceremony had already started, so they sat in the back unnoticed. Catching the end of the reverend's speech, they listened as he asked, if anyone wanted to speak on his behalf.

Kelly's brother, whom John had never met, stood up and walked to the podium. As he did, a piece of paper dangled from his fingers. Reaching the podium and facing the crowd, he stared out at their tear-filled faces. Raising the paper he held, he began to read from it.

"He who is to judge, please be lenient. Forgive my brother, for he ran with those that live without souls; those that choose to benefit at the cost of our children, our future, those that envision true riches as being money, instead of that which dwells deep in the heart. He has come and gone before me. Now he is me; for he shall live in my heart, where I can protect him from the bad element. He's safe now; he's safe forever, thank God!"

Afterward, he stepped down and walked back to where he had been seated. A young female cousin in a blue skirt set got up and sang, "Its

So Hard to Say Good-bye to Yesterday." Leaving everyone in tears, she stepped down in tears herself.

Row by row, everyone viewed the body. John, Tony and the boys finally reached the front and went up to the casket. John, teary eyed, took a long look at him and then walked off.

Just as Tony approached and leaned over to kiss him, Kelly's mother slapped him as she yelled, "I knew he'd end up like this, running with you! You murderer! How dare you show your face here, get out!"

Tony, hurt from this, marched out with his boys and Angie following.

About thirty minutes later, the casket bearing Kelly's body was being carried out of the parlor, then placed into a hearse. As it pulled off, a train of cars followed close behind. Tony and the gang trailed, also.

Arriving at the burial site, the body was carried to the plot and secured. The preacher read the eulogy, as Tony and the gang watched from afar.

During the ride back to Tony's house, not a word was spoken. Everyone was drowning in pain as they arrived. Once inside, the well-dressed clan sat and continued the long silence.

John rose and said, "I need some air," as he headed out the door with Alvin and Angie rising to follow.

While driving, Alvin came from out of nowhere, stating, "I'm tired of seeing these guys I like die! I wish somebody would just smoke Jewels! He's the one that's behind all of dis!"

"Yeah, but proving it is something all together different!" replied John.

"We'll get proof," stated Alvin.

Later on as he dropped Angie off, John drove Alvin home, where they found out that his mother had been evicted. His mother and sister were nowhere to be found. Alvin asked neighbors, but no one knew anything. He had John go from spot to spot, till he found them. Upon entering the apartment where they were, it seemed as if people were everywhere. Alvin's mother was drunk, sitting on the floor. This big, dark woman looked like she was gorgeous in her day.

"Come here, damn it!" she yelled, then added as he ignored her, "I know you hear me!"

Alvin turned and raced out the door, with his mother stumbling behind him.

"Lady, you shouldn't torture these kids like this!" John stated, following the two.

"They're my damn kids! So mind your damn business and go sell some drugs or somethin!"

Alvin jumped in the car and pushed the locks down, so she couldn't get to him. John marched past her as she pulled on the door handle, shaking his head.

"Excuse me, can I get in my car?" he asked.

She backed away, still yelling.

"Keep your sorry ass away and don't come back! Ya just like ya father!"

John rolled the window down, gave her twenty dollars, then told her, "Please feed that pretty little girl of yours." Pulling off as he finished, they left her standing at the curb. He watched her in his rear view mirror. She gave him the finger.

Taking confused Alvin to his apartment, John told him he could stay as long as he liked.

"But what about my sister?" Alvin asked with concern.

"I'll take you to see her whenever you wish," answered John.

The two of them started taking off their suits and put on jeans and shirts, then sat back and took a well-deserved rest, for this last week had been tough on them.

Driving through the strip that night, the head count was down and the police presence was stronger then usual. They were everywhere, walking, sitting in their cars and around back. The strip was officially under investigation.

"I wonder what they're investigating?" asked Alvin.

"Probably the murders and how wide open everything has gotten," responded John.

Seeing this, John called everyone and they all decided to take the day off. They ended up on Forty-Second Street in New York City, in an arcade. Alvin played video game after video game. Afterward they ate and took in a movie, then came back across the water to Newark.

Before going in, John drove back through the strip. The only people they saw were a few of Silk's workers, who now worked for Jewels. As he passed a few stragglers, he called Angie to make sure she was all right.

"Hello Angie, its John, what's going on?"

She told him that the police caught Wallace and Eric as soon as they stepped out.

"Damn, I told them not to come out, there were too many police!"

"No, the police had left, but came back. I guess they just changed shifts and that's when Eric and Wallace thought it was safe. But the police weren't here for drugs; they were looking for a stolen detective's gun. The gun was taken as the detective tried to apprehend a suspect in a buy and bust. It was supposed to have been used to kill one of Silk's runners, Viking (he was given this name because of his rough and rugged look)," stated Angie.

"It figures," grumbled John.

Angie continued, "They eventually found the gun and the guy who supposedly shot him in an abandoned apartment. The guy stated that he was seeing demons and people chasing him. He was totally delusional, they claimed. It just doesn't add up, and as usual, Jones and Michaels were right there! I think the gun belonged to one of them.

"After they left, Wallace and Eric showed up. They asked had you been around, then went straight to work, like everything was okay. I told them not to go out there! It seemed like someone called in on them, because as soon as they set up and went out, the police swarmed."

Excited, Angie just rambled until John stopped her.

"Thanks, John said and hung up.

He called the precinct as he cruised closer to his place, to find out their charges and their bails.

"Hello, Fifth Ward police station, Officer Jenkins speaking."

"Yes, I'm calling in reference to Wallace Johnson and Eric Sawyer. I would like to know what they're being charged with and their bails, if they have any," John rambled on.

"Hold on," the officer answered. There was a long pause before the officer returned. "Sir, Wallace Johnson is being charged with assault and conspiracy to sell narcotics. He has a seventy-five-hundred-dollars bail. Eric Sawyer is being charged with possession and possession with the intent to distribute. His bail is twenty-five-hundred cash."

"Thank you," John stated appreciatively before hanging up.

He quickly dialed Tony's number and after about thirteen rings, it was finally picked up. But all John heard was someone mumbling on the other end.

"Hello, hello. Wake up, Tony!" he shouted.

Tony spoke in a grumpy tone.

"Yo, dis betta be important!"

"It is. Wallace and Eric are locked up! I need ten thousand dollars to bail them out." John blurted out.

"What did they get into, that their bails equal out to ten thousand?"

"Wallace caught an assault charge and they both were caught coming out on the set with drugs."

"Damn!" Tony uttered softly. "They'll just have to sit till tomorrow morning, I'll call you," he added, then hung up.

John and Alvin headed in and called it a night.

The next morning, freezing because he had left a window open, John woke up to a ringing telephone. It was Tony on his cellular.

"Come on; let's go bail out the boys!"

John jumped up after hanging up the phone and headed into the bathroom. He threw some water on his face, brushed his teeth and put on the first pair of pants and shirt he could find. Grabbing his jacket from a chair, he rushed past Alvin, who was sleep, then headed out the door.

Waiting downstairs in a shiny black van, sat Tony. As quickly as John jumped in, they pulled off. After doing so, John noticed that there was a blonde-headed brown-skinned woman sitting in the rear. Tony, seeing this, introduced them.

"Yo, excuse my rudeness. John, this is Shanelle. Shanelle, this is John."

The two exchanged hellos, then John turned back around and stared out into the streets.

"She's going to bail Wallace out, as his girlfriend and you can do Eric, if that's all right with you," Tony went on.

"Sure," stated John.

Shortly after their release, Wallace started telling his story, as they walked from the precinct to the van.

"You know detectives Peters and Brown, they ran down on us with a few regulars' cops, too. I didn't know what was going on, I honestly thought they were stick-up kids and they were trying to rob us! When I saw them pull out their guns and badges I knew, but it was to late. I had already started swinging and punching! I gave as well as I took. I almost got away, until this big fat white cop grabbed and held me!"

"What about you, Eric?" asked Tony.

"I didn't have a prayer. Before I knew anything I was face down on the pavement," he explained.

They all laughed about the incident as Tony pulled in front of John's place. He climbed out and headed up the stairs as they drove off.

Entering his apartment, he found Alvin bathed and combing his afro out neatly. John, seeing that his hair was uneven, said to him, "You need a haircut!"

Alvin quickly replied, "I'm not getting my hair cut! Plus, it's Sunday, there's no barber shop open!"

"My buddy Mike has a shop and he's open," stated John.

"I'm still not getting my hair cut!"

"Okay, let's go get it shaped up. Afterward, we'll go through the mall and do a little shopping," added John.

Alvin finished getting dressed as John went to the back to shower. When John was finally ready, he walked into the living room and said, "Let's go."

Alvin jumped up and the two of them walked out.

After Alvin got his hair trimmed, they went shopping, then came back to the apartment. The phone started to ring.

"Hello," said John as he picked it up.

"Hello, big brother. They're freeing me!" stated Rick, overly excited.

"Okay, I'll be there in a few," John told him as he looked around the room and put his bags down.

He and Alvin headed back out once again. When they arrived at the hospital, Rick was sitting in a wheelchair in the lobby area. The two crept up behind him.

"What's up?" they harmonized as Rick turned around and smiled.

Rolling him out to the car, Rick looked up at the sky and down at the small portions of snow on the ground. He stared as if he had missed being outside The breeze felt good to him. Closing his coat as he started to get cold, he smiled as they approached the car.

"New car, huh?" Rick asked as John opened the door.

"Yeah," stated John as he helped him out of the chair and into it.

"I'm all right, I can do dis myself!" Rick stated as he climbed in.

Once everyone was in the car and they had secured themselves, they drove off.

"So how's business?" Rick asked.

"Kinda touch and go right now," answered John.

"So, how's my little friend?" asked Rick as he reached out to give Alvin a pound.

Alvin looked at him then smiled as he reached to slap his hand. Alvin embraced him and told him, "I'm happy you're alive. Let's keep it that way!" He laughed as he pulled away.

"What do you mean, you little runt!" Rick returned, laughing also.

It was evident that everyone was happy. So as they joked back and forth, tears could be seen in Rick's eyes.

Shortly after driving Rick home, he and Alvin drove around aimlessly. Ending up at Tammy's place, they climbed the stairs, but as they did John noticed some flowers in front of her door.

"Who are those for?" asked Alvin.

"I think they're for Tammy," John replied as he opened the note that was with them.

"Your Tammy?" Alvin questioned.

"My Tammy!" answered John as he read the note.

> Dear Tammy,
>
> I know I barely know you, but seeing you every day drives me wild. I wonder if you're free, would you like to go to dinner with me one evening.
>
> Signed, Larry

Closing the note, John placed it back neatly on the flowers before knocking on the door. As Tammy opened it, he picked up the flowers and handed them to her. She kissed and hugged him and told him how sweet he was. He then told her that he didn't bring the flowers, that they had been left by her door and that they were from someone named Larry.

"John, now he's a guy at work who has a crush on me. I think nothing of him. Now how is your brother?"

"He's okay; we just dropped him off a little while ago." The thought of the flowers was still on his mind. But he knew he could trust her, so he forgot about it.

"Come here, baby, I apologize," John stated, feeling guilty for not trusting her.

"For what?" She asked.

"For even thinking that of you, period! It's just the thought of losing you, that bothers me."

"Who's your little friend?"

"That's Alvin; he's like my little brother. His mother's having some problems," John answered, holding her tightly.

3 THE INVESTIGATION

It all started with a gathering at Tony's home.

"Look, I want to secure information that it's Jewels who's ordering these hits. I also want to find out who he's paying to do them. We know he's not working alone!" stated John.

Alvin cut in. "I overheard a conversation back in December, they called a guy named Hits! Remember, we thought that was a cover for whoever Danny is?"

"I'm going to gather as much information as I can, along with names and dates. Then we can nail that slippery sucker!" added John.

Night fell on this warm, but breezy evening and everyone maneuvered into position on the strip. They all seemed to be keeping close watch on Jewels and his every move, but he didn't hang around that evening. To John's advantage, he had written down his license plate number.

Monday at work, John called Tammy and asked her if she could have some plate numbers run for him and she agreed. He read the plate numbers off: "B-K-K-3-6-G and G-M-G-7-6-K, that's it. I'll see you later."

Later at Tammy's, John found out the plates on the champagne BMW belonged to a Patricia Gable. She lived at 1667 Northfield Road in West Orange. The plates on the Acura Legend belonged to a Kevin Gibbs of Chestnut Street in East Orange.

John picked up the phone to call Keith and relay the information that Tammy had given him. He asked Keith if he could process them and get him birth dates, family members and whatever else he could dig up. Keith told him he'd do his best, and called in a favor from a friend who worked in vital statistics.

Back at Tammy's, John thought about the new information he had gathered, until she seduced him. They carried on till about nine that night.

Arriving late on the strip, the fellows had almost finished. John stood staring out the window in thought. He decided to try to lure one of Jewels' boys to their side of the street.

Pondering longer, he still came up blank. He pulled a piece of paper from within his pocket, which had names and addresses on it and looked them over.

Walking out the door, he headed to one of the addresses, 1667 Northfield Road.

Upon pulling up, he sat across the street looking into the driveway and then pulled off. Next, he arrived at 10 Chestnut Street, East Orange, and noticed the champagne BMW sitting out front. Outside of that, he saw nothing out of the ordinary so he left and headed home.

At ten-thirty the next morning, a fax came through onto Keith's desk. He sat processing information from the day before, but then suddenly took notice. Grabbing the sheet from the fax, he begin to read to himself: "Patricia Gable, born March 30, 1964. Birth name Patricia Parks, daughter of Catherine Parks. Kevin Gibbs, born January 10, 1961, son of Michelle Gibbs."

During his lunch break, Keith ran down to the Hall of Records. After making sure all the information was accurate and correct, he relayed it to John.

After work, John headed to a nearby camera shop, where he purchased a small 35-millimeter model. Hopping back in his car, he drove to Northfield Road. Once there, he took pictures of the house and all of its surroundings. He did the same at 10 Chestnut Street.

Just as he headed home, his pager beeped. He pulled over briefly to return the call.

"Hello, John, this is Wallace. I've found out where Jewels lives. He stays on a dead-end street in Montclair, 115 Seabright Terrace, off Bloomfield Avenue."

"How do you know about this?" asked John.

"I followed Slim. I'll talk to you later about everything," Wallace finished as he rushed to hang up.

John resumed driving, now in deep thought.

Later on that evening at Tammy's, John pulled a shoebox from her closet. Inside was all the information he had collected: newspaper articles, plus bits and pieces that he thought might be helpful. He laid everything out on a desk Tammy had against a wall near her bedroom window. As he viewed it all, he still figured he had nothing.

About ten o'clock, a stolen car's brakes had locked up and smoked up the entire strip, then raced away. John and Eric had everything in motion and moving steadily.

A voice came over the headset. "Get out of there now, here they come!"

The police came running through 207, from the back.

John and Eric ran up the street and through a vacant lot to avoid them. The police followed, but stopped as John and Eric continued. They ran till they spotted a patrol car, coming around the corner in front of them. Ducking into an alleyway, they avoided them as they passed.

Back in the apartment, Angie, Wallace and Alvin waited to see if the police caught John and Eric, but they knew after the police had searched and returned empty-handed, that they were all right.

About two hours later, the two of them came through the door, laughing. "Damn, dat was close, they almost had us!" stated John.

Wallace spoke. "Have you guys noticed that the police always mess with us? They never run down on Jewels' boys. I think their paying them off, because when they chased you, they didn't look across the street. Something's definitely going on!"

Disregarding what just went down, they sat back up and continued to make their money cautiously. Slowly easing back into position and trying not to be in the opening, they let their helpers do all the work. After the last of everything, the two of them headed back through 207, then into 210 and up to Angie's apartment.

Sitting, counting up the money, Wallace asked, "How's your investigation coming?"

"Well, it's not going good, I can't get any strong leads!" replied John.

Wednesday, as John sat at work thinking, something occurred to him. Did Catherine Parks or Michelle Gibbs have any more children?

He contacted Keith again and Keith told him he'd get right on it.

John waited patiently, when suddenly the phone rung. Keith told him, "Simon Parks has a brother named Robert Parks and Kevin's an only child."

John thanked him and told him that he owed him one.

After hanging up, John added this information to his puzzle. With still no real connection, John felt if he could infiltrate Jewels' operation, he could save his own ass.

Day in, day out, for the next four days, they made money on top of money, but John gathered no additional information. At work he sat, and he decided to take a different approach.

Later, as he left work, he pulled out a pad, turned to the page that Jewels' address was on and headed up Bloomfield Avenue. When he finally reached Seabright Terrace, he drove through, but there was no house with the number 115. Turning around and driving back through, he noticed a dead-end street and turned into it. Not long after, he spotted a large white house with the numbers 115 on it as he passed slowly. He made a U-turn and headed back past it again, even slower. He copied down the plate number of a Honda and another car in the driveway.

Back on Bloomfield Avenue, John headed back down toward Newark. Arriving at Angie's, he sat down while she cooked. Thinking of how hard it was to make things link up, he immersed himself in thought. Angie placed a plate of food in front of him, bringing him back instantly.

"Mmm, this sure smells good!" stated John as he attempted to grab the skinless baked drumstick and dropped it back onto the plate. "Ow, hot!" he shouted as Angie grinned.

Picking up the fork, he focused on the macaroni salad and string beans smothered in butter. After sampling the meal, he asked her, "Where did you learn to cook like this?"

She smiled and waved her hand, as if to tell him to stop. She blushed.

"I'm serious, this is really good!" he added with his mouth filled. He paused to chew and swallow, when Wallace, Eric, Rick and Alvin walked in. John, not being able to speak, because his mouth was full, reached out to shake their hands instead. Angie chased them to the bathroom so they could wash up and join them at the table.

As everyone sat eating, they discussed the past as well as the present. John slowly drifted back into his own world, when suddenly Alvin tapped him.

"John, did you hear what your brother asked you?" Alvin asked.

"No, sorry, I drifted off," John answered.

Rick repeated himself. "What have you put together so far?"

"Well, I know the BMW is registered to Patricia Gable, daughter of Catherine Parks, who also has two sons, Robert and Simon Parks. Now I need to find out exactly who Simon and Robert are!"

Pausing for a second, he continued, "Now check this. I took a drive up to Montclair. You know, Wallace, to the address you gave me, where you told me Jewels lived. I saw a few cars in the driveway there, so I took down the plate numbers and I'm having them checked as we speak. The other plates, on the Acura Legend, belong to a Kevin Gibbs of Chestnut Street, East Orange, but the house belongs to a Steven Arch. Tomorrow, I'm going down to the Hall of Records and check out Seabright Terrace."

Sounding hopeful, John rambled till Alvin spoke out. "What does any of this information have to do with your case?"

Rick agreed and spoke out next. "Yeah, all this address searching and plate running isn't leading anywhere and if it is, your running real short on time!"

"Man, let's just murder them all! We're sure to get the killer that way!" stated Eric.

John, knowing this, but he also knew he had no other course or plan to execute. He just prayed that between he and his lawyer, they could build some kind of case.

Two hours later, John and Eric worked the streets, making money, while Rick and Wallace sat with Angie watching TV and discussed bringing Jewels out into the open.

Across the street, Jewels talked on his cellular phone. "She lives in building 210 take care of things like we discussed."

As he pulled back the shade to look out the window, he noticed John and begin to take great interest in him. As John hustled back and forth, Jewels watched as it came to him.

"That's that joker, Johnathan! What the hell is he doing out here! I knew I knew him! Yo, find out all you can about him. That joker just don't learn!"

Slim left as he finished.

As the rain poured relentlessly, the next morning John rushed into the Montclair's Hall of Records. He was drenched, though he had his jacket pulled over his head. Scanning through one of the books, he finally came upon the address he was looking for, 115 Seabright Terrace. He found out that it belonged to White Picket Fence, Inc. and noted it in the pad that he brought with him.

"Who the hell is White Picket Fence, Inc.?"

He headed for the door, but as he rushed back out, he was stopped cold by a flash of lightning. He stared for a moment, then continued on, till he reached his car and pulled off.

When he arrived back at work, his father told him Keith had called, leaving him a message that the plate on the Honda matched that of his colleague, Karen Wells.

Keith, now knowing that Karen had something to do with Jewels, started watching her very carefully. She did nothing out of the ordinary. He thought about going through her belongings, but knew it was impossible, because of all the others in the office. He mumbled to himself about all the loose ends. At the close of the work day, he looked around as the office emptied out. Mr. Krasdale was looking over some documents, when Keith stretched to peak at some papers on Karen's desk. He was disappointed because they were faxed sheets of statements and other miscellaneous papers.

Keith on his way to nowhere as the rain came to a halt, drove around burning gas and thinking. What is her connection? Girlfriend, Family, what? He ended up at his apartment, where he sat puzzled.

Meanwhile, at John's, Alvin sat on the couch playing Sega Genesis games with his sister. John walked in with a big smile as he noticed them.

"What's up?" asked John as he sat across from them.

"I brought my sister over because my mother was drunk. On my way, I bought dis video game, check it out!" Alvin offered, as he rose and pulled him over to the couch where they sat. John watched them play awhile, then headed to the back to his bedroom. Taking notice of the newspaper articles taped to his wall, he took them down and put them in his back pocket. Grabbing a few dollars he had left on his dresser as petty cash, he headed back through the house. Telling Alvin he'd see him later, he left in a rush.

At Tammy's, she and John compiled all the information from the articles to the names and addresses, but they still had nothing.

"Damn, I have to find out what Jewels' real name is, then I'll have something, I'm sure of it! Then I'll work from there."

He sat, still seething with frustration as Tammy came over and sat on his lap, hoping to distract him and cool him off.

"Don't worry baby, it's going to be all right," she stated as she hugged him and smiled.

As the afternoon slowly went by, Keith watched Karen once again. Now that he did so, he noticed how extremely sexy she was. He really never paid attention before, because of his workload. But as the day came down to its last seconds, Karen rose from her seat and headed to the ladies' room. Keith quickly knocked some papers from his desk onto the floor. Kneeling down to pick them up, he tried to peak at some papers that were on her desk.

A voice startled him. "What's up, Keith? Did you lose something?" It was Karen.

Shocked, he jumped back to his feet, gathering all his papers in the process. He nervously responded, "No. I was just making sure I hadn't missed any of the papers that flew from my desk!"

Smiling now, Karen sat, then reached into her drawer and pulled her purse out. She told everyone good-night as she made her exit.

Keith got up and headed out the door shortly behind her.

Meanwhile, Tony paged John. He quickly returned the call on his cellular phone.

"Hello, Tony, it's John. What's up?"

"John, Jewels' real name is Simon Parks," stated Tony.

"How did you find that out?" asked John.

"Come on, man, that's easy, though I didn't grow up with him, we do have mutual friends."

Hanging up, John breathed a sign of relief. He thought to himself, I need a criminal history on him.

Ringing his lawyer afterward, he asked him if he could supply him with such. He told John he'd try and get back to him. John also asked, "Are there any other new developments?"

Mr. Sharpe replied, "Well, we pretty much haven't been able to find a witness. So I guess I'll try to find out what they have evidence-wise besides the gun, they're not budging. Your only defense is your word against theirs right now. The main thing that works for you, is the fact that you have no violent criminal history. You do have a job and the fact that you're left handed, not right! No one saw you do the actual shooting, either. I'm waiting for the medical examiner's report now. Call me tomorrow!"

John quickly fell into a depressed state, thinking that things didn't sound promising at all and that his whole future was riding on what he could find out.

That night on the block, John sat on a crate, in his usual disguise and scoped Jewels' operation. But as usual, he found out nothing new, so they made their loot, packed up and called it a night.

As the sun gleamed through the window the following morning, John's newly bought alarm clock rang. He woke up from his coma-like sleep and then tossed the clock against the wall as it continued to ring. He rubbed his eyes and yawned, as he sat up on the edge of his bed. He slid his feet into his slippers and attempted to take on the new day. He rose, picked up the clock from the floor, turning it off as he headed to the bathroom to shower.

Hearing the loud sound of the television playing, he dragged himself to the front of the apartment. There he saw Alvin fast asleep, as the television echoed throughout. John flipped it off and marched back through the apartment and into the bathroom, where he prepped for work.

Stepping from the building, John was greeted by a warm breeze, which made him feel like it was going to be a good day. He felt refreshed and ready to take on the world. Climbing in his car, he pulled off as the radio played the sounds of 101.6, a jazz station. Within twenty-five minutes, he had arrived at work and opened up the store, ready for the day.

Elsewhere, Keith sat at his desk at work in serious thought. Then, shaking himself free of his newly found fascination with Karen, he remembered that he needed to find out what her connection with the notorious Simon Parks, better known as Jewels, was. Trying to push everything he had on his mind to the side, he started to focus on what was important. Glancing at an old dusty clock on the wall to the right of him, he noticed that it read seven forty-five. Sitting still for a moment, he was still engulfed with the presence of Miss Wells. Now wondering what had come over him, he thought about asking her out, but didn't know if she was Jewels' girlfriend or not. He really didn't want any problems from Mr. Bigtime himself. He couldn't see straight for the obstacles in his path. So as the day progressed and the sunshine turned to rain, it was time for lunch.

Karen turned and asked him if he had an umbrella that he could loan her. He reached under his desk and surfaced with a small black one.

"Here you go!" stated Keith as he handed it to her.

"Thanks," she said, as her smile made his heart race uncontrollably. He couldn't help but to be captivated by her beauty, for her smile was as warm and subtle as a summer's breeze and her body could bring a grown man to his knees. She was beautiful all right, but for months he hadn't noticed. As she left the building along with the rest of the staff, Keith saw that she had left her briefcase behind. He slowly scanned the room to see who had remained. Seeing only one other person besides Mr. Krasdale, he eased out of his seat. He checked to see if the briefcase was locked by hitting the latches. It popped open.

"Yes," he softly said to himself as he looked around again. He pulled it over to his desk and fingered his way through it. Sitting in his chair, he fumbled, looking up every so often.

"Simon Parks, Simon Parks, Simon Parks," he kept saying to himself as he flipped through papers, then through folders. Suddenly, right before his eyes, there it was, Simon Parks, as plain as day on a manila folder. He quickly grabbed it from the briefcase and rushed over to the copier.

Making one copy after another of all the documents, he then put them back in the folder, then back into her briefcase, which he placed back alongside her desk, as if nothing had happened.

Wiping his face, which was full of sweat, he smiled. With copies in hand, he read them over thoroughly, quickly noticing the heading on the stationary: White Picket Fence, Incorporated.

Linking Jewels with the corporation now, Keith continued to read. Learning more and more, he was impressed by the amount of real estate and businesses Jewels was tied in with, jewelry stores and so forth. His partners were Glen Robinson and Kevin Gibbs.

Flipping through expenditures, profit and loss sheets and a long list of investments, Keith had a new respect for this man. After a few more minutes of reading, he put the papers into an unmarked folder, as some of the staff came back in laughing loudly. He sat still afterward, running the new information through his head with the old that he had compiled. Keith sat still, lost in thought. Simon Parks and Kevin Gibbs are more then just partners in crime, they're business partners as well. They live as well legally as they do illegally. Karen must be acting as their financial advisor and organizer, as well as their accountant. He couldn't have found a better person.

An hour later, after Keith had faxed the information that he had discovered to John, John called his lawyer.

"Sharpe, Simpson, and Smith, attorneys-at-law, Jeanette speaking, may I help you?"

"Yes, I'd like to speak to Mr. Sharpe, please," John said politely.

"He's not in at the present time, can I take a message?" she added.

"Yes, can you tell him that Johnathan Jackson called?"

Remembering that Mr. Sharpe had left a message for a John, she checked to see if it was he. She told him to hold on as she put the phone down for a second. When she returned, she relayed it to him, as he was the right person.

"Hello, John, Mr. Sharpe says that the person you asked about has no criminal history."

Pausing for a moment, he thanked her and hung up.

Hours later, as the rain pounded against the windows, John and Tammy read over the new information. They started with the long list of expenditures, which included company vehicles, business trips, etc. They went through profit and loss sheets for the last two year and a list of investments that all seemed to have been in the amount of four thousand dollars to the same sportswear company, Team Players. There were community functions and projects that he gave donations to for the purpose of tax write-offs. According to the documents, John gathered that they were well established as businessmen and had no reason to be hustling at all!

He thought to himself, all that money and power and they still choose to sell drugs. That's crazy, but Tony, on the other hand, is no better. Putting the documents back into the folder that Keith had given him, John handed it to Tammy so she could put it away. She walked to the closet, as John watched.

Noticing that his pager was flashing, it reminded him that he had to meet the boys on the strip. Kissing Tammy good-night, he headed out into the cool night air.

As he drove, he thought of his life as it stood and how drastically it had changed and how quickly it had happened. But as the rain continued, he drove home first to change his clothes, then arrived at Angie's. John became more and more concerned about saving his butt, but also enjoyed playing the roll of an investigator.

Gazing out at his surroundings from Angie's window, he saw nothing but a few people that were working for them. The streets were empty. So they weathered the storm, sold out and packed it up.

John drove Alvin to where his mother was staying, because that was where he wished to go, then he picked up Rick and they headed out to a club. The two danced the night away.

On Friday, April 27, 1990, the rain had let up and the new day set in as the sun started to shine. John woke up looking for his alarm clock, then started to laugh as he thought about what he had done with it. Heading into the bathroom to shower, he grabbed his towel from the foot of his bed. Beneath the warm water, he hummed and sung a old ballad. After about thirty minutes, he rinsed himself off, then went into his bedroom to get dressed. After sitting on the bed, drying off completely, he proceeded to put lotion on. Once fully dressed, he stepped out and headed to his car.

Noticing a note under his left windshield wiper, he retrieved it. It read:

John,

> The kids at the community center miss you. Please, stop by and at least talk to them.

Your
friend forever,
Cherie

John smiled, as if it had made his day. Starting his car, he sat while it idled, then drove off. Before he headed to work, he decided to stop at the coffee shop.

There, he sat down, ordered breakfast, his usual eggs, grits and beef sausage. Jewels and Slim came in right behind him and sat at one of the booths along the right wall. A waitress walked over to them and asked, "What would you gentlemen like?"

"Your phone number!" they both responded, as they laughed and continued to flirt.

After they finally gave their order, John sat eating hoping to go unnoticed. They talked loudly and John seemed to hear it all. All they spoke about was women. Karen's name came up.

"She's nice, very well shaped and just talking to her gets me horny as hell!" stated Jewels.

As their conversation jumped from one woman to another, the waitress put the check face down on the counter in front of John. Picking it up, he placed a tip in the center of the table. He paid the cashier, and rushed out to avoid being seen.

The workday went quickly, but it still wasn't moving fast enough for John. He had an idea and couldn't wait to get paid and get off work. He watched the clock, counting every minute. He thought he had a plan that would top all of his prior ones. Impatiently, he waited for the clock to reach three-thirty. When it finally came, he was out and on his way across the water to New York.

He had planned to purchase some surveillance equipment, voice activated recorders, etc. This idea came to him as he remembered seeing a billboard above one of the buildings along the West Side Highway. The sign read: "We carry all types of surveillance needs, recorders, bugs, mikes, etc."

John couldn't remember the exact location and address, but would recognize it when he saw it, so he drove till he stumbled across it.

It sat back off the street, hidden from plain view. He had to walk down, then under some stairs to get to the entrance. Once inside, he noticed that they had everything that one could imagine and more. Knowing exactly what he wanted, he bought it and quickly left.

Two hours later at Angie's apartment, John paged Wallace, Eric and Rick, telling them to come to her place as soon as they could. Within an hour or so, they were all there and eager to know what was so urgent.

John began to explain. "I want to plant this voice-activated recorder in the hallway that Jewels and his boys operate from. But first, I want someone that they're not familiar with to move in over there, preferably a woman!"

"Now, who would want to live there, in that drug-infested building, except a dope fiend or a homeless person?" said Wallace, seeing a major flaw in John's plan.

John, on the defensive, quickly replied, "Pay somebody to put it in their mailbox then!"

"Who?" Rick asked.

John, unable to think of anyone to use, decided to give it up for the time being. So he left the equipment in the bag, then pushed it under the couch, till he could come up with a sound plan.

"Being that we all are all here, we might as well get some work done," stated John right after.

Wallace responded, "I didn't bring it, because I didn't know what you had planned. I can go get it. It'll only take twenty to thirty minutes." At that precise moment, Wallace left with Eric to get the product so that they could get down to business.

While they were gone, John who was lost in thought, tried to figure a way to infiltrate Jewels' operation. There came a light knock at the door.

"That's Alvin!" Rick shouted.

Opening the door, Rick picked him up and said, I love this little guy!"

Alvin pushed away, then Rick puts him down, as he fought to break free. Alvin headed over to the couch and took a seat. As he did, his foot hit the bag John had placed there.

"What's dis?" asked Alvin as he reached down to touch it.

John grabbed the bag, opened it and showed him. He explained it to him, the same way he had to everyone else.

As John got down to the gloves and mask, Alvin cut him short.

"What do you plan to do with all that?"

"I had planned to put the recorder in a mailbox or something in the hallway that Jewels operates from. But I don't know anyone that lives there," replied John.

"Don't worry about it, I'll take care of this!" Alvin stated as he grabbed the recorder.

Alvin headed out the door, walked over and through the crowd of people, hoping to go unnoticed. But waiting in the hallway was Smoke (one of Jewels, boys), sitting on the stairs with a submachine gun in his lap.

"Well, well, well, what do we have here? What's up?" he asked.

Alvin stopped in his tracks, looked at him, then tried to march past. Smoke put his arm out to prevent this.

"Where are you going?" he asked with sinister grin on his face.

151

"I-- want to work with you again," stuttered Alvin as he couldn't come up with anything else to say.

"Oh yeah, right, like he's gonna trust you after you've been running with those cats. Man, you're just wasting your time. What happened with you and those kids anyway?"

"They're too cheap, plus, they're not treating me right. They treat me like I'm a little kid!"

Smoke spoke after a short pause.

"I doubt that Jewels will want anything to do with you, but I'll ask him. You wait right here!" Smoke stressed to Alvin as he got up and headed up the stairs.

Alvin listened as a door opened and shut, then rushed to plant the recorder behind the staircase. Jamming it into place, he hoped it was in a good spot.

Suddenly Smoke came running back down the stairs.

"He said for you to get your little ass out of here, before he wipes the sidewalk with you and them fags across the street."

Smoke escorted Alvin from the building, not sensing a thing.

Alvin thanked him for his effort and then dragged himself back across the street. He carried on with a sad face as he kept his head down to add drama to his little show. Reaching the other side, he looked back and then proceeded into Angie's building. He laughed as he ran up the stairs and into the apartment.

"It's not in the best spot, but it's there! Smoke was sitting in the hall, so I had to lie. I told him I needed work and he ran to ask Jewels; then I put it under the stairs," Alvin stated as he smiled, then bounced down onto the couch.

"I guess that's good enough, considering that they stay in the hall most of the time anyway!" added John.

A loud knock at the door silenced everyone.

"That must be Wallace and Eric," stated Rick.

Peeping through the peephole, Rick snatched the door open after he was certain who it was them. The two of them rushed in.

"There's a whole lot of money out there! Come on, let's get to work," stated Wallace as he rushed to get prepared.

John pulled his hat down to his eyebrows as usual and started to prepare himself.

John and Eric left to get to work. As fast as they put the product in their workers' hands, they sold it. They called through the headsets for more and Wallace met John in the hallway of 207. John gave Wallace the money he collected and in return, he was given more product. Wallace headed out the back, as John walked toward the front to resume business. Just as he approached the front entrance, Eric stumbled in, as John noticed patrol cars pulling up everywhere. John turned around and the two of them raced up the flight of stairs. Shortly after, Wallace came running up behind them.

A voice came over the headsets. "Don't come out, they're all over the place! They even ran up in the building Jewels operates from!"

John, Eric and Wallace sat on the steps breathing heavily from their short run. All of a sudden the sound of walkie-talkies interrupted them. The trio eased up another flight, trying not to be heard. Their facial expressions looked worrisome, as the sound of police radios seemed to get closer.

Just as one of the wooden planks in the floor creaked, one of the officers announced that it was all clear. The officers then walked down the stairs and out of the building. John and the fellows' faces showed great relief.

"Damn, that was close!" Eric whispered, still kind of out of breath. They sat and made themselves comfortable, until the police had left.

"Alvin," Wallace whispered through the headset.

"Yeah, stay put! They're still out there and they're searching the area. Hold up! Now an ambulance is pulling up and they're going in the building that Jewels operates from," Alvin responded, then stopped talking.

Wallace and the gang hung on for further information. Then after a few minutes passed, they heard, "They're bringing somebody out. It's Tasha! She probably overdosed again," added Alvin.

As the ambulance pulled off with its flashing lights on and sirens going, it disappeared as it turned right. One at a time the patrol cars left, all but one. It remained to slow or detour drug sales.

Alvin spoke again.

"It's all clear, there's just one car out in the front."

The shook trio walked down the stairs and out the back, when an officer in a patrol car noticed them as he rode by, then backed up. They ran into 210, where Angie lived, yelling through their headsets, "Open the door, now!"

After reaching the top of the stairs, the door stood wide open.

Once everyone was in, Alvin closed the door quickly.

As they all fought to catch their breath, Eric spoke. "They're not going to let this be easy, are they?"

John walked over to the window and peaked out. Suddenly everyone got quiet, as the sound of a walkie-talkie echoed in the hall. So they all sat in silence, until they were sure that the officers had left. Figuring that they had made enough and didn't want to be caught, they decided to shut down and call it a night. The police presence remained strong for the rest of that evening.

Wallace pulled the money from the safe that was bolted to the floor. He placed the drugs within, then closed it back up and brought the money up front into the living room. They all sat around as it was being counted. It amounted to five thousand, three hundred and thirty-three dollars.

Placing elastic bands around each of the stacks of fives, tens, etc., he then put it into a shoulder bag and slid it under the couch, leaving it there till they were ready to go. For the next hour or so, they sat around drinking beer, while Alvin sipped from a soda can.

At eleven-forty, John looked out at the street and all he saw was emptiness. He figured, no time better than the present to leave. Noticing that John was ready, Wallace jumped to his feet, grabbed the bag, kissed Angie and headed for the door.

As they all marched through the hall area, John asked jokingly as everyone listened, "What was that all about?"

Wallace just smiled. "She's sweet, I like her," he admitted.

Upon reaching the car, they all piled in and raced down the street to a red light.

Saturday morning, April 28 had finally arrived. A beautiful day it was, from the cool summer breeze, to the green leaf-filled trees. Yet it was another trying day in the life of Johnathan Jackson. As surely as the day started, he expected it to test him. He just didn't know from what angle. So on this day he walked through his apartment, barefooted, in his boxer shorts. When he reached the front, he woke Alvin up.

"Get up, little brother!"

He then walked into the kitchen to pour himself a cup of tea. As he sipped from the mug, he spoke again.

"Look, it's nine o'clock. Let's get an early start. Here's some money for you. Go spend it on your sister and give your mother some, so she'll keep her mouth closed."

"What are you going to do today?" asked Alvin.

"I'm going to search out a few things, then I'll be at Tammy's."

By eleven, o'clock they both were dressed and on their way. John drove Alvin to where his mother stayed, now on Ninth Street.

Arriving at their first destination, which was the park, John got out and opened the trunk, where he took out some sweats and begin to get dressed right where he stood. Jogging alongside the roadway in the park, he started to analyze the last few months of his life and decided to give it all up: the drugs, the hunt for evidence, everything and let his life go back to normal, or close to it. He figured he'd let his lawyer handle it from there on.

Later, as he tried to tell Tammy this, she told him that she understood, but his lawyer knew no more than he did. She also expressed how much she didn't like him out there, either, because it left her worried.

"What the hell am I paying him for! I can't believe he can't find a loophole. There's got to be somethin'!"

John carried on as he paced back and forth with a look of angry confusion on his face.

Dropping to his knees, he yelled, "Please help me, Lord!"

Placing his head in his hands, he sat still as Tammy looked on, feeling his pain. Watching him drown in his misery, she felt helpless. Minutes later, he stood up and seemed much calmer.

"I need to take a nice long vacation, somewhere beautiful and relaxing," he stated.

Tammy nodded her head as if to agree.

"Honey, I know it looks bad. But you've got to be strong, turn this thing around, upside down, whatever! Don't let it beat you!"

John smiled and hugged her.

"What would I do without you?"

Walking over to the window, he recited a poem.

> "I stand before the world a man,
> neither perfect in my past or present.
> But I refuse to be blamed for those that have killed,
> when it is them that I refuse to shield.
> But if one must continue to murder our African seeds,
> kill me, for it is easier.
> For I play the front line,
> bearing my heart on my sleeve, as always."

He slowly placed his right hand against the glass of the window, as if to feel the warmth of the sun.

"All these years, I've been wearing my heart on my sleeve. Just when it is I who needs a little love in return, the community turns its back. Now I'm part of the blame that I speak of shielding our children from," he rambled.

"No!" Tammy blurted as she interrupted.

"So explain to me why I participate in drug dealing? I can't do it any more!" stated John as he stormed out the door.

Back in his own living room, stressed out, he stared at the ceiling. Then he pulled it together enough to call Tony, to tell him he was finished.

Tony said, "Yo, I know you're feeling kind of unsure, but it'll pass."

John shouted, "I'm serious. I don't want nothing to do with nothing no more!"

"Yo don't have a choice, have you forgotten," Tony returned.

"Do what you have to do, then! I'm not slinging nothin!" instructed an angry Johnathan.

"You know what? You got dat. I'm going to let your brother run things. If you change your mind, you're always welcome."

"Thanks, but no thanks. But as far as finding Darryl's killer, I've still got to pursue that!" responded John.

Seconds after John hung up the phone, he felt as if someone lifted about eighty pounds from his shoulders. In those few seconds, he decided to call Tammy to tell her the news.

"I quit!" he announced, sounding relieved and cheerful. "Now all I got to worry about is the murder trial!" he added without pause.

He apologized for all he had put her through, then not long after, he was on his way to the community center.

Once inside, where he watched the kids play, he begin to feel like he hadn't felt in a long time. As he walked through the place, he noticed a few volunteers, and begin to approach one of them who stood in the center of the floor.

"Hello, I'm Johnathan Jackson, a former volunteer," John stated as he extended his hand.

The counselor looked at him then smiled, shaking John's hand as he began to speak.

"Hello, I'm John Hammond."

John said, "I just stopped by to speak with the kids and to play ball with them."

"Mr. Jackson, Mr. Jackson!," one of the kids yelled, as he came to a halt in front of John and the counselor. "We miss you here! When are you coming back? Mark's in the hospital. He got hit by a car yesterday, when we were playing football in the street." Pausing to catch his breath, the kid just stood there waiting for John to respond.

Now concerned, John asked, "What hospital is he in?"

"The university," the kid replied.

"What's his last name?" John asked.

"Anderson, Mark Anderson," he answered.

"Thanks!"

John stayed long enough to play a few games of basketball, then at six P.M. he glanced at his watch and made his way off the court. As he did he said good-night to the kids.

Heading to the hospital, he asked for Mark Anderson when he arrived at the front desk. The receptionist gave him a blue pass, then directed him to the Intensive Care Unit.

Reaching Mark's room, John noticed two older people standing over his bed. John assumed they were Mark's parents. The two didn't even notice John as he entered. He watched them. They were obviously happy that Mark was all right as they held his hands tightly.

"Hello," greeted John, hoping not to startle them.

Mark's parents looked up with tears in their eyes, but happiness was in their expression. Mark, who looked up also, introduced everyone.

"Hey, Mom and Dad, this is John, the guy I always tell you about!" With his usual perkiness, he had a spirit that couldn't be killed.

"Hi, how are you?" they politely asked, almost in unison.

"Our son speaks very highly of you!" Mr. Anderson added.

John smiled and then directed his attention to Mark, who was lying in the bed.

"How are you, champ?" John asked out of concern.

"I'm okay, but the kids at the community center miss you a lot," Mark remarked.

"So I've heard. I'll stop in periodically to check on you guys, okay?" John told him, because he knew Mr. Myers wouldn't take him back due to the turmoil surrounding him.

Then he looked at the clock on the wall behind him. It read seven-thirty. "I've got to go!" John told Mark as he bid the Andersons a good-night. Before he left, he also told Mark he'd see him tomorrow. He walked from the room to the elevator, from the elevator to the car.

As he drove, his pager started beeping. He looked at the number, then returned the call.

"Hello," John said.

"Yo, John, this is Tony. I need the car."

John was disappointed, but knew it was coming, so he told Tony he could come and get it at ten that night. He figured to be home by then. Tony agreed and hung up.

At ten that evening, John sat watching television and eating Chinese food. Suddenly there was a knock at the door.

"Who is it?" he asked.

"Wallace!"

John opened the door, shook his hand and invited him in.

"So you're giving it up? I understand," stated Wallace. "No need for explanations," he added, cutting John off as he started to respond. "You're still all right with me!" he finished.

Knowing why he had come, John walked over to the lamp table, picked up his keys and removed the car keys from the chain. After giving them to Wallace, John hugged him and then Wallace headed back out the door.

He turned and said, "I admire you, you're a strong brother." Then Wallace walked out.

John closed the door, sat down and finished his meal in front of the television.

Later, as John slept, Alvin came in, tired and worn down from spending the day with his mother and sister. He just dropped across the couch and went to sleep, also.

Two days later, as morning rolled around, John had woken up and gotten out early. He was back to catching the bus. On his way to the bus stop, he stopped at the coffee shop to get a newspaper and a bite to eat. While waiting for his food, he fumbled through the pages. He unknowingly stumbled onto an article, entitled:

DRUGS SEIZED, DEALER KILLED.

Right below that one, was:

TWO SOUGHT IN DEADLY SHOOTOUT
TWO KILLED, TWO INJURED

"Your food, sir!" a waitress announced as she held the plate in her hands. John quickly put the paper to the side, as she placed his plate in front of him and he began to eat. After he had finished and had paid his bill, he headed for the bus stop.

Looking at his watch, which read six twenty-eight A.M., he hurried because he was cutting it close. Figuring the bus should be there or on its way, he fumbled through his pockets for change, as he started to trot. Five minutes after he arrived at the bus stop, it came flying up and threw its doors open. John stepped on, then fought his way to the back of the bus. As he embraced the daily grind, once again he smiled. He felt that all the good that he had killed within, had been revived.

At that same time, Keith also arrived at work at the firm. He noticed that Karen hadn't come in yet. About eleven-fifteen she walked in with a frightened look on her face. Walking straight past everyone, ignoring them as they spoke, her focal point was Mr. Krasdale's office.

After exiting his office, she grabbed a few papers and folders from her desk, then left. Something was definitely going on, thought Keith.

Back at the Sandwich Spot, John called his lawyer, while it was on his mind.

"Hello, is Mr. Sharpe in?" he asked.

"Yes, he is, Mr. Jackson. How are you today?" asked the polite and now familiar voice of the receptionist.

After a brief pause, Mr. Sharpe picked up.

"Hello, John, I've found out from ballistics that all the bullets came from the same gun. They all were fired at close range, execution style."

"I told you it was an execution!" John aggressively mentioned.

"So our defense is, one man is all they saw running from the park. We know one man couldn't have possibly held three guys at bay, then shoot them square in the head, one at a time. At least one of them would have tried to run. On top of that, you, the alleged killer, picked up a basketball, then takes flight. It just doesn't make sense. Not only that, the gun was found in a dumpster three blocks from your house. In most of the statements I've read, everyone said they saw you with a ball, not a gun! Then there's the fact that you did report the shooting. Now why would someone report a shooting, if they did it? It's all crazy; it makes no sense at all. Don't worry, I can't really see them convicting you."

Hearing all of this, John forgot what it was he called for. Then it came back to him.

"Mr. Sharpe, I'm bringing you some money this week, as soon as I get a chance."

"Fine," he replied.

As the day passed and work had ended, John stepped outside. He had forgotten how much he missed by sheltering himself in the confines of automobiles and buses. He enjoyed everything around him, so much that he decided to walk to the hospital to see Mark, then head home.

Later, just as he arrived home, Alvin was sitting up playing a video game. John, glad he was still around, decided to sit down and talk with him. He sat beside Alvin, as he picked up the other controller.

"What's up?" John asked as he stared into the television and Alvin reset the game so the two of them could play it together.

"What's up with you?" Alvin returned as he put down the remote and spoke.

"I'm glad you asked," John stated, then continued. "I've stopped hustling. That's not what I wish to do with my life. But you, on the other, need to figure out what it is that you want to do with yours. If you wish to stay here, you have to go to school in September. No more hanging out all night, no more drug dealing, and I promise you, I'll help you as much as I can."

Alvin smiled and agreed.

John, thought as he hugged the little guy, he's not bad. He just needs someone, who cares enough to reach out and help, someone to point him in the right direction.

Shortly after, at the supermarket, the two of them picked up some much-needed groceries. On their way back to the apartment, they walked past a few young guys smoking weed. Alvin knew them.

John, noticing the expression on Alvin's face, asked, "Are they friends of yours?"

"Yeah, but now they're getting high, they're being stupid. Ain't nothing cool about dat! I've seen my mom; high all the time, her friends high, I've seen people do crazy stuff for drugs, you know. I'll never get high!," Alvin stated as he took it personally.

John smiled, because he thought he had made a difference in someone's life. He thought, as the saying goes; if you can reach one lost soul, you have made a difference.

Putting his arm around Alvin as they headed home, John enjoyed the night air.

As the evening progressed, they made a home cooked dinner for their invited guest. Finishing up, they set the table, as a knock at the door alerted them to her presence.

"It's Tammy!" Alvin shouted. He walked over to the door to let her in.

"Hello, Tammy," Alvin greeted as he opened the door to allow her to come in.

She entered and took a deep breath.

"Umm, something smells good in here!" she expressed with a smile.

"Your table awaits you, madam," Alvin told her.

He escorted her into the kitchen, then to the table, where he pulled her chair out for her to be seated. She smiled, then laughed, as she wondered where John was. He came out from the back, nicely dressed in a silk shirt and dress slacks. He was carrying a bottle of wine in one hand, flowers in the other.

Before he sat down, he gave her the flowers, kissed her on the mouth and told her he loved her. She smiled, then leaned over and kissed him again, then thanked them both.

Alvin lit the candles and turned off the lights and sat down to John's left. They all ate, watched television and talked. Alvin dozed off. Tammy kissed him on the cheek as she and John headed to the back, into the bedroom and closed the door.

Morning came, as Tammy rested asleep against John, and the breeze blew back the curtains. The pigeons played on the window ledge. John, who had woken up, picked his head up from his pillow. He looked at Tammy, smiled, then went back to sleep, forgetting about work, finally able to really relax.

The next thing he knew, she was up and yelling at him.

"Get dressed before you're late for work!"

John, tired, suggested to her that the two of them should take the day off, and they did. About eight-thirty, after Tammy had notified her boss, and John had called his father, John ran out to get a newspaper. When he came back, he burst in yelling, scaring everyone to death.

"Look!" he shouted as Alvin jumped up and Tammy came running from the back, wearing his green robe.

"Look!" he said again, as he pulled the paper wide open.

Tammy and Alvin both looked around each side, at the article he wished them to see:

MAJOR DRUG DEALER SOUGHT

After a series of raids, twenty-nine,-year-old Simon Parks was nowhere to be found at a building on the well-known Clinton Avenue, a.k.a. The Strip, yesterday evening.

One hundred fifty decks of heroin were recovered, estimated street value, fifteen hundred dollars. Two nine-millimeter handguns were also confiscated at that same location. At 150 Avon Avenue, two more guns and fourteen grams of cocaine were confiscated.

Seven persons were arrested: Kevin Gibbs, 29; Timmy Kates, 21; Andre Atkins, 23; Jamie Roberts, 19; Kim Hollands, 27' William Walker, 18; Cathy Spears 44.

A few other locations were raided, but there was nothing found, not even Mr. Parks.

John, pacing back and forth, decidedly happy about the turn of events, thought to himself, What's my next move?

Meanwhile in a suite, in the Pocono's, Jewels sat in a Jacuzzi with two lady friends of his. Laughing and sipping from a cocktail glass, he was unaware of what was going on back in the streets, and that was a lot.

By being his usual self-absorbed self, Jewels didn't think to check on anyone. He just played with his two playmates, enjoying the afternoon.

Hours later, as he drove up the turnpike heading home, he continuously tried to contact Slim. But on every attempt, he failed. He thought to himself, something's got to be wrong. He tried paging other employees, but again he received no answer. Frustrated, he called a few others, then Karen. Finally he got in touch with someone, Karen, who quickly blurted the news as soon as she knew it was him.

"Have you read today's paper?" she asked.

"No," he quickly responded, waiting for her reply.

"Well, the police raided the strip and a few of your other spots. Now they're looking for you!"

"Karen, call my lawyer! His name is Mr. Goodman. His number is 705-6615. Tell him I want him to find out what's what! Tell him I'll meet him tomorrow at eight in the morning, in his office."

Jewels hung up and raced to a nearby hotel.

Wednesday morning came. Jewels and his lawyer met as planned. His lawyer explained the situation to him.

"They say they have you on tape and have phone conversations and deals that you were party to. They're assuming that you run the whole strip and you're moving everything from soup to nuts. They want you to turn yourself in and I think it might be best. I don't think they really have a case."

"I say what's best! You do as I say, you hear me?" Jewels shouted.

His lawyer finally convinced him to turn himself in. He was locked up immediately, as one of the detectives handed a list of charges to him and his lawyer:

Conspiracy to violate New Jersey narcotics' laws
Illegal distribution of cocaine, heroin, etc.
Organizing
Kingpin

The detective from the Bureau of Narcotic (B.O.N.) went on, only to be interrupted by Mr. Goodman.

"I hope you guys have all that you say, because if not, I'll have you lying in your own shit!"

The officer stood up and said, "He's under arrest as of now! If there's something else you wish to discuss with him before we put him away, I suggest that you do so!" Then he walked from the room, slamming the door behind him.

Later; as Jewels sat in a cell by himself, he laughed hard and loud.

Meanwhile, at Tony's, Jewels' competitor gathered everyone around. He told them to shut down for a few days, just till things cooled down and he knew exactly what was going on. He got no arguments from anyone.

Back at Tammy's, she and John sat, thinking. A few minutes later, he picked up the phone to call his lawyer.

"Hello, Mr. Sharpe, I know I asked you this before, but I know there has to be something on Simon Parks, the drug dealer arrested after the raids."

"I'll see," answered Mr. Sharpe. "I'll ask my partner. He's a former member of the D.E.A. (Drug Enforcement Agency). He can probably contact one of his buddies and find out something."

John expressed his thanks and hung up. As he sat on the couch staring at the articles and documents, it came to him. Maybe he could creep into Jewels' home while he was locked up.

Eagerly he jumped up, as Tammy asked, "What's up?"

Hesitantly he told her and then quickly made his way to the door. She ran behind him, refusing to let him go without her. He paused to tell her no, but knew she wasn't going to listen, so he turned and continued on.

Rushing down the stairs, John called Rick's place to see if he was home. Maria answered and told him he wasn't there. So he called Keith, who told him he'd be right there. Once he had arrived, they climbed right in, with John in the front and Tammy in the back.

"Where exactly are we headed?" asked Keith as he pulled away from the curb.

"Montclair, 115 Seabright Terrace, Jewels' house," stated John.

"What's up at his place?" asked Keith.

"I just want to see what's what. Maybe I can slip in while he's away," explained John.

"You're crazy, that guy will have both of us killed if he thinks were in his business!"

"If you're not with me, drop me off, I'll do it myself!"

"No, John, let's just wait for another time," interrupted Tammy.

"No! I'm not waiting. There might not be another time!" John shouted as he started to get angry.

"Okay, John, if you must, I'll be right there with you," added Keith, not wanting John to go by himself.

John smiled and then patted Keith on the back.

Keith stated to John, "I don't think this is at all sane!"

John looked at him, then at Tammy as he said, "I know, but I got to do what I got to do!"

"Now what do you hope to find there?" Keith asked curiously.

"I'm hoping there's something that can help me, or should I say, my case. A failure beats the hell out of not trying at all!"

Once on Bloomfield Avenue, they drove as Keith stated over and over to himself, "This is stupid."

After a few lights, they turned onto Seabright Terrace, then onto the dead-end street. After parking near the corner of Seabright and the dead-end street, which for some reason didn't have a sign, Keith and John both climbed out. They walked across and down toward Jewels' house.

In front of it, they marched through the grass and up to the door. John rang the bell, but no one answered.

Heading back through the grass, the two peeked in the driveway. Suddenly the front door opened and a woman peaked out.

Shook up, they slowly turned to see. As they did, Keith noticed it was Karen standing in the doorway, as beautiful as ever. Keith caught himself drooling. He quickly straightened up and tried to play it off.

"Hello, Karen, I didn't know you stayed here," he stated as he smiled and walked back to the porch. John just watched as he smiled, also.

She answered, "I don't. I'm just house-sitting for a friend."

He walked up the stairs, now face to face with her.

"Who's the friend?" he asked.

"Now you're being a bit nosy," she stated as she backed up a step, then two.

Tammy watched from the car, as Keith told Karen that they were just admiring the house. He said that he had seen it one time before and it caught his attention. Nervously, he asked John, "Isn't that right, man!"

John nodded, yes.

Karen looked around and then asked him where his car was. He fumbled for words, as she looked him in the face, waiting for an answer.

Then it came to him. "I have a friend who lives not far from here. He does excellent mechanic's work! He's changing my oil and plugs as we speak. So rather then stand around, we decided to take a walk and here we are."

She smirked as if she didn't believe him, but didn't know what to think.

"Well, it's nice seeing you," she told him, as she stepped back and pushed the door shut.

He stood there with his mouth wide open.

"Bye, Keith!" she shouted through the door, knowing he was still standing there.

Knowing that she didn't believe a word of what he told her, Keith started cursing to himself, as he and John walked back to the car.

Tammy opened the door to allow them to get in. After hearing them arguing back and forth, she told them both to get in. Upon pulling off, she spoke again.

"You guys didn't really believe a guy of Jewels' power and stature would leave his home totally unprotected, did you?"

John sat still lost in thought.

4 THE CONFLICT

FRIDAY, MAY 25, 1990

Jewel's runners were all out on bail. He had made bail that first week, one hundred thousand cash. Everything slowly eased back to normal, but Jewels came nowhere near the strip. For that matter, neither did Slim. Karen had told Jewels about the incident concerning Keith. Thinking that he was snooping, Jewels figured he'd have his boys pay him a visit.

Night fell on this unusually hot day. John was sitting in his living room, under the air conditioner, playing video games and laughing with Alvin. The phone rang.

"Hello, John?" the voice requested.

"Yes, this is he," he replied.

"This is Mr. Sharpe. I had my partner check out the name Simon Parks. He found out that, as we speak, his friend is investigating several drug-related murders. He thinks your Mr. Parks may have ordered them, all of which have him baffled. Keep this to yourself, because he believes there's a leak within the precinct."

"Thanks a million!" John said, then added, "Do you think you can get the dates of these murders?"

"Yes, I have them right here. Come in tomorrow and I'll give them to you," stated Mr. Sharpe as their phone conversation came to an end.

After hanging up, John looked at Alvin.

"Let's take a walk," he suggested.

Alvin shut everything off and the two of them headed out the door.

"Where are we going?" asked Alvin as he stared at John, waiting for an answer.

"Just for a walk," he answered.

Walking now, they come across a former customer from the strip.

"Hey, what you got?" asked the poorly dressed man.

John quickly responded, "I'm not in that line of work no more!"

They walked away as the drug addict watched, then stumbled over him self.

In stride Alvin stated, "I don't understand why people do drugs." He looked to John for an answer.

John told him as he smiled first, "They do them for the same reason we sold them. They got addicted; it's a habit. Just like making that fast money, it comes so fast and so easy, you become obsessed with it to the point that you're chasing it and will do anything to get more of it!"

There was a long silence, as Alvin absorbed everything that was said. Then, just as they turned the corner, from Fifteenth Street onto Clinton Avenue, they walked into a store. They brought a bag full of junk food, then headed to the video store, to rent a few movies.

Afterward, they went home and enjoyed the rest of the evening.

For the next month, John just relaxed and tried to spend as much time as he could with Tammy. They went to carnivals and amusement parks. He was happy, at least for the time being. They walked along beaches, letting the sand cover their feet. What a month, he thought to himself. The trial and the streets seemed to be the last thing on his mind. But he knew that it was still there. He felt that if he had to go to jail, he'd better enjoy himself now. So as the sun beamed in each day, he lived them as if they were his last.

The 4th of July crept up. John, Alvin and Tammy all headed to New York to enjoy the fireworks. As all the fireworks and explosives echoed for miles, everyone yelled and cheered for more. Slowly, as the evening passed away, they headed back home.

After dropping Alvin off at John's place, he and Tammy went to hers.

The next morning, Keith was off to work, but the Karen that he encountered would be a lot less sociable. She rolled her eyes and looked through him as if he was the worst person alive. As the work day progressed, then ended, she left in a hurry. Keith took his time. As usual, he was the last to leave.

On the steps to his home, Keith opened the door, only to find out that someone had broken in. He couldn't help but notice the inscription on the living room wall. It read: "Stay the hell out of my business or I'll kill you!"

After reading that and stepping over a broken lamp and some scattered papers, he realized that he had gotten into a little too deep. In a panic, he paged John and waited for him to call back. As he looked around he saw that his leather loveseat had been cut up and that they left the entire place in shambles.

But as he sat, the phone did not ring. Keith tried again, calling John's apartment and, once again, there was no answer. Now even more shook up, he decided to leave a message.

"Hello, John, this is Keith. Man, they've got me scared. Jewels had someone come to my home and they trashed it! I love you, man, but I can't get involved anymore. I think I'm going to take a little time off and go see my family or something. Love you, man." The dial tone sounded, as the trembling voice of Keith rambled as if he was convinced that his life was in danger.

Later, about six that evening, John walked into his place, sat down and listened to his answering machine. As soon as he heard Keith's message, he called him, but he didn't pick up. John called again and again, but there was no answer. Worried, he looked in his address book for Keith's address. After finding it, he decided to pay him a visit. But just as he prepped to leave, the phone rang. It was Keith.

Alvin walked through the door at that same instant.

John grabbed the phone as Alvin stood there listening.

"John, my place was trashed; these people you're messing with mean business!"

Detecting the fear in Keith's voice, John tried to calm him down.

"Listen, man, I understand. Get yourself together."

"I knew going to his home was a bad idea, I knew it! John, I'm scared, I'm scared I might be next!" Keith babbled on.

John, hearing this, told him, "You've got to pull it together, go somewhere safe. I don't need to lose anybody else!"

They talked a little while longer and then hung up.

John faced Alvin, who had a puzzled look on his face.

"What's wrong with you?" John asked.

"Who was that, acting like they were scared to death?" Alvin asked.

Not really wanting to elaborate, John answered, "We have enough problems of our own. No need to concern ourselves with others and theirs."

Alvin, sensing that John didn't wish to tell him, left it alone. John, remembering he had an appointment with his lawyer, called him to tell him he'd be a little late. After which he headed to his office, dragging Alvin along with him, for his own safety. Fearing that Jewels might have figured it was him behind it all.

Arriving finally, he sat for about twenty minutes, while Mr. Sharpe talked with another of his clients. As the person exited, he told John to come in. After they exchanged greetings, Mr. Sharpe handed John copies of a few documents on his desk. These documents contained the dates and times of a few drug-related murders.

John quickly looked them over, but focused on one date in particular, the murder of Kenneth Tombs. Who, according to the documents, was murdered on December 2nd.

Waking from thought, he handed Mr. Sharpe a check in the amount of two thousand dollars. Placing the list back in the folder that was given to him, John made his exit. He and Alvin walked out together and headed to Tammy's.

Reaching Tammy's, she let them in. John rushed into her bedroom, grabbing the rest of his papers and clippings, as Alvin and Tammy wondered what he was up to. He came back and sat on the couch with them on each side of him, as he opened a folder marked expenditures. He made comparisons, but could not see a connection. Disappointed, but still determined, he looked through investments and compared them to the dates in question. The investments included a beauty salon in which Jewels had invested nine thousand dollars on January 17, 1989, a sportswear company in which he had invested five thousand dollars on August 25, 1989, and a grocery store he had invested twenty thousand in on November eleventh, 1989. Another, for four thousand, went to True to Life Sportswear on August nineteenth, 1989. Then another deposit to True to Life Sportswear, on December 10th, 1989. Looking at the article on

Darryl Ward, who was murdered on August twentieth, 1989, he eagerly shuffled through the papers to find an article on Silk. He found it, as Tammy and Alvin looked to see what it was that he noticed.

The article stated that Kenneth Tombs expired December second, 1989. Looking back and forth from the articles to the list of so-called investments, John stared as he thought.

"What is it, baby?" Tammy asked. "Nothing, it's just that the dates of the murders and the disbursements of funds to this sportswear company are quite close."

He looked for the owner's name, which was Kenneth Gates. He also noticed that there was a payment made, November nineteenth, 1989 and another to this same company more recently, on April fifteenth.

John began to search for the article on Kelly's murder.

"Bingo!" he stated to himself as he noticed that Kelly was shot and murdered on November twenty-fourth, 1989, the day after Thanksgiving. But he could not link anything to the date in April. He searched and thought, but came up with nothing. He figured either Jewels murdered someone else already or intended to. But, why the long wait this time? Could it be that, whoever it was, he changed his mind about, or was all this just plain madness?

Confused, he decided to let it go, at least for the moment.

"He'll slip up eventually!" John said to himself.

Elsewhere, Jewels was on the phone talking.

"You owe me because you botched up that job. I'll leave the information in an envelope, you know where!"

The mysterious voice responded, "For the record, I didn't botch up shit! You told me to hold up, let it rest."

"Well now, this one's for sure!" stated Jewels.

The operator interrupted, asking for a deposit of a nickel, so they hung up because there was nothing else to talk about.

On Friday, July 6, John and Tammy walked through the park after a long day's work. They sat on a bench, enjoying each other's company. John promised her he'd never leave her. As the two lovers held hands and walked from the park, they were engulfed in each other, never noticing that a small burgundy car was following them. They walked for blocks with the car not far behind. It eased past them and parked, with the occupants just watching. Then, as they walked past a vacant lot, the car quickly shot up alongside them. Two of the guy raised guns and begin to unload, hitting John in the shoulder and the jaw. As he fell, Tammy was shot in the center of her head and she tumbled over with her eyes wide and motionless. Still holding John's hand, she struck the pavement as another bullet hit John in the chest area. The car sped off, as the two lay still, somehow managing to hold onto each other's hand.

The people who saw the shooting ran to help Tammy and John as they lay drenched in their own blood. John lay choking in serious pain, unable to move. Tammy was still with a hole through her head and blood all over her face. He squeezed her hand and prayed for the best, as a mouthful of blood stopped him from calling out her name. People began to crowd around to see what was going on and couldn't believe what they saw.

Finally the police arrived, along with detective Jones and two ambulances. The officers asked everyone to back up, as they put up the yellow tape to close off the scene.

Seeing that John was still alive and barely conscious, they rushed him to one of the awaiting ambulances, as the sheets that his limp body lay on became soaked with his blood.

Tears ran from the faces of some of the onlookers, as the ambulance pulled away with it s lights flashing. Tammy, in the midst of this, lay still on the pavement, with a sheet covering her lifeless body.

The crime lab pulled up, inspected the scene, picking up all the bullets they could find, along with their casings. They marked the spots where they were found and even took statements from the few eyewitnesses. But the most anyone saw was a burgundy car with tinted windows. No one could give a good description of the shooters.

As everything wound down, two guys in black jumpers with big bold letters on the back that spelled CORONER, jumped from a blue van. After putting on their gloves, they removed Tammy's body from the dried blood on the pavement, placing it in a body bag, then onto a gurney, then into the blue van. As it disappeared, so did the remainder of the crowd.

Meanwhile, at the hospital, John fought for his life, as he was being operated on. They removed the bullets from his chest and shoulder without any complications. They were not immediately concerned about the one to the face, being that it went in one side and out the other, shattering teeth and shredding gums in the process. He survived the surgery and was placed in I.C.U. as they searched his belongings for identification. The only piece of identification they found was a business card, which read:

Johnathan Jackson
624-2234

This matched the identification the police had provided. One of the nurses was told to call the number, but got no one, so she left a message for whomever to get in touch with University Hospital.

Elsewhere, Rick sat at Angie's with the gut instinct that something was wrong. He looked outside and saw Dre, Slim and Jewels sitting on a wall conversing. He watched Eric, who sat outside also, keeping his eyes on things.

Uncertain about things, Rick walked over to the phone and called his brother. Alvin answered.

"Hello!"

"Is John around?" Rick asked rudely.

"No."

"Have you seen him?"

"No. Why, is something wrong?" asked Alvin, now worried himself.

"I don't know, it just feels like..." Rick cut the conversation short and hung up. He tried paging John, but received no return call.

Wallace stopped cuddling with Angie long enough to ask, "What's up?"

"That's just it, I don't know!" stated Rick as he grabbed his gun from one of the kitchen cabinets, placing it along the waistband of his pants, while pulling his shirt over it. He walked out as Wallace looked at Angie, then followed him with a confused look on his face.

As the two of them left, Angie rose and walked over to the window. She looked out and around, but saw nothing out of the ordinary. Then she saw Rick's car go flying through the intersection. She wondered to herself what was going on.

Rick drove to Tammy's place, but there was no answer. He stopped at their father's business, but again, nothing.

Their father told him that John might have stopped to see his lawyer. Rick tried to calm down for a minute, wanting to believe the best. He decided to page John again and he used the business phone to make this desperate call. He paged him four times consecutively, but there was no return call within the entire thirty minute period he waited.

"Dad, something's wrong! He always calls me back!" he shouted as he raced out and jumped back into the car with Wallace.

Driving, Rick pulled his gun from beneath his shirt, snatched out the clip to make sure it was full and secure. He quickly slapped it back in, as Wallace tried to watch him and drive at the same time.

"Drive through the strip!" Rick stated, as he stared blankly through the front windshield.

"Hold up, if you're planning to do something stupid, I'm not going through there!" warned Wallace.

Hearing this, Rick placed the gun on the floor of car between his feet.

"Look, John never disappears without somebody knowing something. Plus, he has a cellular phone, so why isn't he returning my calls? I paged him and put in 9-1-1."

All of a sudden Rick received a page and so did Wallace. It was John's home phone number that appeared.

Wallace quickly pulled over near a phone booth, as Rick barely let him come to a stop, before he bailed out.

Just as he did, Wallace shouted, "See, and you were worried. That's probably him right there!"

Rick relieved now, dialed John's number. As soon as the phone was picked up, he blurted, "John!"

His voice went from excited back to worrisome, after Alvin spoke.

"John got shot! He's in the hospital!" Alvin explained hysterically.

Rick slammed the phone down and then ran back to the car, leaving Alvin hanging. He told Wallace with tears streaming from his eyes. "My brother's been shot! Please get me to the hospital. Please, God, let him be all right!"

Wallace raced down South Orange Avenue toward the hospital. He parked and they sprinted through the emergency entrance, stopping at the desk, out of breath.

Rick asked for Johnathan Jackson, who was recently brought in with gunshot wounds. The receptionist checked, after which she asked them what their relationship was to him. The two of them simultaneously said, "His brothers."

She told them he was resting in I.C.U., then handed them passes.

Heading up the corridor, Rick and Wallace followed the signs that led them to the elevator. Once on it, Rick looked at the pass, which had Fifth Floor written on it.

Exiting the elevator, they approached the desk where the nurse sat. They asked for Johnathan Jackson and she began explain.

"He's lucky to be alive! He was shot in the face once, but it went in one side of his jaw and out the other. He was grazed on the top of the head, took one to the chest and one to the shoulder. She then added, he was also lucky no major artery or veins were severed. He'll be all right. He won't be able to talk for a while, we had to wire his jaws shut," she added.

She told them they could see him, but to make it brief, because he needed his rest. She came from behind the desk area and led them to his room. As they approached his doorway, she stepped aside and they walked in.

At the sight of John with tubes and bandages everywhere, Rick's eyes became glossy as he trembled as if he was about to explode. Rick told John he loved him as he walked over to the bed and picked up his limp left hand.

At that moment, John moved his head back and forth, mumbling something. But with the harness about his face along with the pain and anesthesia, he went right back out.

Rick and Wallace stood, wondering what it was he was trying to tell them. Realizing that he needed his rest, they headed out and back to the desk.

"Was there anybody with him?" asked Rick with a concerned look on his face.

"I don't know," answered the nurse, as she paused from writing to do so.

Back downstairs, Rick called Tammy's place again and again, but received no answer. He hoped that she wasn't with John when he was shot.

As he and Wallace approached the car, Wallace asked, "What do you want to do?"

Rick stated, "It's not like Tammy to not come home, unless she was out with John! Her parents are dead and the rest of her family lives down south somewhere."

Rick's concern for her was that of a brother. Angered once again, he told Wallace to drive through the strip.

Sitting at a traffic light, they noticed that there was no one out, except Dre. Their side of the street was empty, also. Assuming that Eric must have left to get more product, they didn't worry.

Rick thought to himself, Jewels and Slim are nowhere to be found, as usual. He envisioned himself driving through and shooting them all the first chance he got, then figured he'd creep up and make sure, by putting bullets in their heads at close range. Coming out of this vengeful thought, he told Wallace to forget about it and just park in the lot in the back of Angie's. Afterwards, Rick picked his gun up from the floor of the car and made his exit.

In the building, while they walked through, he held his gun in plain view as a tear rolled down the right side of his face.

Wallace, seeing this, told him to put the gun away, as he assured him they'd get them. At Angie's door, Wallace unlocked it and the two of them walked in. Angie jumped from the couch to her feet, inquiring about John. Rick, distant, walked over to the window, leaving Wallace to explain. The two of them walked into the kitchen, as Rick stared out and across the street. He watched everything, but still no Jewels. Suddenly, he marched straight for the door and out he went.

Hearing the door slam, Wallace yelled from the kitchen. Not getting an answer, he came into the living room area, looked around, then ran out behind him. Rushing down the stairs and out into the street, he didn't see Rick anywhere. He ran through the building to the back, still without seeing Rick.

Shots rang out, and Wallace quickly ran back to the front, yelling, "No!"

Thinking Rick had gone and done something stupid, he looked around for him out front. Noticing people running for cover and from the building that Jewels worked from, Wallace assumed that was where Rick went. Wallace raced across the street, hoping to catch him before it was too late. Figuring he was after Dre or Slim, or both, he rushed into the hall area. Here he, too, pulled his gun from his waistline, then removed the safety. Hurrying through the building, listening to shot after shot, Wallace prayed that Rick would still be alive when he found him.

Meanwhile Rick, who was one flight above Wallace, ignored him as he called out his name.

Wallace raced to get to him, Rick shot; holes through a door to an apartment that Dre and a few others hid behind.

Suddenly, after the repetition of shots, a solo shot rang, then all was quiet, except a loud thump that could be heard as Wallace climbed the stairs to where it all took place. He was not prepared for what he saw. He stood there in total shock.

Rick lay at his feet, lifeless, with a single shot to the head. Out of rage, Wallace yelled and kicked open the door, unloading his gun into anything that moved. As the sound of sirens filled the air, Wallace hurried down the stairs and out the back. Running now, he heard the police yell, "Freeze!"

He continued to run as the officers gave chase. They threatened to shoot, but Wallace hopped a few fences just as they did. After a thorough search, Wallace was no where to be found and they gave up.

Searching the scene, they found three dead bodies and two others hiding in the same apartment. The crime lab and the coroner pulled up, not long after they dragged out the two living souls.

Angie stood in the window, wondering if Rick and Wallace were all right. She headed downstairs to get a closer look. Staying calm, she walked up through the crowd of noisy onlookers. As the two men from the coroner's office brought the bodies out one at a time in body bags, everyone wondered who they were. Angie pushed her way through, her emotions driving her to yell and cry.

"Please let me through! Those might be my brothers!" Shouting hysterically, she made her way through and was met by Detective Jones. He told the men to hold up and pulled back the sheet on one of them.

Angie didn't respond, but leaned against the officer for strength. He walked over to the van and unzipped the second one and she cried out.

The detective tried to comfort her.

"What made you assume that it was your brother?"

"I saw him go in the building right before the shooting took place," she answered.

"Did he enter alone?"

Not wanting to give Wallace up, she told the detective yes.

"Does he know anybody in there?"

"No," she answered, as she was tired of his questions. She went on to tell him that she wasn't sure what went on, just that she saw him go in the building.

Detective Jones told her to go to the coroner's office to positively I.D. the deceased. He offered her a ride, but she declined. She told him she had left her door open because she was in such a rush to get down the stairs. She added that she had a friend that would take her, when he said he would wait.

She headed back to her building and up into her apartment. When she entered, Wallace stood by the window with a tear running down his right cheek. She walked toward him, relieved that he was alive, but crying for the same reason he was.

"They killed him! Why couldn't he wait? Why?" asked Wallace as he turned and hugged Angie. Then he turned away to bang his head against the wall, as his face became flooded with tears. She rubbed his back, as he agonized in his pain.

"Baby, I know it hurts, I know it hurts!" she stated as he began to calm down.

She told him that she had to go to the coroner's office to identify the body. The two of them gathered themselves and headed to the only car there, which was Rick's.

An Integra pulled into the lot, horn blowing, trying to get their attention. It was Eric, who asked them where they were going, then noticed that they had tears in their eyes. Climbing out of the car, he asked what was wrong.

Wallace put his arm around him and told him he'd tell him on the way, as he asked him to give them a ride. Once in the car, Wallace directed him.

Eric asked, "Why all the tears?" As Wallace continued to direct, he tearfully told Eric about the incident. He told him that John had been shot and that Rick was dead. Eric, not wanting to believe what he was hearing, stopped the car in the middle of traffic. Cars blew their horns, then raced past, cursing and calling him stupid. But he paid no attention, because he was numbed by the news.

When he awakened from his trance, he hit the steering wheel and yelled.

"Damn, what happened?"

Pulling over to let the other cars pass, Eric climbed from the car and told Wallace to take the wheel. Eric walked around the car, punching his fist into his hand. Once back in the car, Wallace pulled off and they continued their journey to the coroner's office.

Upon entering they told the examiner that they were there to identify a body recently brought in. The examiner led them into another room, where a few dead bodies were laid out on tables. He pulled the sheet from one of the John Does, as they all looked on in shock. Angie ran from the room, crying. It was definitely Rick, they assured the examiner, who asked for his full name, along with a list of other questions. Wallace explained to him that he'd have Rick's parents come in, because he didn't have the answers that were needed. As he turned to leave, he noticed a toe tag on a petite foot.

"Tammy Jenkins," he mumbled to himself, as he read it. Refusing to believe it was the same Tammy that Rick was searching for, John's girlfriend, he walked out to where Eric and Angie were sitting.

"Let's get out of here!" Wallace stated with a spooked look on his face, as if he had seen a ghost.

On their way to the car he spoke.

"We have to stop by Rick's place and tell Maria. That way she can tell their parents.

At Rick's place, Wallace rang the bell. Maria lifted the window and asked, "Who?"

"It's Wallace."

She shut the window and came down to the door. She looked for a minute, noticing that he had Rick's ex-girlfriend and someone else with him. Not seeing Rick, she automatically thought the worst. She snatched the door open and quickly asked where Rick was.

No one rushed to answer. With a saddened look, Wallace told her Rick had been killed. She fell into his arms screaming, as they all stood mourning with her. After letting her cry awhile, he asked if they could come in. There was more, he had to tell her.

Wallace hugged her and helped her climb back up the stairs, while Eric and Angie followed. As they all got comfortable, Wallace told her the rest.

"John was shot earlier, too. I think Tammy may have been with him. Could you call their parents and relay this?"

With tears in her eyes, she sniffled continuously before, during and after she spoke.

"Tammy's parents are dead and the rest of her family live in Georgia."

She got up and headed into the kitchen. She looked on her calendar for Rick's parents' number. She called and the phone rung, but no one answered, even after the tenth ring. She hung up and called right back. There was still no answer, until she got ready to hang up again.

"Hello," said the distorted voice of Mr. Jackson, sounding as if he was asleep.

"Mr. Jackson!" she shouted, as she couldn't bare to tell him this horrific news.

Feeling that something was wrong, Mr. Jackson cleared his throat and asked her what was wrong. Hearing the shaking in her voice, he could tell it was the news that he dreaded.

She gathered the courage and began to spit it out. "Rick and Tammy are dead! John's in the hospital!" He said nothing for a few minutes, then loud screaming and yelling followed. Mr. Jackson never returned to the phone.

Saturday morning set in like the calm after the storm. Everyone sat in Maria's living room, as a cool breeze blew through, awakening Wallace. He woke Angie, who lay resting on his shoulder. Eric, who slept in the recliner, opened his eyes and yawned. Maria lay still on the couch. Knowing that they had to wake her, Wallace walked over and called her name.

"Maria, Maria."

She opened her eyes, which were bloodshot from all the crying. Wallace asked her if she wanted to go see Rick. She told him no, but she said she'd like to see John.

Time passed and it was ten o'clock. They were still waiting while Maria got dressed. As she entered the living room, fully dressed, they all got up and walked out. Maria trailed and locked up behind them.

At the hospital, exiting the elevator, they all walked toward John's room. Upon entering, he heard them and turned to look in their direction. Painting on smiles, they all walked in and greeted him. Maria walked to his bedside and grabbed his hand and held it, with tears racing. John, seeing this, cried too. While this took place, Wallace grabbed a napkin from a nightstand near John's bed and wrote something on it.

After putting the pen down, he held up the napkin and called for John's attention. The napkin was inscribed" "WERE YOU AND TAMMY TOGETHER, WHEN YOU WERE SHOT?"

John, seeing the note, closed his eyes as Maria held his hand tightly. Tears emerged as he opened them and his face wrinkled up like a prune. He nodded his head up and down, not being able to speak, due to the fact that his jaws were wired shut. Seeing how painful it was, Wallace crumbled up the note and threw it in a nearby garbage can.

Rage consumed Wallace, as he sat quietly thinking. Watching Eric and Angie standing to John's right, as Maria stood holding his hand from his left; Wallace sat, trying to keep from exploding. Within seconds, he rose and marched out to the phone booth in the hall area. Thinking only of revenge, he pictured Rick falling to the floor after he was shot. Calling Tony, he waited for an answer. But as he waited, Tony passed him, heading toward John's room. Wallace, seeing him, chased him, yelling his name. Tony turned around, as Wallace walked up to him.

Waving the newspaper in the air, Tony asked, "What's this madness I'm reading about in today's paper?"

Wallace tried to explain, but he was so hyper he was hard to understand. Tony told him to calm down and take it a little slower. He took a deep breath and tried again. He told Tony everything and it made him furious.

After the conversation, they walked the few paces to John's room. But right before their entrance, Tony stopped and told Wallace,

"We have to get Jewels and whoever else that's involved. He's gone much too far!"

Throwing the paper on the table outside the room, Tony greeted everyone as he entered. Wallace followed after picking up the paper and flipped to a page where one of the articles was printed. It read:

NEWARK COUPLE GUNNED DOWN

On Friday, July 6, at about 5:30 P.M., a burgundy car, as described by one onlooker, drove up, stopped and started shooting, leaving one dead, Tammy Jenkins, 26, and Johnathan Jackson, 32, critically injured.

Wallace flipped to the next page, looked toward the bottom and there he noticed the other article that he was searching for.

TWO KILLED, TWO ARRESTED

> Yesterday, a young black male, possibly intent on revenge, was murdered after chasing some rival drug dealers into a building. He murdered one of them in his rage. Among those killed were Ricky Jackson, 31, and Linwood Smith, 23. Arrested at the scene were Andre Green, 28; Keith (Jugs) Littles, 34; and Kevin Gibbs, 30.

Wallace closed the paper and held it tight. He stared at the wall above John's bed, as he leaned against a window sill. Shortly after, they all headed out and walked toward the elevator. Right before they all piled on, Angie expressed the fact that she couldn't bare it any longer.

"I don't want to see anyone else get hurt or killed. I don't want anything to do with this anymore!"

Tony and everyone else looked at her, understanding exactly why she felt the way she did.

The elevator doors opened, as they all headed through the lobby and toward the front entrance. But as they did, they bumped into Rick and John's parents. Now up in each other's faces, Mrs. Jackson leaned on Mr. Jackson, drying her eyes with a tissue. Maria hugged her, as she let go Mr. Jackson. Maria broke out crying.

"It's going to be all right. He'll be all right. He's in a better place!"

While this took place, Wallace, Tony and Eric expressed their deepest sympathies to the Jackson's. Mr. Jackson stared blankly at them, not really acknowledging them at all.

Seeing this, Angie told them to come on. They started walking as Maria told them; she would catch a ride back with the Jackson's.

Outside, walking to their vehicles, Tony told Wallace to meet him at the house later. Wallace agreed, and they jumped in their cars and pulled off.

A half hour later, they pulled into the parking area in the rear of the apartment building where Angie lived. Wallace pulled up alongside Rick's car. He just stared at it, as he thought of him.

He said, "Later we have to take Rick's car to Maria."

Climbing out from the Integra, they walked up into the building. Eric and Angie climbed the stairs to her apartment, while Wallace walked out toward the front.

Out front it was empty; there was nobody around, except a few fiends looking for drugs. Wallace headed back through the building and up the stairs, also, fighting the urge to go to Jewels' house and kill everything and anything that moved.

Once inside the apartment, Wallace sat in complete silence, Eric stared out the window and Angie sat at the table, nibbling on a sandwich. There wasn't a sound, until the phone rang. It rang and rang, but not one of them picked it up.

Later, at Tony's house, they all discussed what their next move would be. Wallace expressed his angry thoughts about Jewels.

"We've let him get away with too much! Whether he did it himself or not, he's got to pay! We know he had something to do with all their murders."

Tony and Eric agreed, as Tony continued. "We can't do this out of anger. We have to think this one out.

"Forget thinking, I'll take him out myself!" stated Wallace.

Tony grabbed him and looked him in the eyes.

"Yo, look, I understand how you feel, I'm hurting, too. But we must do this right! I want to catch him just right! We don't need for anyone else to die or get hurt."

They all paced around barefooted, back and forth on Tony's plush carpet. Eric began to speak.

"Look, I think we should give him a taste of his own medicine."

"What do you mean?" asked Wallace, now standing at the bar, fixing a drink.

"What I mean is, we should scope him out and make it look like some type of accident," finished Eric.

They all agreed, but Wallace wanted to go straight to his face and get it over with. So as he and Eric put on their shoes and headed out the door, Tony told Wallace to keep cool.

Shortly after leaving Tony's and arriving at Angie's, they took Rick's car to Maria's, parked it and put the keys through the mail slot. As the two of them drove through the strip again, once again it was empty.

They then headed up to Montclair and sat not far down the street from Jewel's home.

Noticing that the house was dark, Wallace pulled from the parking space and drove up closer. Cruising past, they peeked in the dark and vacant driveway. Seeing this, they assumed that there was no one home. Turning around, they eased up into the driveway, shutting their lights and engine off and letting the car roll to a stop. Climbing from the car, the two of them drew their guns and headed around back.

Creeping, they noticed it was totally dark, except for a dim porch light. As they approached the porch, the whole yard lit up. They pressed their bodies against the side of the house, hoping if someone came out that they wouldn't be seen. But to their surprise, no one came out. Not even to the window. Not sure of what they might be walking into, they decided to retreat. They jumped in the car and let it roll out of the driveway, before starting it up. As they pulled off, a shadow of a figure appeared in one of the front windows.

As arrangements were being made by the Jackson's, for Rick and Tammy's funerals the very next day, John was moved from I.C.U. to a regular room.

"Alvin knocked at Angie's door and she quickly pulled it open to let him in. He told her that he tried to call and he stopped by, but nobody answered either time. He started to cry, because of what he heard and desperately wanted it not to be true. Angie explained it to him the best she could, then held him tightly and told him to be strong.

Tears began to slide down his face as he told her, "I want to see John."

Angie agreed to take him as soon as Wallace arrived.

"I want to see him now," he shouted. He pushed away and left her with a shocked look on her face. Hopping up, he raced toward the door, but she told him to hold up, she was going with him. Together they headed down the street to where the number twenty-two bus ran.

In another part of town, Mr. Sharpe had his investigator checking a lead on Mr. Gates, who was documented as the owner of True to Life Sportswear. His investigator, Mr. Woodson, was a short, older guy in his mid-sixties. His hairline was set back and it had thinned out. He had a fat face and wore a poorly made suit. Anyway, he drove up the street comparing addresses to the one he had written down on a piece of paper. Looking at the homes facing both sides of the street, he figured Mr. Gates was well to do.

These homes had to be worth at least three to four hundred thousand dollars each. Repeating the address to himself over and over, "407 Ridgewood Drive," he finally found a match. He stopped instantly in front of the house with that address. Climbing out, he proceeded up the walkway. Upon reaching the door, he rang the bell, then from the other side someone shouted, "I'm coming."

As the door opened, the slender, but fit-looking Black male looked surprised, as if he was expecting someone.

Mr. Woodson said, "Hello, I'm James Woodson, private investigator. I'm looking for a Mr. Kenneth Gates."

The man at the door stood still for a few minutes, as if he had seen a ghost, as if he sensed something about Mr. Woodson.

He said, "He's not in right now," shutting the door in his face. Mr. Woodson knocked again. He needed to ask a few more questions. This time when the door opened, he quickly asked, "Well, do you know when he'll be in?"

The man standing in the door stated, "He doesn't really stay here any more. He spends most of his time at his girl's place. Where that is, I don't know!" He closed the door, which was partially open to begin with. As Mr. Woodson pulled off, a curtain was pulled back and someone peeked out.

Back at the hospital, Angie and Alvin stood on each side of John's bed. As they proceeded to ask questions, John could do nothing but nod. Alvin asked where Tammy was and John's whole face tightened up. Angie held his hands tightly with both of hers.

"It's all right. It's all right to let it out!" She said to him.

Seeing the hurt in John's face, Alvin knew something wasn't right. He dashed out the room, down the hall and onto a waiting elevator. Angie called out to him, but he disappeared as the doors closed.

Later, on the strip, Alvin turned the corner and saw a few new faces in front of 215 (the building that Jewels hustled from). Knowing they didn't know him, he walked right past. Once up in the building, he looked around to make sure no one was watching. Ducking behind the stairs, reaching through the filth, Alvin found what he was looking for. Placing it inside his pocket, he headed back out the building. But on his way, he bumped into Slim, who grabbed him, forcing him back into the building. He searched him, finding nothing but a small tape recorder. He tried to make it play, but it didn't work, the batteries were dead.

Smiling, Slim thought nothing of it and threw it back to him. Alvin left the building, shaking as he headed up the street.

Elsewhere, around the same time, Maria paged Wallace. Once she came in contact with him, she told him Rick's wake was the next day, and that Tammy's would be in four days, just so some of her family could attend.

Wallace hung up and then stood near the phone booth, which sat outside the poolroom. Walking inside, he watched some older guys playing a game for money. Drifting in thought, he pictured Rick falling again and again, seeing Kelly in a casket, John with tubes in his nose and a toe tag with the name Tammy Jenkins on it. The anger boiled within him as he walked out the hall to his car.

"He's got to die! He's got to die," he said to himself over and over, as he pulled off and ran a red light.

A patrol car flew up behind him from out of nowhere, with its lights flashing. Wallace pulled over and rolled down his window, as the officer approached his car, with his right hand on his gun.

"License, registration and insurance," demanded the officer.

Reaching for his wallet, Wallace asked, "What are you stopping me for?"

The officer responded, "You ran a red light back there!" referring to the intersection he had just passed through.

Wallace glanced back and saw the light and the intersection, acknowledging that he didn't stop. He pulled his papers out of his wallet and handed them to the officer. Walking back to the car, the officer sat within and ran a check. Wallace patiently waited, hoping he didn't have a warrant or any outstanding tickets. As he did so, he took a deep breath. Then before he knew it, the officer was giving him back his papers, along with a ticket.

The officer told him, "Watch the red lights!"

As the officer marched back to his patrol car, Wallace looked in his rear view mirror and pulled off slowly, with the patrol car close behind. But as he turned right, the patrol car continued straight. Wallace, feeling like things might get ugly on this night, decided to go home and relax.

Eight-thirty that same evening, just as visiting hours were almost over, Mr. Sharpe appeared in John's doorway.

Keith, who was leaving, smiled and hurried on.

"Hello John," he greeted. "I heard the news. You have my deepest sympathies," he added. Concerned, he also asked,
"How are you doing?"

John nodded his head up and down as if to say fine.

Mr. Sharpe then went on to say, "I want to brief you on what's going on. I sent my investigator out to the home of owner of True to Life Sportswear. He was told, by someone, that he didn't really live there. So I figured I'd send the list of murders, along with the document you gave me, to my source inside the police department. Maybe with a little effort, they'll catch Jewels up in something big."

John nodded again, and then smirked. Mr. Sharpe expressed his deepest condolences once again and told John to get better soon, as he headed out the room.

Midnight approached, as Wallace and Eric stood on the strip collecting money from all their workers. Not thinking it was wise to be out there anymore, they then strolled across the street. Now up in the faces of the members of Jewels' new squad, Wallace spoke, as he pulled his .380 automatic from his waistband. "You guys are lucky I don't just rob and shoot all of you!"

One of the guys smirked and Wallace smacked him in the face with the gun. On the ground now, blood running from his mouth, he looked up, startled. Eric quickly pulled his gun out and told the other two to walk into the hallway. Wallace grabbed the other one from the ground and dragged him along.

Inside, Wallace and Eric robbed them and then made them strip down to their drawers and run from the building. They followed, as people passed by, laughing at the half-nude posse. Wallace and Eric walked across the street, carrying the men's clothes. Reaching the other side, they told their workers to leave, as they went into the building.

Twenty minutes later, Slim arrived with three others. Wallace watched from the window as he walked into the middle of the street yelling. "Bring the noise, you cowards! Come on!"

Angry now, Slim walked up into the building to gather up his half-nude squad. He brought them out to the car, after giving them each a pair of jeans. They were quickly packed in the car like sardines. After watching them pull off, Wallace walked away from the window and joined Eric on the couch. Angie fumbled in the kitchen making a sandwich.

Wallace said, "Look, I can't sit around waiting for the so-called perfect time! I'm going to find Jewels and take him out myself!"

Eric looked at him, then told him, "Let's scope out his movements and roll from there." Wallace agreed, but Eric didn't trust his word. They both stood up, Wallace kissed Angie good-night and then the two of them marched out the door.

The next morning, July eighth, John jumped straight up in the bed, sweating, for he had had a nightmare about the shooting.

"My baby, my baby!" he cried out in a muffled voice, as the pain shot through his face. A nurse rushed in to calm him down. As she did so, she noticed that he was having a bad dream.

"It's all right, Mr. Jackson, it's all right!" she stated, plumping his pillow so he could lay back.

He calmed down and did as she suggested. As soon as she left the room, he hopped out of the bed in tears, crying for the loss of Tammy. The nurse saws this and rushed back in to aid him once again. She tried to take him back to his bed, but he refused. She called for assistance and a few others come to her aid, then together they carried him back to his bed. They strapped him in to prevent any further episodes.

At two o'clock, at Terry's Funeral Home, people had started to arrive and view Rick's body. Family and friends from all over came in tears, as they looked at his corpse. His sisters and brother, who all lived in other towns near and far, cried as they hugged each other. Even Tony, Wallace and Eric cried for their fallen friend.

Wallace boiled inside, as he continuously pictured the incident that took his friend. Tony grabbed him and told him, "It's time!"

At that precise moment, Angie and Alvin walked up to the casket. Alvin looked at him without shedding a single tear, for he had witnessed so many die, especially those who were so young. He just walked away in silence, his face showing anger.

After everyone had viewed the body, they stood around to comfort Mrs. Jackson and Maria. When the service was concluded, everyone dispersed and went their separate ways. Most of the immediate family headed to the hospital, to see John while Tony and his boys discussed closing the books on Jewels.

Sending Angie and Alvin home with Eric, Tony told him, after he dropped them off. to meet them at the Chicken Shack on Springfield Avenue at seven P.M. Tony and Wallace drove off, heading to Tony's place to get ready for whatever.

While standing in Tony's basement, Tony pulled three automatic submachine guns, a few vests and two grenades from a suitcase that was buried beneath a pile of miscellaneous junk sitting in a corner. Loading the clips and locking them in place, they put the guns into a duffel bag they had brought in with them.

Walking up the stairs from the basement, Tony grabbed some gloves to ensure they didn't leave any prints.

In the car, they decided to go to Jewels' home first, after meeting with Eric. Wallace pulled one of the guns from the bag, then looked at his watch for the time, telling Tony it was six forty-five, but it made him drive no faster.

Tony thought; we don't need any encounters with the boys in blue. Reaching their designated meeting spot, Eric had not yet arrived. They parked and waited patiently. At seven-thirty, he still hadn't arrived, so Wallace, who became worried, stepped from the car and walked over to a nearby phone booth, where he paged him. As he leaned on the booth, the phone rang and he grabbed it quickly.

"Hello, Eric?"

"Yeah," the voice responded, sounding like he was in pain.

"What's wrong?" Wallace asked out of concern.

"I just had another run-in with Peters and Brown, walking from Angie's back to the car. They were in the lot searching and as I ran, I twisted my ankle."

Wallace listened, then stated, relieved, "As long as you're okay. Tony and I will take care of this job."

Eric quickly disagreed. "I'm all right! I'll be there in about fifteen minutes."

Wallace calmed him down and told him they'd wait, then hung up and headed into the Chicken Shack to place an order, just to kill time. As he walked from the place with a bag, he saw Eric flying down the street in the Integra. Reaching the car in which Tony sat; Eric pulled alongside, as the two of them rolled their windows down and begin to talk.

Eric told them to follow him after Wallace climbed in the passenger side. He wanted to put his car up. Following closely, Eric spotted Jewels' BMW going in the opposite direction. With his hand out the window, Eric pointed, hoping Wallace and Tony saw it, too. He ripped around with Tony following, heading in the opposite direction to pursue Jewels, who constantly looked in his rearview mirror. He made a right turn, sped up to make his escape.

By the time Eric and the fellows hit the corner, they slowly cruised, as they wondered where he could have disappeared to. Driving down the dark street, they saw nothing: no cars, no Jewels, nothing. Looking in every driveway, they turned around and then drove slowly out the way they came. Back on the avenue, they made a right and headed toward the parkway. On the parkway, they get off at exit 150, Bloomfield Avenue. Driving up the avenue, they finally came to the street connected to the dead-end, the one on which Jewels resided. Turning right, then driving past the street, they parked two blocks away.

Tony and Wallace climbed from one car, as Eric did from the other. They walked down Seabright Terrace, then down to Jewels' home, and this time the lights were on.

Entering the alleyway, Tony opened the bag while it was still on his shoulder. Handing Wallace and Eric both submachine guns, Tony took the grenades out also and placed them in his left pocket. Remembering how the lights came on when someone entered the back area, Wallace told Tony as they approached, "Hold up. If you step back there the lights will come on!" They all stayed alongside the house, awaiting Wallace's next move.

Tony shouted; "Damn this!"

He ran up to the back door and kicked it in, as Wallace and Eric followed, after looking at each other. Just as they all entered, the alarm sounded. Wallace shot it off the wall, but it continued wailing loudly. Tony quickly ran through the house, then back to where Eric and Wallace stood. Hurrying out to avoid the police, Tony threw one of the grenades through a side window, shattering the glass as it did. They all ran back up the block, when "BOOM!" a loud explosion sounded. Debris and flames were everywhere. It lit up the area, as Wallace noticed flashing lights coming, as they reflected off a nearby building. Leading the pack, he stopped Tony and Eric, and they all ducked into an alley to avoid being seen. A dog behind a fence near where they stood barked as the patrol cars rushed past and down toward the blazing house. Creeping across a few lawns, they eased around the corner unnoticed.

People stepped from their homes to see what made such a loud noise and lit up the sky. Fire engines sped onto the scene, as did additional police vehicles. They closed off the street to pedestrians and automobiles.

Back in Newark, Tony and the gang drove through the strip slowly. Slim saw them and eased back up into the building. They continued driving up the avenue, then turned off, driving from spot to spot, club to club and every known hang-out. They found no signs of Jewels.

Looking at his watch, which read ten-thirty, P.M., Wallace suggested going back to the strip. Once there, they pulled into the back. Jumping out of their cars, they walked through 207. The three crept up to the front and looked through the glass portion of the door. As they did so, they observed Slim running from the building across from them. He hurried around the corner and then his car could be heard racing away.

Sensing that they had Jewels and his boys shook up and running scared, Tony and Eric headed back to their cars, and Wallace went into 210 and up the stairs.

Day broke, as Wallace lay snuggled up with Angie in her bed. Alvin bust into her bedroom yelling, as loud banging could be heard throughout the apartment. Wallace, assuming it was a raid, jumped into his underwear and pants and raced up front. As he did so, he told Angie to get dressed. Just as he and Alvin got to the living room area, the police had made their way in. They Rushed in with Peters and Brown leading the way.

"Everybody on the floor! Nobody move! We have a warrant to search these premises for drugs and guns," stated Peters, as he held up a document. Angie walked from the back, screaming.

"What the hell's going on?" she demanded to know.

Detective Peters showed her the warrant, then told her to be seated. After about an hour, they had concluded their search. Brown came from the bedroom and asked, "What's in the safe in the bedroom closet?"

"Nothing but a few hundred dollars," Angie answered.

"Open it!" demanded Brown. She told Wallace to open it for them.

He rose from the floor and walked through to the back, with the two detectives following. Coming back to the front disappointed, the detectives told the remaining officers they could leave, after which they warned Wallace, Angie and Alvin.

"We've been watching you guys, and trust us, you won't keep slipping through our clutches. The day will come, when we get the last laugh!"

Watching the detectives as they walked out, Wallace thought to himself, someone gave us up. Lucky for us we didn't work last night. He looked at the doorway and decided to get a new door, a drill, plus a lock. He asked Angie to get him a measuring tape. She went into the kitchen and returned with it. He measured the doorway, then headed out to get one.

When he came back up the stairs, stumbling, he had a new one in his hands. Laying it against the wall in the hallway, he started to remove the old. In that same instant, a man came marching up the stairs.

"Hello," he stated, as he reached the second level where Wallace stood.

"Do you live here?" he followed up with.

"No, I don't, I'm just repairing a door for a friend!" returned Wallace, as the two of them stood face to face.

Already informed about the raid, this person who was the landlord, begin to ask more questions.

"How did it get torn out of the frame like that?"

Angie approached the doorway, then joined in.

"Hello, Mr. Johnson," she greeted him. "There musta been a mix-up, they raided the wrong apartment!"

The landlord listened to her and then made a statement. "Because I've never had any problems with you, I'm going to let this incident go. But if there's a next time, I'll evict you for sure!"

He headed back down the stairs, as Wallace removed the old door, then propped and screwed the new one in place. He cut and drilled a hole for the lock, as Angie stood and watched. Alvin sat in the living room staring at a wall, thinking. Once Wallace finished and checked it to make sure it was secure, he closed and locked it.

Afterwards he sat down as he looked at Alvin, who seemed lost. He then asked, "You miss John, don't you?"

He replied, "Yes. But I'm happy he's okay."

Wallace smiled at Alvin and for him it felt good, being that all he felt was pain lately. He grabbed Alvin and held him close as he told him, "It's going to be all right."

Then Wallace sat back, picked up the remote and switched the channel, being that no one seemed to be watching it. Flipping through, he came upon a news broadcast. He left it there and sat the remote on a nearby table. The newscaster went from subject to subject, until finally the talk was of an explosion. Capturing their attention, Angie quickly sat down next to Wallace as Alvin sat up to listen.

"A house was blown up as it blazed out of control. It was said to have been a grenade that caused this travesty. Luckily, there was no one hurt, but it did burn two homes to the grounds. The one it was thrown in and another alongside it. Burning debris was everywhere."

Shocked, Angie thought to herself, what is this world coming to? Alvin just looked around the room, then hopped up and walked to the window.

About the same time in a suite in the Holiday Inn, Jewels sat with Slim, Dre, Jugs and a few new members. They discussed retaliation, blaming Tony and his boys for blowing up Jewels' home. Furious, he ranted and raved.

"They blew up my castle. They stole from me. Who the hell do they think they are? Who the hell do they think they're dealing with?" Jewels asked as he looked around the room at everyone's face. "Don't they know I could have them murdered before night falls if I want? They want to play, the gloves are off now!"

He turned his back as silence filled the room. Then told them he needed to be by himself and they could leave.

After hearing the door close, Jewels picked up the phone and could be heard dialing.

"Hello, Danny?" Jewels asked as someone picked up.

"Yes," the voice responded.

"It's me, Jewels. I have something we need to discuss. Come to the Holiday Inn off of 1 and 9, by the airport; Room 101A, as soon as you can get free."

He agreed and told him he would be there as soon as he finished at work. He abruptly hung up. Jewels looked at the phone as he frowned and also hung up. Before he knew it, it was three twenty-five and there was a knock at the door. Kind of shook, due to all that was going on, Jewels took precautions before opening the door. He grabbed his gun as he approached the door and asked, "Who is it?"

Relieved to hear that it was Danny, he relaxed and opened the door slowly and allowed him to come in. The two shook hands, embraced, then Jewels offered him a seat. As he sat, Jewels explained his problem and how he wished it to be solved.

"Look, I have a problem and you're the person that can solve it. You see, my rival, Tony, and his boys are hurting business. They're putting pressure on my staff, plus someone blew up my home. But I have my partner taking care of that."

Danny cleared his throat to speak.

"This whole thing is getting out of control! I don't want anything else to do with this!"

Jewels walked across the room with his fingers massaging his chin, thinking.

"One more hit, I promise, I'll make it worth your while," added Jewels, trying to convince him.

"I'm listening," stated Danny.

"The job is worth fifteen grand to you," blurted Jewels as he leaned on the back of the couch behind Danny. "Now here's the deal. I need you to scope out Tony and find out where he lives. Take him out and anyone else that gets in the way! This one's off the books, I'm paying you face to face."

Danny spoke, as Jewels awaited his response.

"I normally get my money up front, you know?"

"Well, this job is different, it involves more money. Plus, I refuse to pay this until I know he's dead for sure!" stipulated Jewels.

"Well, I must have at least half up front, for my own insurance purposes," Danny continued.

"You've got that, I'll have it for you tomorrow," finished Jewels.

The two shook on it, as Jewels walked him to the door and let him out. Walking back to the couch, Jewels sat down, lighting a cigar in the process, as he leaned back, laughing.

After returning from seeing John, his father walked into the store in thought. His employees greeted him and discussed the day's business. Mr. Jackson walked to the back where his office was and sat down, dropping his head and holding it in his hands. Then the sound of two kids arguing brought him out of thought.

"What's all the cursing for?" he then asked.

"Excuse me," they both shouted, surprised to hear Mr. Jackson's voice. He rose from his seat and began to help as the store became crowded.

Now as the day drifted away and it had reached six o'clock, Slim sat in the building as his boys stood out front gathering the money as it came in, just waiting for Wallace or one of them to show their faces, but they never did. It grew later and later as they stood armed as they made money and the police made them clear out every now and then.

Slim decided to shut down and head home after awhile. But in the process of counting the money up in one of the empty apartments, he heard gunshots and a car speed off. He ran to the window, pulled back the old worn shade and looked out. He saw nothing, nothing but his boys, who seemed all right as they began to step up into the building. Walking back to the pile of money in the center of the floor, he put it all into a bag. He grabbed his gun from the floor also and headed toward the door. But as he pulled it open, Jugs and the rest of the gang came running in.

Breathing hard, Jugs shouted, "The police!"

Closing the door, Slim told them to go to the back as he looked out the window. Counting the police cars, Slim thought, damn, six cars. They all showed up right away; that's odd.

Watching their every move, he noticed that they searched the buildings on both sides of the street. Then noticed that they rushed off on what was probably another call, due to the fact that they had on their flashers and their sirens going.

Slim yelled to the back, where they had all hid, and told them that the coast was clear.

They all left the apartment and went back down the stairs, out to their cars. They all headed in their separate directions. Slim headed back to the hotel.

Entertaining two women, Jewels laughed and joked as they cuddled up to him on the couch. As he got ready to kiss one of them, there came a knock at the door.

"Go away!" yelled Jewels.

Frustrated, Slim shouted out; "It's me, Slim, open the door!"

Suddenly the door opened and Jewels spoke.

"This had better be good!"

Slim peeked in, then understands why Jewels didn't want any company.

"Jewels, get rid of your hoochies, we need to talk!"

Jewels gave them some money and told them to go have a few drinks downstairs or something. As soon as they left and the door shut, Slim locked it and threw the bag of money at Jewels.

"Here's your money! Look, man, I don't know if you've noticed, but this shit we're up against is serious. You act like you can wash away everything with the snap of a finger or the wave of a hand. It's not that easy!"

Jewels quickly replied, "Take it easy."

"Take it easy! Well, I tell you what, you move the drugs then!" angrily stated Slim.

Jewels laughed, then cut it short as his expression changed, like that of Jekyl and Hyde. Angered now, he shouted, "Listen, I lost my home and everything I owned, so don't tell me I think I can wash it all away, because I can't! I just refuse to let this get me down, especially when the outcome will be in our favor!"

Slim listened as Jewels' cocky attitude overwhelmed him. He then told him, "You're a danger to yourself. You think you're invincible, listen to you! Do you ever think you could be killed as quickly as you kill others? I understand we have no choice this time, but there have been times when we did."

"Oh, damn, is your conscience bothering you?" asked Jewels sarcastically.

Slim realized there was no talking to him, rose from where he sat and stormed from the room.

Meanwhile, driving through the strip, a blue pickup truck cruised past the building where Wallace and Eric resided. Seeing the lights out, the truck continued on. During this search they were unable to be pinpointed. After driving around a little longer, the pickup disappeared.

Tuesday, awake early, Wallace looked in the refrigerator and saw that there was no breakfast food, and quickly rushed out to a nearby store. The summer breeze felt good to him as he raced up the street. A patrol car slowly drove up alongside him and two officers looked him up and down.

As they pulled away, Wallace thought to himself about how the police try to intimidate people.

In the grocery store, he purchased some eggs, sausage, grits and a few other goods. Back at the apartment, he was cooking as the smell awakened Angie. She marched into the bathroom, rubbing her eyes as the smell captured her senses.

"Umm, somebody's after my heart." she stated. She closed the door as Wallace placed plates of food on the table.

"Alvin!" he shouted as the boy had slept nearby in the living room area. Alvin just turned over and put his head under the pillow.

Angie walked from the bathroom, wrapped in her robe. She hugged Wallace from the back and told him that she was really starting to like him.

Noon came and John's lawyer, Mr. Sharpe, sent the documents along with the list of murders and dates, to his source in the Fifth Ward police department. This task was carried out by his investigator, Mr. Woodson.

When Mr. Woodson reached the precinct, he asked for directions to the homicide squad.

Back at the hospital, John was making a good and quick recovery, walking around, washing himself, and getting a grip on what had happened. Though everything he had been through hardened him and made him somewhat cold, he fought to stay peaceful. But even so, the John of yesterday was no more; murdered. When the nurses came in to attend to him, he motioned for them to leave, figuring whatever he needed, he'd do himself or just do without.

Going in and out of angry cycles caused by Tammy and Rick's deaths, he stared aimlessly out the window through the blinds. He wondered how things would have turned out if they hadn't taken to the streets, blaming himself for his brother and Tammy's deaths.

"It's because of me that they no longer live, so in their absence I shall make things right."

Closing the blinds, he headed back to his bed, where he lay across it and turned on the television. Tired of being in the hospital and equally tired of the braces and wires in his mouth, he began to buzz the nurse's station repeatedly. Some one quickly answered over the intercom.

"What now, Mr. Jackson?" the voice asked.

"I want to see my doctor," he said in a muffled voice.

"I'll relay the message," the nurse replied, then the intercom was silent.

He sank down in the bed and relaxed.

Across town, Jewels met with Danny and gave him the deposit inside the hotel room. After their business was taken care of, the two shook on it and smiled, as laughter broke out between them.

"Consider it done," stated Danny as he headed out the door.

Later, as Danny rode from one location to another, Wallace still sat in Angie's apartment.

5THE WAR

Morning came, as Mr. Sharpe had his investigator check the address of Kenneth Gates again. As before, he found him neither there, nor at a forwarding address. So his next stop was True to Life Sportswear, where he arrived at about eleven o'clock. He was trying to catch him either coming or going to lunch, but he came up empty handed once again.

Sitting in Mr. Sharpe's office, Mr. Woodson told him, "We have to somehow find this mystery man, follow him around, so we can pinpoint exactly where it is he lives."

From the conversation Mr. Woodson had with two of his employees, he learned that Gates periodically stopped by, but doesn't hang around long unless something is wrong. They also told him that he's not been around much lately. Mr. Sharpe, thinking perhaps he took a business trip or vacation, told Mr. Woodson to give him a few days and then watch the house thoroughly. So just as Mr. Woodson left, Mr. Sharpe called on his source inside the precinct, asking him if there was any substance to what John pointed out.

He responded, "It's a long shot, but if he could come up with something to solidify his theory, it would be a start."

After hanging up, Mr. Sharpe reviewed copies of the documents in question, then thought to him self, the dates were close, but a good prosecutor would eat right through it.

At the hospital, John was doing much better, but still unable to talk clearly, due to the braces and wiring within his mouth.

Alvin asked him, "When will you be able to leave the hospital?"

John said in a muffled voice, "I'm waiting on the doctor to okay my release."

As if he knew they were talking about him, the doctor walked in and greeted them. "Hello, Mr. Jackson, now what is it you wish to know?"

He wrote it out on a pad: I WANT TO GO HOME, OR KNOW WHEN I CAN.

The doctor replied, "In another couple of days or as soon as the swelling is down. The braces will remain on for at least another three to four weeks, though."

The doctor left the room, as Angie told John of a raid and an explosion featured on the news. John's eyes widened as he sat on the side of his bed, listening. Suddenly he closed his eyes, as if something was eating him. Easing back beneath the sheets, he dropped his head back onto his pillow, and Angie and Alvin sat watching him drift off to sleep. Figuring something was bothering him, the two of them left his bedside and headed home. Meanwhile, in John's mind, he pictured Tammy through all their good and bad times. He also envisioned his brother and faithful friend.

Upon opening his eyes, John looked up toward the ceiling, as he thought, I know not your reasons for taking them, but they'll forever dwell in my heart. He closed his eyes once more.

About ten o'clock that morning, Tony sat in a diner with Wallace and Eric. The blue pickup truck was parked up the street and the driver stared down toward them.

Twenty minutes later, the pickup pulled off, after the driver looked at his watch.

Fifteen minutes after that, Tony and the boys came walking out. Rubbing his stomach, Tony bounced down the stairs to the car with a toothpick wedged between his teeth.

Rushing into the precinct, Detective Michaels raced down the corridor and into the room labeled Homicide. Upon entering, Jones asked him to take a run with, and so he did. After driving awhile, they came to a spot, the spot where John and Tammy were shot. Jones pulled over into a nearby parking space.

Michaels, wondering why they had come to this old crime scene asked, "why are we here?"

Jones answered, "I honestly don't know, it's just something about this shooting that has me puzzled."

"What is there to be puzzled about? We see these kinds of cases every day," said Michaels.

Jones spoke again, after a brief silence. "I believe he was hit, as in hitman."

"Maybe he was, but there's nothing to support that. So let's keep it simple, unless something dictates otherwise! Michaels stated, ending the discussion.

Pulling from the parking spot, they headed back to the precinct and didn't say another word about the shooting.

Back at Jewels' suite, there was a phone conversation between him and Detective Peters. "Look, Dave, stop harassing my people," stated Jewels sternly.

"We will when your bill is paid!" answered Peters.

After telling him where they would meet to handle their business, Jewels ended the phone call. Walking from a phone booth on Springfield Avenue and Twentieth Street, Peters headed back to his unmarked car. As he and Detective Brown rode off, they crept up on some drug dealers a few blocks away.

It was early on the strip, so there was no one crowding the open sidewalk. Nevertheless, there were still people purchasing their drugs, as they eased in building 215, one behind another. Wallace watched this activity from the window.

"I need some money; my cash flow is getting slow," he stated as he walked away from the window. Passing Alvin, he walked to the back of the apartment, where Angie sat on a bed doing her hair. As she sat in front of the mirror, he entered the room. She smiled and blew him a kiss. He smiled too and then told her, "Baby, I've got some business to attend to!"

She asked him to come closer. Just as he did, she turned and ran her hands around his waistline. Rising, she kissed him, then told him he could leave. Wallace laughed and walked out and back through the place as Alvin asked if he could tag along.

"Not this time," Wallace told him.

The door closed slowly behind him, as Alvin watched with a slight pout. Outside in the car, Wallace began to head to the hospital, then suddenly detoured and headed to Tony's instead. Pulling up, he noticed Raymond's green BMW as he and Tony sat outside, talking. Wallace climbed from his car and joined the conversation.

"Yo, just the man I want to see. Ray needs you to run a few people off the block," stated Tony.

"Where?" asked Wallace.

"Walnut Street," added Raymond.

"What's up Ray? Someone trying to muscle in on your money?" asked Wallace.

"Not really, it's just that we need to make more there, to supplement our shortcomings on the strip," clarified Raymond.

Wallace angrily replied, "I'm not letting Jewels and his posse of cowards stop us from getting our usual numbers! I refuse to! If he wants to go to war, let him bring it on!"

Raymond and Tony both agreed, as they smiled almost simultaneously. Then Tony spoke.

"We have to step to him hard and direct! No more playing! Tonight is the night we put a stop to his reign."

At five o'clock, Mr. Sharpe sat in his office, looking over the articles one by one. Trying to make heads or tails of this theory of John's, he read each one thoroughly. But the only major link was that the murders were all done with a nine-millimeter handgun. If what John said about the documents and the articles was true, then what they had to do was force his hand, set him up, thought Mr. Sharpe.

As he tried to figure out a way to catch Jewels, his investigator was watching the home of Kenneth gates. Down the block, in his brown '79 Ford, Mr. Woodson stared, but the only people he saw were two kids and a lady, who seemed to be their mother, going in. He decided to walk up and ring the bell minutes after the door opened. Woodson stumbles for the appropriate words.

"Hello, I'm Mr. Banks, C.E.O. of Rahway Sports. I'm supposed to meet with a Mr. Gates here at five-thirty."

She smiled then said, "I'm sorry, but I don't know a Mr. Gates."

"Kenneth Gates," he added.

"Sorry, never heard of him," she stated as she smiled, and shrugged her shoulders.

"Sorry to have bothered you," Mr. Woodson finished and walked from the porch.

Now for the life of him, he couldn't understand why the guy he spoke with the first time, at the same house, told him we wasn't in, and she had said she never heard of him. It made no sense to him at all. Walking back to his car in a fog, he questioned himself: What's their last name? Turning back toward the home, he read the mailbox, but it had nothing on it but the house number, 1407. Abandoning his glimmer of hope and small lead, he headed back toward his car once again. This time, he got in, started it up and pulled off. Thinking the address that was given to him must be a mistake or been misread. So as he drove, he decided to call it a day and see Mr. Sharpe in the morning.

Later on that night, Wallace pulled up in the parking area behind the building in which Angie lived, with three cars of angry soldiers. As they climbed from the cars, most of them had guns and the remainder of them just came along to act up. Together, they all marched through the building and out the front.

Jewels' entire clan eased into the hallway, as they all stepped from within. Wallace led the mob as they crossed the street, stopping traffic in the process.

They went through the building searching each empty apartment on every floor, coming up empty; Wallace figured they all ran out the back. Heading back across the street, they all scattered as gunshots rang out from a rooftop. When the shooting stopped, Wallace and his boys cautiously stood up, then hurried on as sirens got louder. Racing through the building, Wallace and the boys hurried to their cars. Just as they all pulled off and were about to exit the lot, a few patrol cars flew past, heading to the front area.

Sitting in the parking area of a local fast-food restaurant, Wallace and the gang considered going back, but decided to let it rest.

The next afternoon, as John demanded to be released from the hospital in time for Tammy's funeral, his doctor signed the forms. Walking into the room next to his, he gave the person lying in the bed a written note. Just as John left the room, the person called John's parents' home and read it to Mrs. Jackson.

"He wants his father to come and get him; they have just released him and he doesn't want to miss Tammy's funeral." His new friend stated, as he said good-bye and hung up.

John entered the room again, thanking him with a smile and a handshake, then rushed back into his room to get ready. In about forty-five minutes, his father arrived and was standing in the doorway, watching John, as he sat bent over, tying his sneakers.

His father said, "I see somebody's tired of this place, just as tired as they are of you!"

"Yeah, well," John mumbled, still messing around with his laces.

His father helped him gather his things and placed them into a brown bag that he pulled from the closet. Finally on their way out, John waved to a few people in their rooms and to a few nurses on duty.

In the car, John managed to ask his father if they could stop by Angie's. He told him yes, as John directed him. Halfway, he mumbled, "Call her." Writing down the number that he wanted him to dial on a small piece of paper he found in the car, John gave it to his father. At the next light he pulled over, as he spotted a phone booth on the corner inside a bus shelter. He hopped out and made the call as John sat in the car waiting. When he returned, John continued to point and direct. His father spoke again.

"Alvin said he'd be sitting on a porch around the corner from Angie's, on Bergen. Riding down Bergen now, getting closer, John noticed him swinging his legs on the stoop of an abandoned building. Pulling right up to him, John pushed the door open as Alvin jumped up and got in. The big blue car pulled off as he got comfortable in the back seat. Alvin told John that Wallace and Angie said they'd be at the funeral at about three o'clock. John listened and then nodded to tell him okay.

As they pulled in front of the building in which John lived, he looked around as if he missed the place. He and Alvin climbed from the car as Mr. Jackson told them he'd be back to get them at around two-fifteen. After watching his father pull off, John followed Alvin, who was already at the top of the stairs. In the apartment, John looked around, then headed to the back to his bedroom. He looked in the bathroom, noticing how much of a mess his place was. Alvin raced past him and began getting ready for the funeral. While the shower ran, John pulled a suit from his closet and laid it across the bed. Then he pulled out the ironing board to iron the wrinkles from a shirt that he pulled from within a closet.

Meanwhile, at Mr. Sharpe's office, Mr. Woodson told him that he had spoken to the lady of the house in which he had been given the address to. But she convincingly told him that she knew of no one named Kenneth Gates.

"So what was the guy talking about you spoke with at first?" asked Mr. Sharpe.

"That's just it, their stories are totally different; somebody's lying!" responded Mr. Woodson.

"Try to find out what the family's name is and I'll run a check," answered Mr. Sharpe.

Woodson agreed, but had something else up his sleeve.

Back at the apartment, John and Alvin were fully dressed and heading out the door as Mr. Jackson blew his horn. Walking down the stairs toward the car, John saw his mother on the passenger's side, staring at him. His father quickly unlocked the rear door, to allow them to get in. Climbing in, John kissed his mother on the cheek as he sat down.

Just then she stated, "I loved her like one of my own. First Rick, now Tammy! John, please don't be next, please, baby." She was crying, so

Mr. Jackson pulled over, stopping the car and comforting her. John patted her on the shoulder, as if to tell her not to worry.

Arriving at the church, they all entered as Tammy and Rick's caskets sat in the front near the podium. People sat around crying and talking, some just awaited the minister. As the minister approached the podium, the entire church got quiet.

"Hello to those of you that were blessed to make it here safely; some of you have come a great distance to say good-bye to your loved ones. They have now left us, but will never be forgotten by us." The minister wiped the sweat from his forehead and continued. "It's sad when we can't enjoy life without wondering if we'll be shot or stabbed, mugged or raped. This is not God's way! Those of us who live our lives like that which I speak, shall be judged as it says in the Bible."

He asked God to take them into His care, as the choir started to sing. Row by row, everyone started to rise and view Rick and Tammy's bodies, one at a time. After the last person sobbingly walked past the caskets, the paw-bearers carried them from the church.

John and all those who stood around him stared with tears in their eyes, as the caskets were loaded in hearses. After that, everyone hopped in their cars and headed to the burial site.

Later, back at John's place, he sat in complete silence, while Alvin flipped through the pages of a Jet magazine, just to have something to do. John, now up, went into the kitchen and noticed his set of keys to Tammy's apartment, hanging on a hook above the sink. Grabbing them, he decided to go to her place. He called a cab and it was there in less than thirty minutes.

Upon reaching her dwelling, he and Alvin climbed the stairs and he unlocked the door. The smell of potpourri and perfume filled the air, reminding him of her. Looking at a picture on the mantelpiece, John remembered what a good woman she was. Awakening from his daze, he raced to her bedroom, then to the closet where they stored their records pertaining to the case. After pulling the files from the closet, he kept having flashbacks of Tammy, so he hurried to get out of there.

In Jewels' hotel room, he talked with Karen about financial matters. Karen sat in the center of the loveseat, explaining.

"Look, I think I do a pretty damn good job, Simon. I make sure there's no flaws that you can be caught up in and so forth."

"And," Jewels replied.

"A figure for my services I deserve a few dollars more than what you're throwing me," Karen went on.

"Why is that?" Jewels asked.

"Because I take care of your accounts! I keep your businesses legit. I've helped you with investments. In short, I'm getting in too deep. So if it's not worth it, I want out!" Karen yelled.

Jewels laughed as he moved from the sofa to the loveseat, where she was sitting.

"I like you, but don't push your luck!" he stated as he squeezed her cheeks hard, then kissed her, as she fought to get loose.

"You creep! You, drunk creep! You better wake up and stop thinking the world revolves around you!" she yelled.

He laughed as she stormed out the door.

The blue pickup was parked in front of Tony's house after following Wallace. Watching from a block away, the person within it just sat and ate a sandwich. Seeing Tony walk from the house, he whispered, "Bingo."

He pulled off, making the first left to avoid being seen.

Sitting on the porch, John and Alvin breathed in the fresh air, something John had missed. He remembered watching the moon and stars with Tammy. Alvin woke him from his thoughts. "John! John, look, that cop was in that pickup truck that went by."

John was trying to catch a glimpse, but couldn't see who was driving.

"Did you see him?" asked Alvin.

"No, I missed him," John replied as he sat back down on the porch.

The following morning, Mr. Woodson was outside 1407 Ridgewood once again, but this time he had a different strategy. He sat hour after hour until seven-thirty, when he saw a lady and two kids running to a small gray car, and watched as they then drove off. Then, about nine o'clock, a car came from around the back of the house and straight at him. He sunk down in his seat so he wouldn't be seen. As the car passed him by, he started his, then turned it around to pursue.

After about twenty minutes of driving they arrived at True to Life Sportswear. Mr. Woodson stopped at an adjacent corner, watching the car as it pulled into the lot where the Sportswear Company was located. Mr. Woodson assumed this person to be Kenneth Gates, so he pulled into the lot, also. As he watched him go inside, he parked. Looking at this medium-built, six-footer, he said to himself, he's the guy who answered the door on the first attempt to get information at the home on Ridgewood. He decided to leave to check a few things out, because he believed this guy definitely had something to hide.

In conference with John, Mr. Sharpe discussed matters as he was buzzed by his secretary to notify him that Woodson was there. Telling her to send him right in, Mr. Sharpe and John awaited his entrance. As he entered, John sat in a chair to the left of Mr. Sharpe's desk, so Mr. Woodson grabbed the one to the right.

"Now as I was telling John, we're following his lead, hoping it takes us somewhere, but we're still pursuing normal channels, too." Mr. Sharpe stated. "Any news?" he abruptly added.

"Well, after sitting in front of the home of Mr. Gates or whoever lives there, I followed a black car to True to Life Sportswear. Get this, it was the same guy who told me Kenneth Gates didn't live there, so I figured I'd check him out thoroughly."

John listened to this carefully. So they went over all the basics, which wasn't much. As John's mouth was still wired shut, Mr. Sharpe entertained the idea of a postponement to stall for more time.

At about twelve P.M. the same day, Jones and Michaels discussed a few things. Going from one subject to another, they ended up on the one of a scorned drug dealer who flipped out (referring to Rick).

"I heard that was the brother of John Jackson, the one we arrested for the playground execution," stated Jones.

"We know Jewels probably had something to do with it, but the evidence is too strong against John," added Michaels.

"John, who also was shot on the same day as his brother and whose girlfriend died instantly, when whoever tried to kill him. This isn't random, this is a small-scale drug war!" Jones bluntly stated.

"Someone shot Rick's brother John, who they thought murdered their people in the playground, but Rick, figuring it was Jewels, ran down on Jewels' boys and gets murdered. This is crazy," added Jones.

"So if he's behind all of this, maybe if we make his boy Jugs an offer, just maybe he'll give him up," stated Michaels.

In a conference room in the county jail some thirty minutes later, they told Jugs they'd cut him a deal if he was willing to cooperate.

He hesitated, then asked, "If I decide to work with you guys, can you promise me I won't do any time in Jersey and that this conversation won't leave this room, until I'm out of here, at least?" nervously asked Jugs.

Jones smiled and said, "We'll do our best, okay?"

"No, that's not good enough! I want your word and what I ask or no deal!" Jugs shouted nervously.

Michaels looked at Jones and then together they told him they'd get back to him, and they called to a guard to have him removed.

Time seemed to be flying on this scorching day, as Wallace raced from Tony's home to Angie's place. In his travels he made several stops to deliver drugs to others that they put to work all over Newark. Finally en route to Angie's, he reached the parking area, then ran upstairs.

Inside, he told her to pack some of her belongings so they could leave and that he'd be back to pick up the rest in a U-Haul later. So Angie went to her bedroom without question. Within twenty-five minutes, she returned and was ready to go. Driving from the parking area behind the building in which she lived, she began to speak.

"I figured it would come to this, I was starting to get scared."

"No one's going to hurt you without hurting me first!" Wallace insisted as he stared out at the road.

Pulling up in front of the building where he and Eric resided, Wallace smiled and said, "Welcome to your new home."

Double-parked, he shut the car down and put on the hazard lights. As the two of them climbed from the car, he grabbed her belongings from the backseat. Upon entering the building, the sound of a crying baby was heard, as they walked past a door on the first level. Wallace caught her glancing in the direction of the door, then told her, "That's a young girl named Jamie's baby. Jamie gets high and neglects her child totally. The Division of Child Welfare has been there several times, but all they've done is threaten her time and time again. She straightens up for a minute, but then goes back to doing the same old things."

Now finally reaching the third landing, he opened the door, then yelled for Eric, but no one answered. Figuring it was all right to bring her in, he held the door open. Following her in, he locked the door behind them. Walking through the apartment, he checked to see if Eric was asleep or, for some reason, didn't hear them. After walking through, he came back to the living room area, where Angie stood by the door.

"You can have a seat," Wallace stated as he pointed to a black leather couch, which was against a wall across from where she stood. She walked over to it and sat as Wallace accompanied her.

Once comfortable, Wallace spoke. "Now I don't know exactly what's going down, but I do know we're basically leaving that spot alone and I don't want you around there. So if it's all right with you, I'd like you to stay here for the time being, till I can find us a nice place, okay?"

Angie agreed after seeing how everyone seemed to be dying or somehow ending up in the hospital. Wallace was temporally lost in thought.

Now after I come in from taking care of my business I'll get a U-Haul truck and then go get her things.

Jumping up, he flipped on the television, telling her to make herself comfortable, and that he'd be right back.

John sat in Tammy's bedroom on his knees, accompanied by her aunt Pricilla and her daughter, Kim. Packing Tammy's clothes as they removed them from her drawers, John drifted away as the scent in them reminded him of her.

"Damn, why Tammy," he shouted, startling the women as they turned and looked as if something was wrong.

"John, we know you loved her, but don't let it break you. Carry her in your heart and she'll live with you forever," Pricilla stated consolingly. She sat on the bed folding blouses. One by one, she put them in a garbage bag.

Meanwhile, in the parking lot behind 210, the building Angie dwelled in for years, she was now moving. As a U-Haul truck sat in the back, Wallace, Eric and a few hired hands carried the furniture from the apartment out to the truck. It took about an hour and a half before they were finally finished emptying out the entire place. Wallace and Angie rode in the truck, while the rest of the guys followed in the Integra. Once they reached Twelfth Street where Wallace and Eric lived, they unloaded the furniture and the rest of her belongings into her new home. Afterward, they all sat in the back of the U-Haul drinking beer, dripping with sweat and laughing loudly about this and that.

At midnight, the blue pickup pulled up not far from Tony's house, and two men climbed from it, dressed in black from head to toe. Creeping up the driveway, they put on their masks as a large black dog ran up to the fence. Noticing the dog, one of the two shot it with a nine-millimeter handgun equipped with an infrared scope, and a silencer. As the dog died quietly, they looked around before climbing the locked fence and proceeding. As they were approaching the house, another dog raced out, barking loudly.

Shocked, but not shook, the same guy aimed and struck this one down, also to quiet the noise. Going back over the fence and out the yard, the two men ran back to their truck and took off. Tony ran out the front door onto the porch with a Tech Nine machinegun in his hand. But he was too late, as he watched the pickup swing around and sped away in the opposite direction. Tony, who stood staring down the street a short while, walked back in the house and put on his shoes. Quickly, he headed through the house to the back door, which led to the yard. Opening it, he saw Spike, his prize dog, dead in the grass. He looked over toward the fence and saw Terminator, the older of the two dogs, lying still, also. As tears ran down his cheeks and he stood in shock, he noticed they had been shot squarely in their heads.

Then he yelled, "Jewels, I'm going to kill you!"

Picking up Terminator and laying him next to Spike in the grass, he heard the doorbell ring, as flashing lights were everywhere. Placing the gun in a cabinet on the back porch, Tony grabbed the rear gate key from a rack that hung on the wall to his left. The bell rang, followed by a loud banging. Tony rushed to open the fence and headed out front toward the flashing lights. Noticing him strolling from the driveway, one of the officers called to him.

"Sir, do you live here?"

Both officers had their guns drawn, and noticing this, Tony quickly answered.

"Yes, I do! Someone shot my dogs."

Cautiously they approached as they told him they received a 911 call from someone, saying they saw two guys dressed in black running from his yard.

"Yeah, they shot my dogs," Tony said, hurt and disturbed.

"Do you have any idea who it could have been or what they might have wanted?" asked one of the officers as he stood in Tony's face.

"No." Responded Tony, as murderous thoughts of Jewels ran through his mind.

The officers then asked to go in the back. As one did, the other went to the patrol car and grabbed a clipboard to make a report. Walking through the open fence, they noticed two large dogs lying in the grass.

One of the officers asked, "Where did they get shot?"

Tony, grief stricken, softly said as he pointed, "One was shot in the head and the other took two to the face and one to the head."

As one of the officers wrote out the report, the other looked at the dogs closely. "Your dogs look strong and well-bred," stated the officer looking over the dogs.

Tony just stared at them.

The officer who was then kneeling, rose to his feet, and said, "I love dogs, too. I'm sorry."

Leaving, they told him to call the humane society and they'd come out to get the dogs. The two officers walked from the backyard, as Tony stood there, just staring at the dogs. Rochelle looked from the porch window, first at Tony, then at his two four-legged friends. Tony marched up the steps, through the porch door, where Rochelle stood, but she moved before it swung in at her. She watched as he grabbed the phone on the kitchen wall and dialed information. He wrote down the number as quickly as it was recited by the recording. Then he repeatedly dialed it till he was given a hotline number. After calling the hotline, he sat outside near the dogs on a lawn chair. While waiting for the humane society, he rotated his fingers in a massaging motion about his temples.

Daylight broke as a fight started in the county jail cafeteria. Inmates rushed to see what was going on, as officers fought to get to the heart of it. But by the time they did, it was much too late. For there, in a puddle of blood, with two deep gashes in his chest, laid Jugs, dead and stretched out on the cafeteria floor. The entire jail population was instantly put on lockdown, no movement till the investigation was completed.

Back at Tony's house, as eight o'clock rolled around, he was still outside in his lawn chair, now asleep. By eight-thirty, he was awake and walking back in the house to call the humane society again. The dispatchers told him they had someone en route, so he went back outside and as he stood over the dogs, a look of anger could be seen in his eyes.

Around noon, a call was made to Jewels from a phone booth somewhere in the Newark area.

"Listen, I had a slight problem, but don't worry, I'll get 'em," said the voice.

Jewels responded, "Look, man, the sooner you finish, the sooner you get the rest of your money! So basically, I don't want to hear from you until you've got something worth listening to, okay?"

The other voice hung up as Jewels shouted, "Hello!" but heard nothing but a dial tone. He smiled and said, "I like that guy!" As he hung up the phone, he hit the remote to turn on the television, and he reclined in his sofa chair.

John, now without his sling, exercised his arm by moving it up and down as he jogged through a nearby park. Lap after lap he ran, as if he was trying to outrun his problems. Then, after his jog, he raced home, past Alvin, who sat on the porch, straight upstairs to the shower. After he had freshened up and was fully dressed, he walked back out the door and onto the porch, where Alvin sat fumbling with some dice he had in his hand.

"What's up, little brother?" John asked.

Alvin, with a sad expression and voice said, "It just seems like everybody I like or love either dies or runs away from me! What's wrong with me? Am I bad luck or something?"

John, who was standing over him, decided to sit beside him, and as he did, he told him, "Don't blame yourself for things you have no control over. Never blame yourself because others refuse to accept responsibility and tuck their tails and run. Just be strong and make sure you don't do to those who love and trust you, what others have to you. Most of all, stay away from that path of destruction called the drug game."

At that moment, John's pager went off. He looked at the number, recognizing it, he rushed up the stairs to use the phone, as Alvin watched, but sat still. Now on the phone, John waited for his call to be transferred by the receptionist to his lawyer.

As soon as Mr. Sharpe picked up, he said, "Hello, John, I have some great news. One of Jewels' boys may want to make a deal. I meant to tell you yesterday, but I was so busy I forgot."

"What makes you think this?" asked John.

"My source told me so! I'm waiting to meet with the kid as soon as he gets back to me," stated Mr. Sharpe.

All of a sudden, John felt much better, as if someone had taken a load off his shoulders, but his face showed no signs of happiness. In the midst of all this madness and murder, how could he? So as the phone call ended, John headed back down the stairs to join Alvin once again. But as he reached the bottom of the stairs, he saw Alvin throw his dice out into the street, one at a time. John, showing a hint of a smile after watching this, sat down and stared out into the streets, along with Alvin. Looking over at him, John told him, "You're going to be all right."

Alvin smiled as tears ran down his tiny face and he wiped them away.

Meanwhile, Mr. Sharpe's was on the phone in his office and became the recipient of bad news. Their newly-found witness and possible loophole had been killed. Cutting the call short, Mr. Sharpe slammed the received down out of disgust. Spinning his chair completely around, he stared out the window into the dimly lit sky, rhythmically tapping the tips of his fingers against the arm of the chair. Pausing to glance at his watch, he noticed it was five o'clock and time to go home. So as he spun around one last time, he rose from his chair, straightened up his clothes, grabbed his briefcase and headed out the door, shutting the lights out on his way.

As the sky darkened, the rain began to fall all along the strip, which was alive as Slim and their new team reeled in all the money. Just as fast as junkies could fill the hallway they operated from, they were served and cleared out. After awhile, when it slowed down, Slim gathered all the money and took it to an apartment in the building. When he emerged, he had a wide smile and told his boys how well they had done. Ready to close up shop, they leaned against the wall of the building in the rain, chatting with each other.

Suddenly a black four-door car sped through the intersection with both left-side windows down. Before anyone could move, bullets riddled the area where they stood. The shooter's car sped off, leaving no one standing.

As lightning lit the sky, Slim struggled to get up, as blood ran from his chest and head. Collapsing, he laid still with his eyes wide open, never to breathe again. The other four lay scattered along the pavement and wall, as blood ran down the sidewalk mixing with the rain.

At Tony's home, around the time of this shooting, he sat in his living room with his Glock submachine gun, pump shotgun and plenty of bullets and shells. With all this laid out across the couch and the rain falling, he sat waiting for any and everything. He also made sure his wife was gone for the weekend, so she wouldn't be caught up in anything violent.

About eleven-thirty, Tony's doorbell rang. He jumped up, grabbed two of his guns then asked who it was. The voice on the other side of the door yelled, "It's me, Wallace."

Tony approached the window first, looking and noticing Wallace and one other, but couldn't make the other person out, because of the hood he had on. He strutted over to the door, opened it, and let them in.

"Damn, man, I thought you loved us!" stated Wallace, as he and Eric entered and peeled their raingear and shoes off. Tony relaxed now.

"Yo, I didn't know who Eric was until he came in, because of the hood he had on and the rain suit."

"I see you're ready for a war or expecting some real nice company," Eric stated as he saw all the guns and ammo.

Hanging their coats on a rack by the door, the three of them walked across the plush carpet and over to the couch.

"So, Rambo, what the hell is going on here?" asked Wallace, direct and to the point.

"Yo, I've been trying to page you guys all day, but I got no answer, so I had to protect my home front and myself!" insisted Tony.

"From what?" Wallace and Eric asked at the same time.

"Listen, yesterday someone killed my dogs, but no shots were heard! So, I figured whoever it was came in silence for a reason. Luckily, Spike made a noise before he was shot dead, otherwise I might be dead, too!" Tony shouted.

"This is the work of Jewels! That you can bet!" stated Wallace angrily.

"We've already started cleaning house, let's finish the job," declared Eric. But for the rest of the night, they all sat around watching the television and conversing.

Early the next morning, John decided to go back to work. When he walked through the front entrance, everyone greeted him as his father smiled and hugged him.

"I'm glad to see you, son, how's everything?" His father asked concerned.

"I'm all right," responded John.

He removed his arms from around John, then placed just his right one around his shoulder and asked, "Ready to come back to work already?"

"Yeah, I guess so," John managed.

His father walked him to the back, then as John took a seat, his father headed back to the front.

During John's hours at work, Jewels sat stressing, having heard the news that his partner, Slim, and his new team had been killed in a drive-by shooting the night before. After throwing things from one side of the room to the next, he began to scream and punch walls, as tears flooded his eyelids and his face. Then came a knock at the door, which got louder and more repetitious, so he ignored it. Jewels, shook up, walked toward the door, but in the process picked up his gun from a nearby lamp table.

"Yes," Jewels said, clearing his throat and shaking in fear.

"Hotel security, is everything all right in there?"

With a sigh of relief, Jewels answered, "Yes."

Nervous, he headed back into the living area, and he decided to call Hits to see what was going on with the job.

Back at Mr. Sharpe's office, Mr. Woodson told him that he followed the same car to the Fifth Precinct that he had followed previously to the Sportswear Company. And when he left, at about eleven that evening, the person in question had not come back out. Curious, Mr. Sharpe asked Mr. Woodson if he would take a trip with him back to the Fifth Precinct. Woodson agreed, so they left. When they arrived, Woodson had Mr. Sharpe stop beside a black Mustang, then he began to take down the plate number. They patiently waited for Mr. Gates to come out. At about four-thirty, three detectives came walking from within. Mr. Woodson shouted as he pointed.

"That's him, right there!"

"Which one?" asked Mr. Sharpe.

" He's the one in the middle with the blue jeans and white shirt."

Not wanting to alert or alarm the officers, Mr. Sharpe decided to get out and approach them alone. Approaching them now, he focused on the one he knew, but by the time he got across the street, they all climbed in their cars and pulled off. Failing to get their attention by yelling, Mr.

Sharpe decided to call the detective that he knew and ask him about the officer in question. Climbing back in his car, he pulled off, also.

Back at his office, as the clock read five o'clock, Mr. Sharpe called John, but only got the answering machine. Leaving a message, he told him that their newly-found witness had died behind bars. Then he expressed the fact that he needed to see him tomorrow, to figure out whether or not to postpone the trial for a month or so, or go on as planned.

Twenty minutes after the call from his lawyer, John, followed by Alvin, walked in to his apartment. Alvin flipped on the lights as John roamed through the darkness into the back, where his bedroom was. He immediately turned on the fan and sat on the edge of his bed, pulling off his pants, then his shirt. As he sat in his boxer shorts, he pulled a set of dumbbells from beneath the bed and began to curl them. He exercised his injured arm to strengthen it and the adjoining shoulder muscles. Alvin walked in and interrupted, handing him a tape recorder and adding, "I almost forgot to give this to you."

John laid the dumbbell on the bed so he could catch the recorder as Alvin tossed it to him from the doorway. After hitting the play button and hearing nothing, John looked up at Alvin, who was now sitting beside him. Remembering how long it had sat in the hall, Alvin expressed that it probably needed batteries. John smiled then asked, "Is there anything on this tape?"

Alvin replied, "I don't know, it wasn't working when I took it from behind the stairs."

John put it down on the bed, figuring he'd get some batteries in the morning. Curling his weights once again, John smirked as Alvin watched, then got up and walked out. Heading back to the living room, where he had left the television on, Alvin entertained himself.

Not long afterward, a sweaty John walked into the living room, breathing heavily, looking down at the answering machine, which had two messages. Hitting the play button, he waited to listen. The first message started within seconds.

(Beep) "John, its Aunt Pricilla. I'm sorry I missed you. Bye, we're leaving at noon. Call us sometime. My number is area code 560-423-5561. Love you; take care."

(Beep) "John, this is Mr. Sharpe. Our new witness was murdered yesterday. Plus, we need to talk about possibly postponing the trial."

After listening to the second message, John's face showed no sign of surprise. He strolled to the bathroom to shower and get ready for bed. Alvin got up from in front of the tube, looked out the window briefly, then decided to take a walk.

Due to the murders the night before, the strip was shut down. As Michaels and Williams investigated, they sat out front, questioning everyone they came in contact with. But the most anyone had seen was a small black car fly up and spray the men, then pull off. The detectives left a few cards behind, hoping someone would call.

Driving off, they headed back to the precinct. But as they did, two patrol cars stayed behind to discourage business and to scare away the hustlers. As they sat, people still drifted into building 215, copped what they needed and left.

Later, Tony, Wallace and Eric sat in Tony's living room laughing and joking. Beside them in easy reach, loaded and ready, laid a few guns. The pump shotgun sat on the center table, as they watched a comedy show on the television. Then a loud noise was heard on the front porch. Wallace walked over to the window and peeked out, but saw nothing. Walking to the door with the Tech Nine submachine gun, he removed the lock then pulled it open. Following him, Tony and Eric walked out onto the porch with their weapons in hand, also. Looking around and around, Tony noticed a brick lying in the grass and walked over to pick it up.

"Yo, someone must have thrown this at the door," Tony said as he looked around again. They all looked up and down the street, around the house and through the yard, but came up with nothing. Tony, thinking it was done for the purpose of a distraction, decided to check again, but again found nothing. They checked the back door, the neighbors' yards, but still came up empty.

Wallace looked around back again to be sure and noticed a slightly opened window, but paid it no mind due to the humidity. He met Eric at the back door, where Eric let him in, and they both walked back into the living room.

As they sat back around the table, a shadow appeared from within a darkened den area, as a red beam of light focused on the back of Tony's head. Looking around, Eric noticed it, but before he could do anything, Tony fell to the carpet, face down.

Eric and Wallace both grabbed their guns and opened fire at the spot where the figure had stood. Hiding behind furniture, Eric and Wallace paused after realizing the return fire had ceased. Running over to the doorway where the person had stood, they both kept their guns up, just in case.

Entering the den they noticed an open window. Wallace damn near knocked Eric over, running to the front door. Snatching it open, he rushed out and saw nothing but an empty street once again, as if this person had popped in and out like a genie. Wallace ran around each side of the house, but found no one, as the sound of sirens filled the air. He rushed back in, then stared down at Tony's still body, as it laid in a puddle of his blood, which stained the clean white carped. Wallace told Eric, who had tears in his eyes, to get the shotgun, as he tossed him the submachine gun, and to put them away, out of sight.

Eric ran up the stairs quickly, then hurried back empty-handed, as the blue and red lights glared through the window and sirens sounded loudly. They took deep breaths as they approached the door to open it before it was kicked in. Upon opening the door, they saw the lawn was flooded with cops with their guns pointed directly at them. Keeping their hands where they could be seen, they walked out slowly. Seeing all the police cars and officers shook them both up. As the officers approached and searched them, Wallace began to talk.

"Someone, somehow crept into the house while we all sat watching television and killed our friend. He's lying inside on the carpet!"

Four officers rushed inside following Wallace's lead, as Eric was held onto tightly by another outside. Standing over the body, one of the officers radioed for the portable crime lab and the coroner, as another began to ask questions.

"Now you guys were sitting here watching television, correct?" asked the officer as he wrote in a pad that he pulled from his pants pocket.

"Yes," replied Wallace as he stared down at Tony's body.

"So why didn't this alleged killer shoot you guys, also?" the officer asked as he continued.

Wallace listened to him carefully, sensing that the officer might be trying to trip him up. But before he could answer, Eric did as they brought him inside.

"We jumped behind furniture out of fear, as he shot at us a couple of times, see," showing the officers the holes in the walls.

"We were lucky not to get hit. Then when the firing stopped, we searched for the killer, but he was gone."

Explaining and pointing, Eric led the officers across the room to the den area. Immediately the officers noticed the bullet holes in the wall on that side of the room, also.

"So if he was shooting in that direction at you guys, who did all this?" asked one of the officers, as he pointed to some more holes in the wall. Not wanting to tell on themselves, Wallace and Eric stood quiet for a minute. Feeling as if they weren't getting the truth, or at least not the full story, the same officer ordered the other to search the entire house.

Outside, a sergeant pulled up and began to walk up the walkway. Just as he did, a neighbor ran up to him in his pajamas, robe and slippers and told what he saw before they had arrived.

"A guy came running from this alleyway!" he said, pointing to the one between his house and Tony's. "Then he jumped in a blue pickup truck with another guy, then they drove off," added the neighbor.

The sergeant asked one of the officers to get his name and address and to have him come in to make a complete statement. After which, he turned and continued up the walkway. As he walked through the open door, one of the officers approached him and began to brief him on the situation.

"These guys here are saying the dead guy is their friend and that someone, somehow crept into this house while they all sat watching television. The person then shot the deceased, then got back out the house without either of them getting a good look at him," stated the officer as he pointed and went on.

"If you want my opinion," the sergeant stopped him right there, showing no interest in his opinions. "We have a witness saying he saw a blue pickup truck pull off after a guy dressed in black ran from the side of this house and jumped in," stated the sergeant.

As their discussion went on, one of the officers who was searching the house came down the stairs with something wrapped in a towel. He approached the sergeant and the other officers standing around and said, "Look what I found in a hamper in one of the bedrooms!" Opening the towel, he revealed a shotgun, a submachine gun and two smaller handguns.

The officer also noted that from the warmth of the weapons he could tell they had just been fired. The sergeant, wanting to get to the bottom of all this, decided to take them in on weapons charges, so he could question them further. As the guns were taken to be dusted for prints, the crime lab pulled bullets from the walls and everywhere else.

"Cuff them!" said the sergeant, as Wallace and Eric looked at each other as if that was exactly what they had expected. After cuffing the two of them, a few officers escorted them outside, then to separate patrol cars. As the car door was opened for Wallace, he was instructed to watch his head and placed into the back of it. Wallace eased in, as the tight cuffs caused him to show how much they hurt in his facial expression. After being seated in the car, he stared through the window into the house in thought.

Both patrol cars pulled off and drifted from sight.

Now finally at the precinct, Wallace and Eric sat in separate dimly-lit rooms that criminals often visit to be interrogated. By this time it was three-thirty in the morning and the entire precinct was quiet, exceptionally quiet compared to the chaos of midday. A doorknob turned and a detective entered the room that Eric had occupied for the last twenty minutes. Closing the door behind him, the detective introduced himself.

"Hi, I'm Detective Williams."

Eric just stared.

"Now from what I've gathered from the sergeant and officers at the scene, there was more than one gun used. So do you wish to tell me the real story, or would you like to sit in a cell until I figure it out myself?" added the detective, as he leaned on a table, which sat between them.

Eric thought for a minute and then decided there was not much to tell, except what was already told. Figuring that he'd just add what little he could put together in his mind.

"Okay, our friend was scared. Someone had recently tried to break in his house and he didn't know whether or not they would try again. The guy shot both of his dogs dead, but lucky for Tony, one of the dogs made enough noise to alarm him and his neighbor. Then when he came out to see what had happened, all he saw was the same blue pickup that the neighbor was speaking about. So today, we stopped by and he asked us to hang around, so we did just that!" stated Eric, who seemed winded.

The detective said, "Okay, let's get to the part pertaining to the time surrounding the shooting. Now you and your partner both said someone crept in the house and shot your friend, then escaped without being seen. What were you two doing during all this shooting? I'll tell you what you were doing. You were shooting back, hoping to nail 'em, weren't you?"

A long pause followed, as the detective was now sitting and looking him straight in the eyes. Eric looked away. Still silent, Detective Williams got up out of frustration and started up again.

"Explain the holes in the wall, opposite where you guys said you were! I'm not stupid! You guys were shooting back, weren't you? Tell me now and I'll cut you some slack, but if I've got to wait on reports, I'm going to stick it to you."

Eric thought, as the detective roamed the room, then cleared his throat as he began to speak.

"I know what I'm getting ready to say is going to hurt me, but here goes. We had those guns for protection, just in case those cowards came back!"

"Now we're getting somewhere. You talk like you may know the guys!" stated the detective.

Catching himself now, Eric said, "I hope not."

The detective smirked, then said, "Look, if your story checks out and there's no bodies on the guns, I'll make sure you guys get a more than fair deal."

He walked out of the room, leaving Eric behind, then across the hall, he entered another, where Wallace sat banging his head on the table.

"Is everything all right?" asked the detective, as he watched him do this repeatedly.

Wallace raised his head and in his eyes he had a look that could kill.

"Wallace Mills, now tell me exactly what happened, every little detail," said the detective as he turned a chair around and sat on it backwards.

"We told you guys what happened!" replied Wallace.

"Well, your partner told me that you guys were shooting, as well as being shot at. Is that true?" asked the detective as he patiently awaited an answer.

Wallace, thinking the detective was trying to play him, just stated, "We didn't kill him, so why are you holding us?"

"Because of the fact that we found guns on the premises, holes at both ends of the room, leading us to believe there was some sort of trading of gunfire. Now I'm very understanding, so work with me and I'll make things a lot easier."

Wallace refused to speak another word.

Then Williams said to him, "Fine, have it your way."

Slamming the door on his way out, he raced up the corridor to where a few fellow officers huddled.

As he approached them, one officer paused from his laughter long enough to say, "The outcome of the ballistics report won't be known till tomorrow.

"No problem, we'll just hold them. Maybe we'll find out a little more," stated Williams as he joined their huddle.

"When one of you gets a moment, could you put them in the holding area?" he added as he excused himself as quickly as he had joined them.

Sitting in a coffee shop, eating and reading the newspaper as usual, John noticed an article which read:

FIVE KILLED IN DRIVE-BY.

Skipping through the article, he realized it was Slim and some of Jewels' boys.

MAN ELUDES CAPTURE

After trading gunfire with police officers, a man escapes. All that is known is that he's six feet tall, about 260 pounds, armed and dangerous.

Calling Tony, he dialed again and again until he realized there was going to be no answer, then he hung up. Walking back to where he was sitting, he ate the remainder of his breakfast, paid his bill, then left. Arriving at work around a quarter to seven, he set up shop as usual.

Back at the precinct, Detective Michaels walked down the corridor with a few papers in his hands, and entered the room labeled Homicide Squad. He walked up to the second desk and stopped as he waved the papers in front of Detective Jones.

"Look who we have here!" stated Michaels with a slight grin.

Jones looked at the criminal file and the identification of the deceased, matching fingerprints and all, then spoke.

"Someone finally took him out and I've got a good idea who."

"Who do you think did it?" asked Michaels with concern.

"I'm not a hundred percent sure, but I've got a good idea," said Jones as he massaged his chin and thought.

"All these drug dealers dying is leading me to believe that there's some sort of drug war going on. So if those two in the cell aren't willing to help us (referring to Wallace and Eric), make sure their bails are high enough where this will be their temporary residence! Charge them with possession of firearms, possession with intent to use, unlawful use and anything else that fits the bill."

About half an hour later, Michaels returned and suggested to Jones that they go to the scene to search the surroundings and yard. Jones rose from his seat and followed him out the door, after grabbing his jacket.

That afternoon, sitting in deep thought, Mr. Sharpe didn't hear his phone until the third ring. It was his receptionist transferring a call.

"Hello, Mr. Sharpe, you have a call on line two."

Mr. Sharpe pushed a button to allow the call to come through.

"Hello," he said after a brief pause.

"Hello, Mr. Sharpe, I'm returning your call. I'm sorry I couldn't get back to you sooner, but I was kinda busy," stated Mr. Sharpe's source at the precinct.

"That's okay," stated a smiling Mr. Sharpe.

"What's up," asked the source.

"Well, yesterday, I saw you and two other detectives walking from the precinct and there was one who had on blue jeans and a short-sleeve, button-down white shirt," described Mr. Sharpe.

"You're talking about Williams, Detective Chris Williams," the voice responded.

Mr. Sharpe wrote this down on a legal pad that he had handy, as he asked him if he was sure. Noticing that his voice was a little scratchy, Mr. Sharpe asked him if he had a cold. The response was, "Sort of." As the conversation came to a close, Mr. Sharpe thanked him and told him he'd get in touch if there was any new developments.

In his hotel suite, Jewels sat in the loveseat, on the phone, lounging in his silk robe, laughing as if what the person on the other end was saying amused him. Still smiling and giggling to himself after he had hung up, with a loud burst of laughter, shouted, "Tony, Tony, Tony," as he headed to the bedroom.

As the skies darkened, at the precinct once again, Wallace and Eric asked each and every officer who passed if they could make one phone call. Finally, a sergeant asked them what all the noise was about.

Responding immediately, in unison they said, "I want to make a phone call and we need to know the charges and the bail."

The sergeant told them he'd have an officer come and let them out, one at a time, so they could make their calls, and he'd personally find out what the circumstances were with their charges and bails. Twenty minutes after the sergeant left, and as they talked from cell to cell, an officer approached, asking who needed to make a phone call. Everyone, including Wallace and Eric, answered and stood up. The officer asked Eric, who stood in the front against the bars, "What's the number?"

"1-908-424-6656," he recited as the officer dialed it and handed him the phone. As the voice on the other end answered, Eric responded,

"Hello, Raymond, this is Eric. Me and Wallace are locked up in the Fifth Precinct without bail."

"I know, I heard. What's going on?" asked Raymond.

"We have to talk, so try to get us out of here as soon as possible I've got to go," Eric finished as the officer told him to cut it short so the next man could make his call.

Meanwhile, John rushed from a bus and hurried down the block that led to his apartment. Reaching the door, he heard the phone ring, so he opened it, then rushed in. Grabbing up the receiver, he hoped the person on the other end hadn't hung up. John out of breath yelled, "Hello."

In a soft tone came, "Hello, John, this is Angie. Wallace and Eric are locked up and Tony's dead."

John, hearing this, was numb for a minute and then came back, catching the tail end of the conversation, as she had never stopped talking.

"...I can't believe how out of hand this whole thing has gotten, can you!" she asked as John didn't respond, at least not right away.

"I agree," he answered, not really knowing what she was talking about, because of his disbelief of the whole issue. He cut Angie short, telling her he'd have to speak with her later.

By five o'clock, he had realized he had missed his appointment with his lawyer, so he called him to apologize and tell him he'd see him the following day. Then he sat back relaxing, as he thought of all those lost to gunplay and the lust for money. As he pictured them, memory after memory raced through his head until he dozed off to sleep.

On the other side of town, his lawyer sat, puzzled, wondering if Williams lived at 1407 Ridgewood and if he was somehow affiliated with

True to Life Sportswear, of if by chance he could be Kenneth Gates. Trying to make a connection between the two, he decided to search out pictures of the two of them. In that instant, he picked up the phone to page his investigator, Mr. Woodson.

Sunday rolled around and a nice day it was. The sun shined and everything had a glow to it, except for the house that Tony had died in. It seemed to have a dark cloud above it. The black Mercedes pulled into the driveway behind the van with his wife, Rochelle, behind the wheel. Ducking under yellow tape, she rushed to the door. Unlocking the door and entering, she quickly spotted holes in the walls and furniture. What caught her attention the most was the dried red stain on the usually spotless white carpet. In shock, she yelled for Tony, but got no answer. She ran through the house, hysterically yelling his name, then tripped as she ran up the stairs shouting, "God, please, no."

After searching the entire house, she staggered back to the living room, grabbing the phone, but so shook up she could barely dial. Finally getting it together enough to call Raymond, she cried uncontrollably.

As someone picked up the phone she yelled, "Hello!"

Crying and praying he wasn't dead, she screamed and screamed. "Where is Tony? Where is my Tony? Please don't let him be dead!"

Raymond, not wanting to be the one to tell her, knew he had no other choice, took a deep breath, then let if flow. "Rochelle, I know what

I'm about to say is far from what you want to hear, because I, too, refuse to believe it happened, but it did."

Her crying seemed to get louder as he told the story in its entirety. Trying to calm her as much as he could from the other end of the phone line, Raymond fought back his own tears. Deciding to go over and comfort her, Raymond kissed his wife and daughter good-bye on his way out.

An hour later, he sat in Tony's house with Rochelle crying on his shoulder. "We'll find his killer, but you've got to be strong! He would have wanted it that way," Raymond stated as he consoled her.

He looked around at the riddled walls, broken windows and then at the bloodstain, which had dried on the carpet. His eyes watered, but not one tear fell as his face hardened and became expressionless.

Elsewhere, John stared out the window into the streets, where he watched people as they walked by, wondering if Alvin was all right. Beside the fact that he hadn't seen him in two days, he just wondered, as he walked away from the window and into the back to the bathroom. After brushing his teeth, he headed out on a Sunday morning stroll. Starting toward Alvin's mom's residence, John walked and walked.

After reaching her place, he found out that she had left them behind and run off somewhere. A tenant in the same building told John that not long after she had disappeared, the kids found a note, then they, too, left. John, hearing this, headed back home, hoping Alvin might call or stop by.

When he arrived, he saw that there was one message on his answering machine. He quickly pushed PLAY. "Hello, John, it's Alvin. My mom, left me and my little sister, so I've got to be a man and take care of things. I'll try to catch you later, or tomorrow. Bye."

John was now really worried, knowing that Alvin was a kid himself, trying to take care of his younger sister, with nowhere to live and nothing to eat. He raced out of the house and all around town looking for the two of them.

In the early morning hours, about two-thirty, after John had abandoned his search and was fast asleep in his bed with the phone resting on his chest, there was suddenly a slight knocking sound in the front of the house. John, in a deep sleep, heard nothing. After a while the knocking stopped, and the only sound heard through out the house was his snoring.

Hours later, John jumped up and prepared for work, but not without worries about Alvin and his sister on his mind. When fully dressed he rushed out the door, but as he did, he noticed two kids cuddled up against a wall in the hallway. He walked over, and after seeing that it was Alvin and his little sister, he shook them, awakening them.

"Alvin, wake up!" John shouted.

Alvin slowly opened his eyes, then said, "I didn't want to burden you any more! My mom left and I'm all my sister has. You've got your own problems."

John said, "Look, as long as I'm around, you can always count on me, and together we'll do what's best. Now what did you do with your keys?"

Alvin told him as he searched through his pockets. "I must have lost them somewhere, that's why we slept in the hallway."

John picked up Alvin's half-asleep sister, then carried her limp body into the apartment and placed her gently on the couch.

He told Alvin, "You know where everything is; I've got to go!"

Once again, Mr. Woodson sat in his car, hidden from plain view, taking pictures of the man they had identified as Detective Williams. He took these pictures with a 35-millimeter camera, so he could get some good close-ups. He also took pictures of the car and the plates as it left the yard. Completing that part of his task, he headed to True to Life Sportswear. After entering and reaching the desk, he asked if he could speak with a Mr. John Hearns. The woman who sat at this desk paged him, as Mr. Woodson waited patiently.

In the county jail, Wallace and Eric sat on separate floors, with their bails each set at fifty thousand cash. Raymond and Rochelle made arrangements to get them out, with the help of a local bondsman named James Johnson. During this time, Wallace had to defend himself against an inmate who approached him, telling him he was finished and that he had orders to kill him and Eric. Wallace beat the big, sloppy, ugly guy down as the other inmates looked on. The guards ran down to him and carried him off to lockup. Word trickled down to Eric, as he sat in his cell on a lower floor, ready for anything. An announcement was made over the intercom that bail had been posted for Wallace and Eric. They both showed signs of relief as they stood at their doors, waiting for the guards to let them out.

6THE TRIAL

The long-awaited trial was finally about to begin.

Prospective jurors were picked through and the final selection was made. John and his lawyer pretty much fought for a racial imbalance (more black than white), while the prosecutor fought for the exact opposite. After the final selection, the jury consisted of six blacks, two Hispanics and four whites. Carefully looking over the jurors that took them two weeks to select, John thought to himself, these twelve people will be the judges of where I'll spend the rest of my life.

The first day of the trial started, and the courtroom became congested with John's family, friends and people who he assumed were officers of the court. At the entrance, there was a metal detector. Security and safety seemed to be a priority for this event. John, neatly dressed in a burgundy suit, sat speechless, his nerves were barely under control.

Mr. Sharpe, noticing the stress in his face, smiled and consolingly said, "It's going to be all right."

John looked at the prosecutor, who sat at an adjoining table, to his far right, a slender, balding white man with cheap wire-framed glasses and a poorly made suit. He looked quite focused as he fumbled through the papers and documents in front of him. As quickly as John could straighten his neck up and look forward, the bailiff asked everyone to rise.

"...The Honorable Judge Strickland presiding." He stated without pause.

The judge got comfortable and then asked everyone to be seated. As everyone sat, he quietly looked through his notes to bring him up to speed. The court reporter sat patiently awaiting his first words. John glanced around the room once again, as if he had missed something. The judge broke the long silence.

"Hello, I'm Judge Strickland. Sorry for the delay, but I needed to clarify a few things with my staff first. I appreciate your patience."

He started the proceeding by instructing the jurors, then heard both the defense and the prosecution's opening statements. All the evidence was introduced and then he was ready to hear the first witness.

"Prosecution calls Mrs. Walker to the stand."

A short, older woman rose to her feet, her thin face hidden by her long gray hair. She was the woman who lived across the street from the playground. Approaching the stand to be seated, she was stopped and sworn in. The judge instructed her to put her left hand on the Bible and raise her right hand. After she was seated, the prosecutor began to unveil his line of questioning.

"Hello, Mrs. Walker," greeted the prosecutor.

"Hello," she responded.

"Now Mrs. Walker, going back to the night in question, the twentieth of August, 1989, tell the court what you saw."

"I saw a young man running scared, as if he had done something wrong."

"Objection, Your Honor, that's pure speculation!" shouted Mr. Sharpe.

The judge instructed her to just answer the question. The prosecutor, who was now smiling at Mrs. Walker, said, "I see you have a good memory. So tell me, is that man anywhere in this courtroom today?" She slowly looked around the room, stopping at the sight of John, who was looking at a pad his lawyer had in front of him.

"That's him, right there!" she stated with sureness.

"Describe for the court what he has on."

"He's wearing a reddish-colored suit, with a white shirt and a reddish tie."

"For the record, Your Honor, let it be noted that she is referring to Mr. Johnathan Jackson. No further questions," finished the prosecutor.

Mr. Sharpe rose to his feet, then approached the stand, where Mrs. Walker sat.

"Now Mrs. Walker, you say you saw my client, Mr. Jackson, is that correct?"

"Correct."

"What was he doing when you saw him?"

"Running from the playground."

"Did you hear shots?"

"No."

"So isn't it safe to say, you could have missed something?"

"Yes."

"No further questions, Your Honor."

The prosecution's next witness, Mrs. Hill, was now being sworn in.

"Hello, Mrs. Hill, how are you today?" the prosecutor asked, as he paraded across the floor. "Now in your exact words, someone almost ran you over, is that correct?"

"Yes."

"Is that person in this room today?"

"Yes he's right there!" she said, pointing to John, as he sat with his hands folded, staring at a wall.

"Let the record show she also pointed out the defendant, Mr. Jackson. Now, as he ran, tell the court what happened next."

"I continued walking home. That's when I heard people yelling and screaming, 'Someone call 911.'"

"How sure are you he's the guy you saw that night?"

"I'm positive, as sure as my hair is gray."

"Thank you, Mrs. Hill, no further questions."

As the prosecutor took his seat again, Mr. Sharpe rose to tell the judge he had no questions. He closed his suit jacket, sat back down and leaned over to tell John not to worry, as he noticed the confusion on his face.

As it grew nearer to eleven-thirty, the judge recessed for lunch. The courtroom emptied out into the corridor and the bulk of people stood waiting for the elevator. John and Mr. Sharpe sat on a bench right outside the courtroom.

At the same time, in another part of town, Raymond, Wallace and Eric sat in an apartment, trying to figure out a way to pinpoint Jewels, while preparing for Tony's funeral. Knowing Jewels was basically out of business, and his boys were dead, they decided to ride about town, but they found no sign of him. It was as if he had disappeared from the face of the earth.

Meanwhile, Jewels sat in his hotel suite puffing a cigar, acting as if he didn't have a care in the world. He puffed away as he listened to the radio, which was set on a jazz station. Laughing to himself he choked as smoke filled the room. Tearing and clearing his throat, he began to laugh again, glossy-eyed.

Court resumed and everyone was quickly seated, including the judge. He instructed the prosecutor to proceed and call his next witness.

"Your Honor, I would like to call Detective Jones to the stand."

The detective rose from his seat and walked up toward the stand. John looked on as he was sworn in, then at the prosecutor, who wasted no time.

"Detective Jones, now didn't Mr. Jackson call you the day after the shooting?"

"Yes."

"What did he say?"

"He said he'd like to report three murders."

"Where did he say these murders took place?"

"In the playground on Tenth Street."

"Then what?"

"Detective Michaels and I asked him to come in for questioning."

"Did he show up?"

"Yes, he did."

"Then what?"

"He gave a detailed layout of the murders and a vague description of the murderers."

"Just how many murderers did he say there were?"

"Three."

"But all the reports show that all the bullets came from the same gun. Now, Mr. Jones, may I call you that, detective?"

"Yes."

The prosecutor approached the evidence table to pick up something from it.

"Is this the gun you found?"

"Yes."

"Exhibit G for the record, Your Honor."

The prosecutor placed it back on the table and continued.

"Now could he explain how his fingerprints were found on the gun?"

"No."

"No further questions."

John's eyes roamed the room. He could see some of the jurors taking notes. Mr. Sharpe rose and continued to stay poised.

"Now, detective, you said my client reported the murders in questions the very next morning, correct?"

"Yes."

"Now it puzzles me, why wasn't the gun found until after the fact? Can you shed some light on this for us?"

"Sure. At the time of his statement the gun was being tested for prints."

"Okay, and isn't it possible that two others could have held them at bay, while the real murdered killed them, one at a time?"

"It's possible, yes."

Ready to object, the prosecutor, for some reason, let that one slide.

"Isn't it also possible that when John was abducted, that someone could have hit him over the head and somehow put his fingerprints on the gun?"

The prosecutor rose in fury. "Objection, Your Honor, he's leading the witness."

The judge heard this and responded, "Objection sustained, please stop leading the witness."

Mr. Sharpe apologized then said, "No further questions, but I'd like to reserve the right to call Detective Jones at a later date."

The judge granted that and adjoined court until the next day.

John sat in his living room, going over the day's happenings, while Alvin played outside with his sister. The day drifted into night and Alvin and his sister came through the door, finding John asleep on the couch with the air conditioner and the television both running. But as soon as they closed the door, he jumped into a sitting position. After yawning and stretching, he asked the two of them to sit beside him.

"Now, we have to find your mother somehow. Do you guys have any family we can get in touch with?" John asked, awaiting a response.

Alvin responded, "Our Aunt Charise, who lives in Elizabeth, but she doesn't have a phone."

"Do you know exactly where she lives?" asked John, concerned.

"Yes," Alvin uttered as his sister nodded her head up and down.

"She lives at 496 Broad Street. There's a Shell gas station on the corner.

"Okay, what bus takes us there?"

"The number 23," Alvin answered.

John got up from the couch and walked to the back, to the bathroom, to freshen up before leaving. When he returned, he looked over at the two of them and told them to come with him.

Sitting on the bus, Alvin began to ask questions.

"John, why can't we just stay with you? I can make enough money to help out."

"It's not that easy. It's not a money issue," John quickly responded.

"Then what is it?"

"The problem is, first of all, both of you have to go to school and I can't enroll you. Second, if one of you gets sick, I can't act as your legal guardian or parents. Third, I know nothing about raising a little boy, much less a little girl. Fourth, I'm on trial and barely holding myself together."

Alvin, pretty much understanding his points, turned away and looked out the window.

As the bus stopped to let a few people get off, he turned to look at his sister, who was just happy to be out and about.

Getting off the bus an hour and a half later, directly in front of the gas station that Alvin had spoken of, they walked as Alvin pointed. As he directed he spoke. "See that green and gray house, the fifth one on this side?"

John paused for a second to look, noticing a shabby old house. The three of them marched toward it. After reaching the porch, John rang the bell. Suddenly a light came on. The thundering sound of heavy feet pounding the staircase could be heard as they waited patiently. A woman opened the door, wearing a flower-patterned dress. She filled the doorway entirely.

"Hi!" She blurted bubbly.

She looked at John, smiling. As she noticed Alvin and his sister, Theresa, she became overwhelmed with joy. Hugging and kissing them, she yelled out, "Calvin and Casey, your cousins are here."

Calvin and Casey were thirteen-year-old identical twins, with close-cropped haircuts, big heads with beady eyes. As quickly as she yelled out to them, they came running. As John, Alvin and Theresa stood in the doorway, Calvin and Casey smiled at them.

Aunt Charise laughed and said, "Excuse my manners. Come in, come in."

John, Alvin and Theresa walked in the gloomy dark house.

"Excuse the mess," she said as she grabbed clothes from the broken-down couch and removed a mattress from the center of the floor, which was lying in front of a dusty television that was playing music videos loudly. Charise rushed to the back with clothes in hand as John cautiously sat with Alvin and Theresa beside him.

Calvin and Casey asked Alvin if he wanted to come out back, but he shook his head from left to right, signifying no.

From the back of the dimly lit dwelling came Aunt Charise, who asked, "Now where is your mother, Alvin?"

Alvin looked up, as if to speak, but John cut in. "She left them stranded, so they came to me."

The smile on their Aunt Charise's face dropped into a blank, emotionless look, then she said, "It's not her first and probably not her last; she'll be back." Sounding sure of herself, she sat down in a chair she had propped against a wall. Then she blurted out, "She's probably in some man's face somewhere; she'll be back as soon as he gets tired of her, which shouldn't be long."

John looked down at Alvin and his sister as Charise said this. Alvin stared at the ceiling, glassy-eyed, as if he wanted to cry. His sister sat smiling, as if none of this affected her. John decided to lay his cards on the table.

"Look, these kids need a place to stay until she returns. Now I'm willing to help out, and from time to time they can come stay with me."

Charise responded, "Why didn't you just call the police?"

"Because of the mess it might have caused. Being that they gave me your name and address, I figured you, being their aunt, would watch over them. I would, but I have too many hardships of my own right now, plus I'm never home."

Charise smirked and then nodded her head up and down, as though she had heard this before.

"I'll take them in, but when I see their trifling mother, I'm gonna give her a big piece of my mind, if I restrain myself from punching her lights out!"

John walked from the porch with Alvin, who rushed to his side. John began to speak.

"Look, Alvin, I know this isn't much better, but work with her until your mother returns or I can find you a better situation."

Alvin agreed as John bent to hug him. Alvin headed back to the house as John hurried to the bus stop. When Alvin reached the porch, he turned to watch John and he stood there waiting.

Morning came as John tossed and turned. He was awakening from a dream which included prison bars and an orange jumpsuit.

"No!" He yelled as he woke up and then calmed down as soon as he noticed he was lying in his own bed.

Miles away, Mr. Woodson was up and out to an early start. He was going to have Kenneth gates of 1407 Ridgewood checked out at the Department of Motor Vehicles, where he had worked in the past. At eight o'clock he entered the Motor Vehicle building, squeezed through the crowd of people in line trying to get their license, registration or otherwise. Once through, he approached a vacant window with no line. He called out to a dear friend, who just so happened to be the manager.

"James," he shouted, as a short, stocky, well-dressed man turned to answer.

"What's up?" he responded.

Walking up to the window area where Woodson stood, he and Mr. Woodson both smiled as if they were glad to see each other. Woodson asked him if he could run a check on a name and address. James agreed, so Woodson passed him a piece of paper with all that he wished to be checked and a business card. Then, as he left, he told James to give him a call later.

Meanwhile, back at John's, he rushed out the door as the sound of a horn was heard throughout the apartment. He raced down the stairs and out toward a parked car, which was being driven by Wallace.

Once John was seated inside, Wallace drove off, asking, "How are you holding up?"

He responded, "Fine."

Wallace started telling John that he, also, had to go to court, in August. He added, "I wish you could have been at Tony's funeral. It was packed; everyone from all over came. His brother was even there. You know he had a serious run-in with the police! I've got to give this life up; it's not at all what I thought it would be. I have enough money to just about do anything I wish!"

John replied, "Get out of it while you're still alive and sane!"

A long silence fell until they reached the parking area of the courthouse. Then Wallace put his arm around John and said, "You're all right."

The elevator door opened on the fourth level, where two others besides John and Wallace stepped from it. Walking to their left, they passed people huddled in the corridor conversing, while waiting for court to begin. As the two of them walked closer to the courtroom that John's case was being handled in, they sat on a half-occupied bench, relaxed and waiting.

By nine-thirty everyone started to walk into the courtroom, filling up the benches row after row. John walked to the front, where his lawyer and the prosecutor sat. Wallace squeezed his way onto the bench directly behind John and his lawyer.

Within fifteen minutes after everyone was seated, they were all asked to rise, as the judge entered the room.

Witness after witness said the same thing. Half of them seemed to have been instructed on what to say. As the morning drifted away, so did John. The prosecutor called on the chief medical examiner, Robert Maxwell. This medium-height, nerdy-looking white guy made his way to be sworn in and seated. Once again, the prosecutor wasted no time.

"Now Mr. Maxwell, state for the record what your occupation is."

"I'm the Essex County Medical Examiner."

"Did you examine the corpses of Darryl Ward, Kevin Chambers and Michael Evans?"

"Yes."

"What did you discover from your examinations of each body?"

"First of all, all of them expired from a single bullet to the cranium, the head area. Second, I noticed that all three expired at approximately the same time, and from the way the bullets shattered their skulls, it had to be a high-caliber pistol, fired at close range."

"So is it safe to say that one person could have committed this horrific crime?"

"Yes, it is."

Placing pictures on an easel, the prosecutor set up for his next question.

"Are these the pictures you took, exhibits D, E and F on the easel to the right of me?"

"Yes."

The prosecutor then gave the pictures to the jurors, so that they could view them. As the gruesome pictures made their way back to the front, the officer collected them and returned them to the evidence table.

"No further questions."

Mr. Sharpe stood just to say, "No questions, Your Honor."

"Next witness," the judge demanded as the medical examiner stepped down.

Back at Wallace's place, Angie sat at the kitchen table sipping tea from a mug, when Eric entered and ran straight through the apartment to the back. Never noticing Angie, he ran right back through with a gun in his hands and continued out the door.

She hurried to the bedroom window to see what was going on, but all she saw was Eric fixing his shirt, as he jumped in a car that sped off. Not recognizing the car, she decided to page Wallace to see if he had an idea. She waited patiently by the phone for about twenty minutes, when she decided to page him again. Finally, after another ten minutes passed, he called back and she grabbed the phone before the completion of the first ring.

"Hello," she nervously blurted out. "Hello, honey," she quickly added.

"What's up?" Wallace asked.

"Eric just ran out of here with a gun, like something was going down."

Wallace, silent for a minute, then asked, "Who was he with?"

"I don't know!" she replied.

"Well, I'll be home in a few minutes; they'll be finished here for the day shortly."

Angie looked at the clock, which read three-thirty, and then said, "Okay."

He hung up, leaving her holding the phone, listening to the dial tone.

In another part of Newark, Eric sat on the passenger side of a stolen Acura, following Jewels in his BMW. Jewels, who was always observant, noticed and quickly made the next right, then left, ending up on

Frelinghisen, where he accelerated with the Acura on his tail. The Acura pulled around to the left side of the BMW, and just as they began to roll the window down, Jewels made a sharp right as the Acura squealed when they hit the brakes. Spinning around to pursue, as they came to the corner and raced down the block, the BMW was nowhere to be seen.

"Damn, that slippery son of a bitch, he got away!" shouted Eric furiously.

Wallace, home now, paged Eric back to back, but the phone didn't ring once.

Just as Wallace started to think something bad must have happened and had jumped up to head out the door, the rustling of keys could be heard on the other side of it. The door opened and Eric rushed in as Wallace stood there in his path.

"Damn, fellow, you don't know how to answer your pager?" asked Wallace angrily.

"I was busy," responded a hyper Eric, as he brushed past Wallace with a look of disgust on his face.

"Busy doesn't cut it with me!" Wallace stated as he turned and followed him.

"I was just plain busy, okay!" he yelled back.

Wallace, figuring Eric needed time to cool off from whatever was bothering him, let him be. Figuring he'd talk about it later, when Eric was much calmer, Wallace went and sat on the loveseat with Angie. She rested her head on his shoulder.

Later, as Mr. Woodson sat at home on his porch, enjoying the peace and quiet of living alone, he thought of his wife, who had died some years ago. He sat in an old wooden rocking chair, rocking back and forth the way she did, in that same chair. As it began to get late, he rose from it and went in the house to get ready for the next day. Anticipating a phone call, he picked it up to make sure it was working, because it hadn't rung the entire time he was home. He put the receiver to his ear to listen for the dial tone. After hearing it, he put it back on the hook. After this, he headed through the darkened hall that led to the back of the house, where his bedroom could be found.

John was just walking from the bathroom, out from the shower. Wrapped in a towel, he walked through his, once again, empty place. Noticing Alvin's video games, which were still lying beside the television on the stand, John sat down for a minute, realizing he missed him already.

The judge had adjourned court until Thursday for personal reasons, so John had the entire day to himself. He began to get dressed and as he did, he went through a drawer which had a small tape recorder in it. He picked it up and remembered he had meant to give it to his lawyer, so they could listen to it together. He checked it to make sure the batteries he had put in it still worked. As he sat down and listened to it, the first voices he heard were that of two people getting high. One asked the other to pass the needle. Fast forwarding through this, he then heard a brief conversation and tried to identify the voices.

The first voice said, "Yo, Jugs, did you collect all that money yet?"

The second voice replied, "Yes, I did, here's most of it; I'll get the rest when they're all finished."

Then, after listening to a lot of unhelpful conversation, John was just about to throw the tape recorder down, when suddenly he heard, "Yo, Jewels, what's up with those guys across the street?"

Jewels responded, "Well, if Peters and Brown don't get them, Danny will! Guaranteed!"

John grabbed the phone and immediately called his lawyer, hoping this might be of some help. After telling him he had something for him to listen to, Mr. Sharpe expressed to him that he couldn't see him until five-thirty. John, figuring this might help his case, at least a little bit, bounced around, doing the odd chores, cleaning and straightening up at home.

About twelve o'clock that night, at Wallace's place, Eric told him of his encounter with Jewels. Wallace pounded his fist into his hand, then shouted, "Damn, that would have made my day." Then he stated, "He'll surface again or someone will see him eventually. That you can bet."

He walked from the room in which they sat, into another, where he and Angie slept. He kissed her on the cheek, then headed back to where Eric sat and told him, "Come on, let's take a ride."

Eric rose from his sitting position and together they walked out the door. To one who knew them, something was brewing.

In the car, they drove endlessly, until finally they ended up at John's place. Once inside, they discussed issues, then John played back the tape in the recorder. They sat in silence, just listening.

Wallace asked, "Who is this Danny?"

"Your guess is as good as mine," answered John.

"Rewind that just a little," asked Eric, as he leaned over to listen more carefully. There was the sound of the recorder rewinding fast, then John brought it to a sudden stop and hit the play button.

They heard, "Well, if Peters and Brown don't get them, Danny will!"

Wallace said, "I sort of thought something was going on between them and Jewels, but who the hell is this Danny?"

A puzzled look appeared on all of their faces. Wallace snapped his fingers as he said, "Danny, Danny, we know he's Jewels' hitman. Remember Alvin overheard one of their conversations and they spoke of him." It suddenly came to them, as Wallace went on to say, "Remember the time Alvin crept up into building 210 and listened from a vacant apartment next to theirs?"

Now that they all recalled the day, it was still a mystery, because not one of them had ever seen Danny. John, looking up at the clock, noticed it was four o'clock. He asked Wallace if he could give him a ride to see his lawyer, whom he had to see at five-thirty. Wallace, still thinking about the subject at hand, paused long enough to say okay.

Across town at Mr. Sharpe's office, Mr. Woodson discussed the fact that he thought Kenneth Gates and Detective Williams were one and the same.

Mr. Sharpe asked, "Do you have anything to support this, any kind of proof or something?"

"Not yet, but the person you have me watching goes to True to Life Sportswear some mornings. Then, on others, he goes to the police station on Bigelow."

"Okay, check it out, but he could be covering for Gates, because he's family or otherwise," stated Mr. Sharpe.

"It's not making sense, one person telling this, another telling me that. Something's just not sitting right with me. Well, as we speak, I'm waiting on an address on Williams."

Woodson paused and asked, "Well, anyway, how does it look so far?"

"Too early to tell," replied Mr. Sharpe. He reclined in his chair as he drifted away in thought.

Mr. Woodson looked around the room. Again at Mr. Sharpe, then once again, he spoke.

"If my theory is right and they are one and the same, then there's something extremely wrong!"

Now with his head in his hands, Mr. Sharpe nodded as if to agree. He then went on to say, "Either way it goes, I smell a rat! A big one! So get the information and the pictures of the two of them, then get back to me."

Mr. Woodson, now standing, headed for the door as Mr. Sharpe reached for the phone. But before he could, his secretary buzzed him, telling him that John Jackson was sitting in the lobby area. He told her to send him right in.

John walked in, holding a small tape recorder as Mr. Sharpe maneuvered around his desk to greet him.

"Hello, John," he said as he shook his hand and offered him a seat. He sat on his backside on his desk and seemed ready to listen to whatever it was John had for him to hear.

John hit the play button on the recorder and let it play. Mr. Sharpe listened, but heard nothing he thought was relevant. John suddenly seemed saddened by his reaction and it was evident by the tone of his voice.

John explained, "You see, Danny is Hits, who is the hitman!"

"I understand where you're going, but it doesn't help your case at all. There was nothing said incriminating pertaining to you or your case." Walking back around the desk, he sat down and began to speak.

"Now what we're working on is a long shot that I think may bring about some answers."

John listened as Mr. Sharpe debated whether to let him testify or not. Due to how things stood, he probably would have to, unless things somehow took a turn for the better.

Mr. Sharpe's secretary buzzed, informing him that his six o'clock had arrived. He rose to his feet and politely escorted John to the door, telling him he'd see him in court the following day. He also told him not to worry, patting him on the back as he did so.

As the two walked out of the office into the lobby, Mr. Sharpe shook John's hand and then smiled as he greeted his next client.

On his way out, John looked back, then turned and continued on his way.

Mr. Woodson could be seen leaving a home on a dark and dreary street. He hurried to his car to call Mr. Sharpe at home on his cellular phone. He explained that he got the pictures and he wanted to meet with him. Mr. Sharpe agreed. Mr. Woodson told him to meet him at the burger joint on the corner of Springfield Avenue and Ellis.

Mr. Sharpe arrived first, then after about twenty minutes, he wondered why his investigator was so late. At that exact moment, he came through the door with a wide smile, and apologized for being late. The two shook hands and then sat down across from each other.

Mr. Woodson unzipped a bag that sat in front of him, pulling pictures, a small notepad and a few miscellaneous items from it. He placed all the pictures on the table facing Mr. Sharpe, so he could view them.

Wondering if he had more pictures to present, Mr. Sharpe waited. But Mr. Woodson explained to him that that was the two of them in front of him. As he pointed, Mr. Woodson pulled another picture from his jacket pocket, placing it alongside the rest. Now seeing the connection, Mr. Sharpe smiled and commended Mr. Woodson.

"So, it's true!" stated Mr. Sharpe.

Mr. Woodson just nodded his head and smiled.

"So if Gates is Williams and vice versa, that explains a lot." Sharpe was thinking aloud.

"Also, the addresses match!" Woodson added.

Mr. Sharpe absorbed all of this, then it dawned on him that John was right all along. He figured it was best to tell Detective Jones no more, at least until he found something concrete to solidify it all.

Outside the precinct, Jones, Michaels and Williams all walked to their individual cars, as the workday came to a close. But on this night an unsuspecting homicide detective would be murdered. So as they drove away in their separate directions, heading home, the one who would suffer this travesty rode about, listening to his radio and whistling. As he came to a red light and sat there, a blue car came around the corner to his left. Dropping the passenger window as it came to a stop; two gunmen sprayed the unmarked patrol car thoroughly. Hitting the gas tank as they U-turned and raced away, they left the car engulfed in flames. The masked men fled the scene as a patrol car arrived at the tail end of this horrific event.

Shocked by this sight, the officers in the patrol car paused briefly and then gave chase as they radioed for backup. Street after street they pursued closely, as they started shooting, shattering the windows and the taillights of the murderers' vehicle. Now joining in on the chase, two other patrol cars helped to corner them.

Two guys bailed from within the car, armed, but had nowhere to run, so they began to spray police cars and everything in their path. More and more sirens could be heard as officers ran for cover. The murderers panicked; two of them were struck down, as a third sprayed two standing officers before he was shot dead.

The remaining four officers, plus the additional ones who had arrived, slowly and cautiously approached the now bullet-ridden bodies, which all lay still, except for one.

People passing looked on, as the officers put up the yellow tape to close off the area. As the night drifted away the bodies were removed. The spots where they had laid remained soiled from the blood as chalk marks outlined them. Not far away, the flames were fully extinguished and the charred remains of the fallen detective had been removed.

The next day, court resumed for Johnathan Jackson. The room filled with the usual faces. Once the judge made his grand entrance, the proceedings were on their way.

The prosecutor called his first witness.

"I call to the stand Detective Ken Jacoby."

As he was sworn in and seated, the prosecutor didn't hesitate, he jumped right to it.

"First of all hello; now after careful examination of each bullet, would you tell the court what your findings were?"

"After carefully examining each of them, I can positively conclude that all the bullets came from the same gun."

"What kind of gun was that?"

"A nine-millimeter handgun."

"Are you sure?" asked the prosecutor.

"Yes."

Picking up a gun from the evidence table, the prosecutor asked, "Is this the type of gun you're talking about?"

"Yes," Mr. Jacoby stated after looking at it briefly.

"Is this the gun you examined?"

After carefully looking it over, he replied, "Yes."

"For the record, Your Honor, exhibit G."

Now picking up some pictures from the evidence table, the prosecutor gave them to his witness to look over as he asked, "Are those photographs that of the bullets the medical examiner gave you?"

"Yes," he stated as he flipped through them.

"Exhibit H, Your Honor," the prosecutor stated as he passed the pictures to the jurors after getting them from Mr. Jacoby.

Walking back over to his witness, he continued, "Now tell the courtroom whose fingerprints were found on the murder weapon!"

"That of Mr. Johnathan Jackson," Mr. Jacoby answered as he reviewed some notes to refresh his memory.

"For the record, that's the defendant, Your Honor," added the prosecutor.

Mr. Sharpe stated to note something in his pad as John looked on.

"Were there any other fingerprints found on the weapon?"

"No, just the one set."

On that note the prosecutor walked away with a confident smirk on his face, as he announced that he had no further questions. Mr. Sharpe rose to counter.

"Now you stated that all the bullets came from the same gun, correct?"

"Correct."

"Now the gun in question was held in which hand? Inform me and the jury."

The prosecutor rose to object, but the judge motioned to allow it. He told Mr. Jacoby to answer the question.

"I can't recall."

"Let me refresh your memory. In your statement you said it was held in the right hand, due to the placement of the fingers. Does that sound correct?" Mr. Sharpe reminded him as he glanced at his statement.

"Possibly, but I can't remember that part."

Approaching him now with his statement, Mr. Sharpe gave it to him as he asked, "Now isn't this your statement?"

"Yes."

"So that makes what I just said correct, doesn't it?"

"Yes."

Mr. Sharpe walked over to his client as he spoke."

"Let the record show that my client is not right handed. He's left handed." He pointed to the hand that John was writing with.

At that instant, Mr. Woodson burst into the courtroom, drawing the full attention of everyone. As he walked in, Mr. Sharpe walked back to where he was seated, as Woodson leaned to whisper in his ear.

The judge and the prosecutor both looked on, then the judge told Mr. Sharpe, "Tell your guest to have a seat and for him not to interrupt this courtroom again, or he'll be held in contempt. And you, being a lawyer, you should know better."

Mr. Sharpe apologized as he told him it would never happen again and then requested to speak to him at sidebar. The judge agreed, and just as Mr. Sharpe walked to the right of the judge's seat, so did the prosecutor. As the three huddled Mr. Sharpe spoke.

"I'm requesting an adjournment until tomorrow, because I've learned that one of the defense's witnesses has expired during the night and I need to rethink my strategy, if that's all right with you."

"If it's all right with the prosecutor," stated the judge.

The prosecutor agreed and the court was adjourned until the following day.

Later, back at the hotel, Jewels and Detective Michaels had a talk.

"Now Jewels, I completed the job, where is the balance of my money?" Michaels asked impatiently.

Jewels smiled and then said, "I said all of them, not one! All!"

"No, you said Tony and anyone who got in my way. Don't play with me! I hit Tony with no complications, so there's nothing left to do but collect," stated Michaels angrily.

Jewels smiled once again as he got up, then said, "I want all those sons of bitches dead, you hear me. So if you're not capable of finishing the job, I'll find someone who will!"

Michaels then told him, "You can do what the hell you want after you give me my money."

"You did half a job, you got half paid! What's the problem?" Jewels replied.

"There won't be as long as I get what's mine!" Michaels shouted.

Suddenly, shots could be heard from within the room as they drew on each other, but only the detective was left standing. He quickly searched the room, grabbing an envelope containing seventy-five hundred dollars from a nightstand in the bedroom area and a briefcase from beside the couch, then exited quickly. As he did, he looked toward the elevator, then toward the stairwell and decided to take the stairs because they were closer. While exiting the building he saw the police running in. He walked to his car, got in and drove off.

Back in his office, Mr. Sharpe talked with Mr. Woodson and John, then his phone began to ring. He excused himself to take the call. After hanging up, he told them Jewels had been murdered in a hotel room, by whom they didn't know. Confused, Mr. Sharpe shortened the meeting. Then, as soon as John was gone, he and Mr. Woodson left. Woodson, wondering what Sharpe had on his mind, followed him anyway.

Getting in the car Mr. Sharpe explained, "I'm going to the police station to see Detective Williams 'slash' Kenneth Gates!"

Arriving at the desk of the Fifth Precinct, they requested to see Detective Williams, but they got a big surprise. The picture didn't match; it wasn't him. Now wanting answers, Mr. Sharpe asked him if they could have a few minutes of his time.

He replied, "Just a few, I have a lot of work in front of me."

After they all sat in a room into which the detective had led them, Mr. Sharpe showed him some pictures.

"Do you know who this person is?" Mr. Sharpe asked with a confused look on his face.

"Yes, that's Detective Michaels," responded Detective Williams.

Mr. Woodson and Mr. Sharpe looked at each other in shock. As they did, another detective came in and interrupted.

"Excuse me, Detective Williams, I have the security tapes from the hotel Jewels was killed at, everyone's prepping to view them."

Both Woodson and Sharpe heard this and were curious as to what was on it. Williams excused himself as the two detectives went into another room. Sharpe and Woodson waited patiently and in a half hour or less they both came back with looks of disbelief and confusion on their faces. Just then, another burst in with the files on each of the guys involved in the murder of Detective Jones.

The next day, 1407 Ridgewood was raided and Detective Michaels was arrested for suspicion of murder. As they searched it, Detective Williams stumbled onto a picture that sat over the fireplace. After a careful look at the picture, he noticed some familiar faces, but couldn't quite place them. Then it dawned on him, as he recalled the mug shots of Detective Jones' killers.

"Damn, Danny, why?" he shouted as he looked at the picture of the four of them on a fishing trip.

In front of the house, the handcuffs were being put on Detective Danny Michaels as he was escorted out and to one of the patrol cars that sat along the curb.

Afterward, Detective Williams returned to the precinct, put things together, then wrote down a few numbers, addresses and headed out the door once more.

At the home of one of Detective Jones' killers' girlfriends, Williams first told her that her boyfriend had died in a shootout with the police. She broke down slightly and briefly. Seeing this, Williams paused, then asked her about the night of August 20, 1990. She eagerly answered.

"He came in ranting and raving about how they did in some drug dealer and how he was about to get paid. He also told me he'd kill me if I spoke a word of this!"

Thanking her for her help and time, Williams rose from where he was sitting and walked to the door. With her behind him, he left and she closed the door.

As he walked from the building in which she lived, he passed a blue pickup to get to his car. His next stop was the hospital, to talk to the only survivor of the group of killers, to get more on Detective Michaels. But as he reached the floor where the wounded man was, Williams was told that he was in no shape to talk, so he left.

The next day flew by as John was cleared of all of the charges, but before he departed he had something to say.

"Your Honor, far be I from perfect. But even farther from perfect is this system. I should charge you for murder, as you've done me, for all that I lived for and all that I stood for and those that I loved and lived through have been assassinated. So you see, you have sentenced me whether you realize it or not, to hell on earth, for you have murdered me and my self-worth."

Leaving the courtroom afterward, he left it and all the people in it, in complete silence. The only noise heard was the knocking of his dress shoes against the hardwood floor.

THE END

PT.2 ONE IN THE CHAMBER

PT.3 PUSHED

EPILOGUE

So John, his reputation and life destroyed by all that had taken place over the past year, secluded himself away from everyone by moving south. He found a job at a nearby plant and never looked back.

Alvin and his little sister, Theresa, were put into foster care, where they were placed in separate homes. Alvin ran away, back to the streets. Their mother died from an overdose shortly after John's trial.

Wallace and Eric both ended up in jail serving time. They made plans to go into business together when they would one day be released.

Angie went on working and living out of Wallace and Eric's place. She and Wallace had planned to get married when he was released.

Rochelle disappeared, and was not heard from again.

Karen Wells and Keith finally started dating, after Keith got over his fear of Jewels. They eventually went into business together.

This novel is dedicated to the memory of Richard "Shorty" Wilson.

PSEG

70380 10018

1800
704
3289